# YOUNG SHERLOCK

## NIGHT BREAK

ANDREW LANE

MACMILLAN CHILDREN'S BOOKS

First published 2015 by Macmillan Children's Books

This edition published 2016 by Macmillan Children's Books
an imprint of Pan Macmillan
20 New Wharf Road, London N1 9RR
Associated companies throughout the world
www.panmacmillan.com

ISBN 978-1-4472-9457-3

Copyright © Andrew Lane 2015

The right of Andrew Lane to be identified as the author of this work has been asserted by him in accordance with the Copyright, Designs and Patents Act 1988.

All rights reserved. No part of this publication may be reproduced, stored in a retrieval system, or transmitted, in any form or by any means (electronic, mechanical, photocopying, recording or otherwise), without the prior written permission of the publisher.

Pan Macmillan does not have any control over, or any responsibility for, any author or third-party websites referred to in or on this book.

7 9 8 6

A CIP catalogue record for this book is available from the British Library.

Printed and bound by CPI Group (UK) Ltd, Croydon CR0 4YY

This book is sold subject to the condition that it shall not, by way of trade or otherwise, be lent, resold, hired out, or otherwise circulated without the publisher's prior consent in any form of binding or cover other than that in which it is published and without a similar condition including this condition being imposed on the subsequent purchaser.

*Dedicated to Richard Boardman, Marshall Lewy, Matthew Faulk, Mark Skeet, Simon Winstone and Georgina Gordon-Smith for helping me move my career to the next level.*

*Grateful acknowledgements to Kevin Reilly for the excellent and invaluable advice on period sword-fighting. I haven't yet taken Kevin up on his offer of lessons, but I fully intend to.*

‘If you truly wish to find someone you have known and who travels, there are two points on the globe you have but to sit and wait; sooner or later your man will come there: the docks of London and Port Said.’

*Rudyard Kipling*

# PROLOGUE

Sherlock Holmes wiped a sleeve across his forehead. He looked at the sleeve as he brought it down. It was dark and damp with sweat.

The sun was high in the sky, almost blinding him, and the heat was like a heavy weight hammering down on his head, even through the scarf he had tied over it. Within seconds his forehead was already soaked with perspiration. It trickled lines of warmth down his cheeks and his neck into his collar, which was sopping wet.

The Suez Canal reached from the horizon on Sherlock's left to the horizon on his right – a deep groove in the sand, a man-made waterway so large that it might have been made by a sword-slash inflicted by the gods. Sparkling blue water filled it from bank to bank. Green bushes and reeds lined its edges. It was so wide that he couldn't have thrown a stone to the far bank, and so deep that ships could be sunk in it and other ships would still be able to pass over their submerged wrecks.

Of course, if he didn't stop the sabotage that was just about to occur: then there would be so many wrecked ships in the canal that they would be piled up above the water's surface, and the canal would be impassable for years to come. The problem was that he really didn't know how he was going to do that.

'Sherlock,' a voice said. 'I'm sorry it had to be this way.'

He turned around. Rufus Stone was standing a few feet away. The breeze blew his black hair back from his face. The sun shone on his single gold tooth. His expression was . . . regretful. Even sad.

And he was holding a sword.

Sherlock felt his strength, his confidence, draining away. How had it come to this? he wondered. How had he ended up in the disabling heat of a foreign country, about to fight one of his best friends?

He raised his own sword in readiness of the fight to come . . .

# CHAPTER ONE

The early afternoon sunlight shone through Charles Dodgson's window. Motes of dust drifted through it, dancing around each other as the currents of air shifted around. Outside, students walked around the quadrangle of the Oxford college where he taught. Their voices drifted through the window along with the sunlight, and just as rarefied.

'So,' Dodgson said from his armchair, which was turned so that Sherlock could see his profile. He was leaning back, staring at the ceiling. 'Have you th-th-thought about that sequence of n-n-numbers that I gave you a while ago? As I recall, it was 1, 5, 12, 22, 35, 51 and 70. Can you t-t-tell me what logic links them, and creates the sequence?'

'Yes,' Sherlock said, 'I worked out what the sequence was. Eventually.'

'Please – enlighten me.'

'It's difficult to describe, but it's all to do with pentagrams.'

'P-p-perhaps you could draw the solution for me.' Dodgson indicated a blackboard on an easel that stood over by the fireplace.

Sherlock got up, walked to the blackboard and picked

up a piece of chalk, trying to imagine in his mind the diagram that it had taken him months to work out. Quickly and neatly he sketched out a series of dots on the board and joined them with lines.

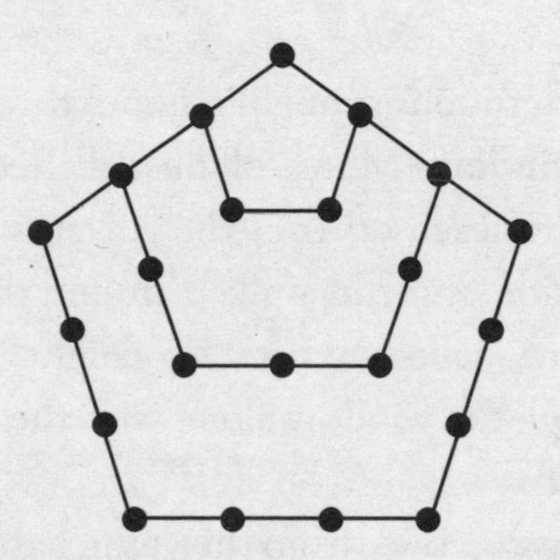

'The first point is the "1", of course,' he explained. 'The smallest pentagram has five points, giving us the next "5". The next largest pentagram has ten points, three of which are shared with the first pentagram, but if you add in the two points from the first pentagram which *aren't* shared, then you get the "12". The third pentagram has fifteen points, of which five are shared with the first and second pentagram, but if you add in the seven points from the first two pentagrams which *aren't* shared, then you get the "22". And so on.'

'Excellent,' Dodgson said, clapping his thin hands together. 'And what d-d-does this tell you?'

'It tells me that working this out took an awfully long time.'

'Yes, but what *use* are these p-p-pentagonal numbers?

What do they t-t-tell us about the world? What *significance* do they have?'

'I have no idea,' Sherlock said honestly.

'Quite right. Pentagonal numbers have no significance that I know about – unlike Fibonacci's N-n-numbers, which seem to crop up in all kinds of circumstances. Perhaps we will discover a use for them, or a m-m-meaning, and perhaps not. Only time will tell. The great mathematician Leonhard Euler did do some very int-t-teresting theoretical work with them, of course, and published his results in a p-p-paper in 1783. He showed that the infinite product (1–x)(1–x2) (1–x3) . . . expands into an infinite s-s-series with the exponents being the pentagonal numbers. What do you think of that, then?'

'I can't really take it in,' Sherlock said evenly.

Dodgson didn't spot the sarcasm, or if he did, then he chose to ignore it.

The tutorial went on for another hour, ranging over many areas of mathematics, and by the time Sherlock left he felt that his head was buzzing. It took a long walk in the cold but bright afternoon air to calm him down.

When he got to Mrs McCrery's's boarding house, where he was staying while in Oxford, he found Matty outside, sitting on the wall. A black-painted cab was parked in the road. Its driver sat reading a newspaper on top, while its horse stood calmly with its eyes closed, relishing the rest.

'You got a visitor,' Matty observed, jerking his thumb at the cab.

'I can see that,' Sherlock said. He walked up to stand beside the wheel closest to the kerb and stared in through the window. Nothing had been left inside, but the cushions had been dented by the weight of the passenger's body – and it looked like it had been a considerable weight.

'My brother,' he observed, amazed. 'Mycroft is here.'

'That was clever. Does 'e have a particular aftershave he uses?'

'Not exactly.' Sherlock decided not to tell Matty that he had recognized his brother by the size and shape of his buttocks. 'Where is he now?'

''E's inside now, 'avin' a cup of tea wiv the old lady.'

'But Mycroft hates travelling.'

'Russia,' Matty observed, holding up a thumb, then, 'Ireland,' as his forefinger joined it . . .

'I take the point,' Sherlock said, 'but what I meant was, he only travels if there is an overriding reason. Mycroft does not make social visits.'

''E does where you're concerned. 'E takes a lot of trouble to make sure you're okay.' He sniffed, and wiped a sleeve across his nose. 'Wish I 'ad a bruvver.'

'You've got me,' Sherlock observed. He gazed at the boarding house. 'I know I ought to go in and find out what Mycroft is doing here, but experience tells me that he only ever turns up when there's trouble or when my life is about to change. Either way, it tends to be bad.'

'You can't put off bad news by stickin' your fingers in your ears an' pretendin' you can't hear it,' Matty said, jumping down from the wall. 'If life's taught me anythin', it's that. Best to get it over an' done wiv quickly. Like rippin' a bandage off a scab.'

Sherlock nodded slowly. 'That's good advice.'

'Hey, what else is a bruvver for?' Matty punched his arm. 'Come an' tell me about it when you get a chance.'

Sherlock grabbed his sleeve. 'What makes you think you're avoiding this? If there's bad news, I want you there with me.'

'Why?' Matty asked.

'Because *that's* what brothers do, as well.'

The two of them walked up the steps and through the door of Mrs McCrery's house together.

Sherlock immediately heard his brother's voice from inside the front room. He stood in the doorway, Matty beside him, and coughed.

Mycroft's voice broke off in mid-sentence, and Mrs McCrery appeared in the doorway. 'Ah, young Mr Holmes. Your brother Mycroft is here. We were just reminiscing about his time at Oxford.'

'I've heard the stories,' Sherlock replied.

'I'll be making another pot of tea. I'd offer you a cake, but your brother's appetite is as good as it ever was and they're all gone. I'll see if I can find some biscuits for you and young Matthew here – I know this young scallywag gets so hungry he could eat a horse!'

'Don't say that when 'Arold's around,' Matty muttered. ''E takes that kind of thing personally.'

'Thank you,' Sherlock said. As Mrs McCrery bustled away, he stepped into the room.

Mycroft had wedged himself into a comfortable armchair near the window. Sherlock suspected that he might need to use a rope and the services of the horse outside to pull him out, when the time came.

'Ah, Sherlock,' Mycroft said. 'It gladdens my heart to see you again. And young Master Arnatt, of course, there by your side like an ever-visible shadow.'

''Allo, Mister 'Olmes,' Matty said brightly.

Mycroft's large head moved so that he was staring back at Sherlock again. 'Sherlock, I need to tell you something, and it is not the kind of thing one talks about in front of relative strangers.'

'Matty is like family now,' Sherlock pointed out. 'I want him here.'

'Very well. Rather than beat around the bush, I will get straight to the point. I am sorry to have to tell you that our mother has died.'

The words seemed to hang in the air like the echo of some vast bell. Sherlock tried to take a breath, but somehow he couldn't get the air into his lungs. Even the light in the room appeared to change, as if a cloud had drifted across the face of the sun, casting the house in shadow.

'Died,' he repeated. 'Mother is *dead*?'

'Indeed. I realize that this comes as a shock to you, as it did to me, but –'

'Mother has *died*?'

Mycroft sighed. 'Yes, Sherlock, that is correct. Take a moment, if you need it, to come to terms with the information.'

In his head, it was as if Sherlock was turning over a selection of different feelings, trying each one to see if it fitted. Surprise? Grief? Anger? Acceptance? He wasn't sure how he should be feeling right at that moment. His fingers were tingling strangely, and he had the impression that he was swaying slightly. He couldn't feel his feet. He opened his mouth, but no words came out. There were no words to *come* out: his mind was empty.

'Matthew,' Mycroft said urgently. 'Help Sherlock to a chair.'

He felt Matty's hands on his shoulders, guiding him sideways. Moments later he found that he was sitting down, although he had no recollection of doing so.

'How?' he asked finally. 'When?'

'As to "how": you know that she has been ill for some time. The disease called consumption, which is better known to the population at large as tuberculosis. It is a disease which attacks the lungs. There are various treatments, including rest and visits to sanatoriums in places with cold pure air, such as the Alps in France and Switzerland, but generally the results of these treatments are not positive. The disease finally weakened her system to the point where she did not have the strength to carry on the fight. She became weaker and weaker, and then she slipped away.' His voice was quiet, and Sherlock could hear within it all the same emotions that he was struggling with. 'As to "when": I received notification this morning that she had died during the night. I immediately took a cab to Paddington, a train to Oxford and a cab here. I did not want there to be any delay in you finding out.'

'What happens now?' Sherlock asked quietly. The various emotions that he had been feeling just moments before seemed to have drained away, leaving an emotional landscape like a beach from which the tide had withdrawn: bare, desolate, and littered with old memories like items of driftwood and sea-smoothed pebbles.

'We need to go home.' Mycroft paused for a moment. 'There will be a funeral, and there will be medical expenses to sort out.'

Sherlock nodded. 'I understand. When do we go?'

'Immediately.' Mycroft put his hands on the arms of the chair and pushed downward. Nothing happened apart from the sound of the wood of the armchair creaking. 'I suggest,' he went on, resting for a moment before trying again, 'that you go and pack for the journey. Assume that you will be gone for a week or so.' He pushed again with his hands on the arms of the chair, but still his body didn't move. 'And while you are doing that,' he said, settling down again, 'I would appreciate it if you, young Master Arnatt, could go outside and bring the driver of my cab in here. I may need his assistance.'

Still in a daze, Sherlock walked up the several flights of stairs to his room and quickly threw some clothes into a suitcase without checking what they were or whether they were suitable. Matty joined him after a few minutes and silently watched. He grabbed his violin case as well, before leaving the room. He and Matty headed downstairs together, and Sherlock found himself wondering as they did so whether he would ever see Mrs McCrery's boarding house again, or any of the students there that had become friends. Perhaps, like Deepdene School for Boys and his Uncle Sherrinford's house, this place was destined to become just another temporary stop on his journey through life.

Mycroft was standing in the front room looking slightly flustered and brushing down the front of his jacket. The armchair looked like it had been in a fight, and not come out too well. Mycroft nodded when he saw Sherlock's bag. 'Good. We are ready to go then.'

Sherlock turned and stuck out a hand to Matty. 'I'll be seeing you,' he said, feeling a catch in his throat. 'I don't know where, and I don't know when, but I will be seeing you again.'

Matty stared at the hand as if he didn't know what to do with it, but it was Mycroft who broke the uncomfortable silence. 'Actually,' he ventured, 'I was wondering if young Master Arnatt would be free to accompany us. I think, Sherlock, that you will need a friend, and my time will be taken up with arranging the funeral and various family matters. I am unsure what state the family finances are in, and I need to assure myself that we are not already destitute. It would be good for you to have someone with whom you can talk.'

Sherlock glanced at Matty, who was looking surprised. 'Me? Come wiv you?'

'If you are free.'

'I'm always free,' Matty said. 'Yeah, I'll come – if Sherlock wants me to.' He gazed at Sherlock appealingly.

'I do,' Sherlock said. He turned to his brother. 'Thank you.'

'Friends are important,' Mycroft said quietly. 'I have realized that through the simple expedient of not having any myself. Master Arnatt, do you need to make arrangements for the care of your horse?'

'Nah – there's people along the side of the canal who borrow 'Arold while I'm not using him. They feed 'im, and look after 'im, and make sure 'e's 'appy. They prob'ly won't even notice that I've gone.' His face fell. 'An' neither will 'Arold, which is a shame.'

'What about clothes?'

Matty stared at Mycroft, frowning.

'Spare clothes,' Mycroft explained.

Matty just kept on staring at him.

'Never mind.' Mycroft sighed. 'We can get clothes for you when we get to the house. At least we will be carrying fewer bags.' He turned to Sherlock. 'And as for your studies at Oxford University, such as they are,' he went on, 'I have taken the liberty of sending a note around to Charles Dodgson, giving him my regards and explaining the situation. He will be very understanding, I am sure.'

The three of them walked out to the waiting cab, where the driver threw Sherlock's case on top to join one that was already there.

'You packed!' Sherlock observed accusingly. 'You said that you took a cab to Paddington Station the moment you heard, but you must have stopped off at your rooms to pack!'

'Your usually sharp mind is letting you down,' Mycroft replied. 'I will put that down to the effects of shock. I did not lie to you – I keep a several bags packed with fresh clothes and toiletries in my office, in case I need to travel in a hurry.'

'But you don't like travelling,' Matty observed.

'That is irrelevant. Firms do not generally like or expect their premises to burn down, but they take out fire insurance nevertheless. I do not like travelling, but sometimes it is necessary to do so in a hurry. As it is now.'

As the cab pulled away from the kerb, Sherlock looked back out of the window. Mrs McCrery was standing in the doorway of her house. She seemed to be waving, but Sherlock's eyes were suddenly and unexpectedly filled with tears, and he couldn't be sure.

The journey to Oxford Station was short, but there was an hour's wait for a train and so Mycroft bought them both tea and cakes in the tea shop there. It took a few minutes for the serving girl to bring them over, but when she had, Matty tucked in with gusto. Sherlock, by contrast, found that his appetite just wasn't there. When Matty had finished his own cake, Sherlock pushed his wordlessly across to the boy.

'What about our sister?' he asked suddenly. 'How is she taking the news?'

'Her mental state is fragile,' Mycroft rumbled. He had eaten two cakes himself. 'Sometimes she is aware of what is going on around her and sometimes she seems to be living in a world of her own. Whatever world she visits, I have a feeling it is more congenial than the world the rest of us live in.' He paused momentarily. 'I understand that she has a suitor – a man whose acquaintance she has made and who seems to have some kind of romantic feelings towards her. I intend meeting with this man and establishing what kind of person he is before we return.'

'Emma – with a man?' Sherlock thought back to the pale girl he remembered. She had always seemed to drift through the house like a ghost, not talking to anyone, immersed in her own thoughts. Younger than Mycroft but older than Sherlock, she had inherited their mother's physical fragility and, apparently, their father's mental fragility.

'You are thinking about our father's problems,' Mycroft observed, 'and how our sister appears to have inherited them.'

Sherlock was amazed. He shouldn't have been – he

had seen his brother demonstrate his amazing deductive abilities before, but this time he was the subject. 'How did you know that?' he asked.

'Was you really thinkin' 'bout that?' Matty asked, intrigued.

'I was.'

Matty looked darkly at Mycroft. ''E read your mind then. I always suspected 'e could do that. The Dark Arts – that's what they're called.'

'That wasn't mind-reading,' Mycroft said, shaking his huge head. 'That was merely observation. Do you see the serving girl at the counter? She is roughly the same age as our sister. When Sherlock mentioned Emma's name his gaze shifted so that he was looking at the serving girl. Obviously he was thinking about Emma, and the girl was merely a mental stand-in, if you will. His gaze shifted to the plates and cups on the table, no doubt observing that the serving girl had got our order perfectly correct, whereas Emma would either have forgotten the order, served the wrong cakes, or spilt the tea. Sherlock's glance then shifted to me, and then to his own reflection in the window of this tea shop. I deduced that his thoughts had similarly shifted to the differences between Emma and the two of us. In particular I noticed that he was unknowingly comparing my hand with his – we both have comparatively long fingers, which is a trait we share with our mother. She, by the way, was excellent at both playing the piano and needlework. Sherlock finished by glancing at the station guard outside, whose uniform would have reminded him of our father's Army uniform, and then upward, to where the Christian Church tells us that heaven is located. It was a simple progression of thought to deduce that he had moved on to thinking about our parents, and how we had all inherited something different from them.'

'Incredible,' Matty breathed.

'Commonplace,' Mycroft said dismissively. 'Even elementary.'

'We've never really talked about Father's problems,' Sherlock said, looking at his brother. 'You know that Uncle Sherrinford and Aunt Anna told me about them?'

'Uncle Sherrinford wrote and told me that the conversation had occurred. I decided that if you needed to talk about it, then you would, and that there was no need for me to needlessly raise the subject.' He glanced at Matty. 'I also know that Master Arnatt was present during the conversation, and I trust him to keep any information he heard to himself.'

Matty nodded seriously.

'Father is a complicated man,' Mycroft observed. 'You were, perhaps, shielded from his mood swings, but I experienced them first hand. There were times when he would stay in his study for days, just staring into space, and other times when he would suddenly decide at three o'clock in the morning to change around all the paintings in the house. His time in the –' he hesitated briefly –

'sanatorium calmed him down, but he will always be eccentric. Fortunately he has taken one of the four career courses where eccentricity is tolerated and rewarded if it is combined with competence – the British Army. The others, of course, are the Church, the theatre and academia.'

'Interesting that Uncle Sherrinford chose to write sermons for vicars around the country,' Sherlock observed. 'He didn't actually join the Church, but he did the next best thing. I suspect his mind was closer to Father's than he would ever have admitted.'

'Interesting also that *you* play the violin and have shown a strong interest in the theatrical life,' Mycroft said without missing a beat. 'I am the exception, of course – I am not a don, or a lecturer.'

'But Charles Dodgson told me that he thought you had the makings of a fine academic, and he was both saddened and surprised that you joined the Civil Service,' Sherlock rejoined.

'It strikes me,' Matty suddenly piped up, 'that I don't even know where your family live.'

'Sussex,' Mycroft said. 'A small town named Arundel. The Holmes family have a large house a few miles outside the town.' He checked his watch. 'The journey will take around three hours, and we will have to change trains several times. Oh, and that reminds me . . .' He patted his pocket, then slid his hand inside and pulled out an envelope. 'This arrived a few days ago. It is from Father, in India. I thought you might wish to read it.'

Mycroft placed the envelope on the table between them. Sherlock stared at it – at the familiar writing on the front, at the strange Indian stamps that adorned it, and at the various creases and stains it had picked up during its travels. A terrible thought occurred to him.

'Father doesn't know,' he whispered.

'I have written a reply to his letter,' Mycroft said, equally quietly, 'in which I break the tragic news.' He paused. 'I have also written separately and privately to his commanding officer, notifying him of the family bereavement and asking him to keep an eye on Father to make sure that . . . that he deals with the news. I have no great faith that his mental state is stable, given his location so far from home, and the privations of the British Army in India.'

*My Dearest Sons,*
*It is one of the responsibilities of a father to pass on to his scions the wisdom that he has learned during his time on Earth. Sadly, given that I am currently many thousands of miles away from you, and am likely to remain in this geographical location for some time to come, I am unable so to do. I have spent much of my spare time here racking my brains for little gems of philosophy that might be of service, but I have come up with nothing that you could not (and probably already) have found in Plato,*

Socrates and the pages of Punch magazine. All that I am able to do is to give you some flavour of the environment, the people and the events here in India - so different from dear England, the land that we all love and which I dream about every night.

I recall that I have, in previous letters, written about the landscape of this strange country - the flat plains, the hills, the rivers and the towns. I remember also writing about the weather, which is either far too hot or far too hot and far too wet. I have also, I believe, given you some flavour of the various people who call this place their home. What I may not have done is to try to explain what my life is like day to day. You may have the impression that, being in the British Army, I am fighting all the time. You may even worry about me. I can reassure you that I spend considerably more time polishing my buttons, my belt and my boots than I do in combat, and that I am more at risk from disease and snakebite here than from a bullet or a knife.

I should, I suppose, say a few words about the strict hierarchy of this society, by which I mean the society of English people living here in India, not the society of the Indians themselves (although we seem to have taken on some of their ideas). The highest of the high here are *called the Brahmins - a word borrowed by the way from the Indians, who have had a very well established caste system for thousands of years. As with their castes, members of our own different levels stick to their own - nobody ever socializes outside their equals. If you try, then you are reported and disciplined, and if you persist, then you may well be sent home in disgrace. The Brahmins are the members of the Indian Civil Service - the ones who actually govern and run this country. Beneath them are the semi-Brahmins - the members of the various other Government departments such as the Forest Service and the Police Service. Beneath them are the military forces, and that is where I fit in. Beneath the military are the businessmen - those who work in commerce - and beneath them are the traders - the shop workers and suchlike. Towards the bottom of the social order you find the menial workers, and at the absolute bottom are those English people whose families have, for whatever reason, chosen to settle here in India and make a life for themselves.*

It wasn't, Sherlock thought, too far away from the various stratified levels of British society. Even in his former school – Deepdene School for Boys – there had been a very definite difference between the boys who came from the aristocracy, the boys whose fathers were in the Army, the boys whose fathers were in commerce and the boys whose fathers worked in trade.

*Given that each level of English society here in India socializes exclusively with its own, I do not get to speak to the Brahmin, the semi-Brahmin or the mercantile class unless on business. I spend a great deal of time here on the cantonment, which is what we call the military base where my regiment is stationed. Here life is driven by the various parades, and becomes not only very predictable but very boring as well. For instance, a month or so back one of the soldiers was carrying a plate of food from the mess to his barracks when a hawk swooped down from the sky, snatched the meat off the plate and flew off with it. We are still talking about it, even now. That is how bored we are.*

*The highlight of our lives here in the cantonment are the formal dinners. The food is certainly not much to write home about, which is why I have not previously done so. Because of the extreme heat and the prevalence of disease, any animal that is butchered must be eaten straight away or the meat will spoil. The meat itself is always tough - tough chicken, tough mutton and sometimes (although it angers* the natives) tough beef - the natives who follow the Hindu religion worship cows, and get very offended if we eat them. The meat is usually 'curried', which means it is cooked with strong spices, and that helps to make it digestible.

The formal military dinners consist of seven or eight courses, and we do, of course, dress up for them - tail coat, boiled shirt with stiff collar and cuffs and a white waistcoat. These conventions are preserved even on patrol outside the cantonment, and I have seen people arrive for dinner out in the wilds on camels, but still wearing their formal dress. In the cantonment the strict rule is that nobody is allowed to leave the table until the Colonel in charge of the regiment leaves, which means in practice that if several bottles of wine have been drunk in the bar beforehand, then there are a lot of increasingly uncomfortable men around the table as the dinner wears on!

It is Sunday here, as I write this letter, although the sun which shines down so heavily on us now has yet to shine on you in England, and by the time it does shine on you it will be dark here. I attended the church service this morning, as we all do every Sunday. The church is exactly the same as it would be back in England, and sometimes, while we are all gathered there singing hymns or praying, it is possible to imagine that we aren't in India at all, but are back home, in Aldershot perhaps. At least, it would be possible if it weren't for the heat radiating from the stones, the insects buzzing around our heads and the fact that the pews have notches cut out of them for us to rest our guns in. Yes, we take our guns into church with us. I wonder what Jesus, with his feelings against moneylenders in the grounds of the temple, would have made of that.

I mentioned earlier the weather, which is either far too hot or far too hot and far too wet. We dream of cold, and of snow. The excessive heat here leads to many problems, two of which are the diseases and the insects. As far as diseases go, I could write a book about them by now, but suffice it to say as an example that there is something called 'prickly heat', which sounds very civilized but in actuality means that your skin is covered so thickly with itching pimples that you cannot slide a needle between them. I have seen a man start off dinner scratching himself lightly and finish by tearing his fingernails down the skin of his chin and neck so hard that he drew blood. As far as the insects are concerned, they go in cycles. One week there will be stink bugs everywhere - in your bedding, in your soup, in *your ink pots. They are innocuous unless you crush them, in which eventuality they give out the most appalling smell. The next week the stink bugs will be gone but in their place will be jute moths which, if you absent-mindedly brush them off when they land on your hand, leave behind some chemical secretion that burns you.*

*They call this place 'the land of sudden death', but there are times when I wonder if death would be preferable to living in constant discomfort, pain, boredom and torment.*

*I must cease writing now, or I will say things that perhaps I should be keeping to myself. Please write back to me - it is your letters, along with the letters from your mother and your sister, that keep me sane.*

*Yours sincerely,*
*Your loving father,*
*Siger Holmes*

Sherlock finished the letter and folded it up very carefully. He handed it back to Mycroft without saying anything. Neither of them had to. It was clear from his words that their father's mental state was deteriorating out there in India. Discovering that his wife, their mother, had died in his absence – as painful as that was to Sherlock, what would it do to his father?

# CHAPTER TWO

The journey to the seat of the Holmes family for generations past took several hours. It wasn't so much the distance – Arundel, where Sherlock had been born and brought up, was, as the crow flew, not that far from Oxford – but it did require several changes of train and a deal of sitting around in small tea shops waiting for the next train to arrive. Matty was as chirpy as ever, and managed to put away a slice of cake in every tea shop, but Mycroft seemed to be in no mood to talk, and Sherlock felt the same. This was not the kind of family reunion he had been dreaming of.

The weather was fine, and when they were on a train Sherlock stared out of the window at the passing landscape. He had become fascinated at the sheer number and variety of people and places that existed in England. Everywhere he looked out of the train window there were people cutting and binding crops in fields, or picking apples or pears in orchards, or driving carts piled high with hay. Every station they passed through, whether they stopped or not, seemed to be crowded with travellers or with people meeting travellers. There were businessmen in suits and hats, labourers in rough clothes, old ladies with baskets or young ladies with extensive skirts and tiny jackets, and everywhere there were dogs, large and small, running around and chasing each other. All human life was there, and Sherlock found himself trying to read the stories of the various travellers from the slight marks on their hands or their clothes. One man they shared a compartment with for a while was a former soldier, judging by the shine on his shoes, the shortness of his hair and the way he sat stiffly upright. A lady who sat down for a few minutes, fussed with the window, and then moved to a different compartment with an audible huff of annoyance, was not as well-off as her clothes suggested, based on the fact that her shoes had been re-soled several times and her jacket repaired by a reasonably competent haberdasher. A vicar engaged them in conversation for a while, but Sherlock was fairly certain that he wasn't a vicar at all. Certainly his knowledge of the Bible was patchy, when Sherlock questioned him, and he kept trying to change the subject to something more general. Sherlock caught Mycroft's eye, and was amused to see his brother suppressing a smile. When the vicar finally left their carriage they both burst into laughter, much to the surprise of Matty.

'Should we call the police?' Sherlock asked, through giggles.

'Impersonating a vicar is not a crime, as far as I am aware,' Mycroft replied, his heavy frame shaking with suppressed mirth.

'But he may be an escaped prisoner in disguise, or a

confidence trickster aiming to fleece a congregation of their offerings in church.'

'Or he might be a sad individual who gets some perverse pleasure from dressing up as a cleric. We have no way of knowing, and no reason to interfere with his deception apart from curiosity. Let it go, Sherlock. Some questions will never be answered – at least, not while we are around, at any rate.'

As they got closer to their goal, Sherlock began to recognize aspects of the landscape. The sights made him feel nostalgic. He had good memories of Arundel – both the town and the large cathedral. Arundel was near the town of Chichester, and so the houses were large and the families well-off. The Holmes family were descended from a line of local squires, and although they had little or no actual power or influence locally, they were well regarded and so invited to all the events, galas, dinners and parties. Sherlock's childhood had been filled with long walks by himself in the countryside, many hours spent in the family library, reading his way voraciously through the classics alongside his brother – each sitting in his own armchair and not talking for hours on end, but enjoying the silence – or hiding things like frogs and caterpillars in his brother's bag when Mycroft went off to university each term. His memories of his mother and father were less clear – they had been caring, but quite remote, leaving the two brothers to get on with their own lives. Sherlock remembered his father mainly as a big man with a large moustache and a booming laugh, but he also remembered that there had been another side to his father as well – a man who would lock himself in the library with a bottle of brandy, and not come out until it was finished, or who would not speak to anyone in the house for days on end. Sherlock had accepted, as children do, that his father had mood swings, but it was only later, talking with his Aunt Anna and Uncle Sherrinford, that he had realized his father's problems went deeper than that. His mother had been a distant presence for a while – unlike his father, whose mood swings were abrupt and difficult, her condition had deteriorated slowly and gradually until she was little more than a ghost moving around the house. There had been a lot of coughing as well, more so later than earlier, and the occasional sight of blood on a handkerchief. Somehow Sherlock had incorporated those things into his memories without questioning them, but it was obvious to him now, looking backwards, that both of his parents had been ill for a long time, but in very different ways.

Eventually the train began to slow on its approach to Arundel. Sherlock realized that his heart was beating faster. It had been a while since he had been home. He wondered which had changed the most – it, or him?

Emerging from the station, which was little more than two platforms and a ticket hall at the end of a small country lane, Sherlock saw that a brougham was waiting for them. For a moment he expected to see one of the family servants at the reins, and was desperately trying to recall the names of the ones he remembered, but he was shocked to see that it was Rufus Stone sitting up there above the horses.

'Mr Holmes,' he said, tipping his hat to Mycroft, then, 'Mr Holmes,' to Sherlock, and, 'Master Arnatt,' to Matty. He was smiling, though.

Matty just smiled, nodded, and moved to make the acquaintance of the horse that was patiently waiting for some order to move.

'Rufus,' Sherlock called. 'What are you doing here?'

'Your brother wanted to have a familiar face to call on in case of trouble,' Rufus said.

'Actually,' Mycroft rumbled, 'I was worried what Mr Stone might get up to if I wasn't around to watch over him. Besides, I, rather than the British Government, fund his activities, and as there was nothing for him to do while I took a leave of absence from my work, I decided that he might as well earn his keep working for us here.'

'And so here I am, a trained violinist, swordsman and actor, reduced to the position of general cab driver, luggage handler, bodyguard, cheerer-upper and whatever else you need me to be.' Stone took off his hat and managed a creditable bow, even while seated on the highest point of the brougham. 'On call at every hour of the day or night.'

'You have secured rooms in town?' Mycroft asked.

'No need – your telegram of recommendation arrived

at Holmes Lodge and the butler, whose name is Mulhall, by the way, arranged for me to have a room in an outlying building. I think it used to be occupied by horses, given the smell, but I've slept in worse.'

'Excellent.' Mycroft gazed at his travelling cases, which had been placed in front of the station by the stationmaster's boy. 'Well, these cases are not going to move themselves.'

Rufus smiled at Sherlock and Matty. 'Given that I'm actually not a full-time family servant, perhaps you two fine lads could assist in getting the bags up on the back of this brougham.'

After the bags were secured with leather straps, the three of them crammed themselves inside and the vehicle set off, clattering along narrow country lanes at a speed that Sherlock considered fast and Mycroft obviously thought was perilous, judging by the way he clutched on to the window frame. Matty leaned out of the window, his hair blowing backwards in the breeze.

'This isn't a pursuit!' Mycroft yelled up to Rufus at one point, but it didn't lead to any slowing down of the vehicle. Once or twice Sherlock thought he heard Rufus laughing from up on his perilous perch.

Looking out of the brougham's window, Sherlock found that he recognized bits of the countryside as they passed. He had once fallen off the roof of *that* barn, and had been saved only by a fortunately placed pile of hay. He had once fallen in love – as a twelve-year-old – with the daughter of the farmer who owned *that* farm. And he had stood on *that* hill and turned through 360 degrees, taking in every detail of the landscape beneath him.

Childhood days. He felt so old now, in comparison. Where had that innocence and sense of infinite possibilities gone?

A rough stone wall appeared on their right, and Sherlock knew that they were getting close to Holmes Lodge. This was the boundary of the estate. The brougham continued along the wall for a while, then turned into an ornate gateway. Black ribbons had been tied around the gateposts, and Sherlock felt a quiver of sadness. This was where it started. No matter how he had tried to put off the process of grieving, of understanding that his mother had died, this was where he would have to find a way of coming to terms with the knowledge.

The brougham moved along the gravel path that led up to the three-storey, two-winged building that Sherlock remembered from his childhood, and had dreamed of going back to every holiday from school until he had been removed from the school system and set on a different course by his brother. Someone must have seen them from a window, because the main door opened as they came to a halt and several footmen rushed out to take their bags. One man, white-haired and dressed in a black suit and a black velvet waistcoat, moved to open the door on Mycroft's side. 'Sir,' he said, inclining his head. 'And sir,' to Sherlock. And then, after a momentary hesitation, a final, 'And sir,' to Matty, as he slipped out behind them. 'I welcome you back to Holmes Lodge. I only wish that it could be under better circumstances.'

'Thank you, Mulhall,' Mycroft growled. He turned to Sherlock. 'Mulhall has been taken on here since you last visited. He has had the complete trust of our mother and, for a brief time before he left for India, our father.'

'Then he has my trust as well,' Sherlock said, nodding at the man. 'Thank you for being here at this difficult time.'

With a few quick gestures Mulhall corralled the footmen and got them to take the cases and bags inside. 'Your rooms are all arranged,' he said. 'There is a small afternoon tea arranged for you. Dinner will be at eight.'

'And the . . . arrangements?' Mycroft asked.

'The funeral is set for tomorrow. Given the circumstances, the family doctor was content to sign a death certificate, and the local coroner did not see a need to become involved. The service will be held in the family chapel, of course, and the . . . the deceased will be interred in the family tomb in the grounds of the house. There will be a reception back at the Lodge afterwards.'

'And Aunt Anna – she has arrived?'

'Earlier today, sir. Oh, and Mr Lydecker, the solicitor, is here. I believe he wished to talk about family arrangements in your father's absence.'

'Very good. Thank you, Mulhall.'

The hall was smaller than Sherlock remembered –

or he was larger. He remembered the smell, though, a mixture of beeswax wood polish and flowers. Odd, he thought, how scent could bring back a memory more clearly than sight or sound.

He glanced around. The reception room was on his left, and the dining room on his right. The door to the library was straight ahead, with the stairs running up the wall on either side of it, and then turning through 90 degrees to form a balcony above the recessed library door. Any panelled space on the wall was occupied by a stuffed animal's head: stags, boar, badgers and the occasional whole fish. There was even the head of a tiger that Sherlock's father had sworn blind he shot just outside Brighton but which Sherlock knew he must have bought at some bric-a-brac shop because he liked the look of it.

Matty stopped, staring down at the striped skin of a zebra that was acting as a carpet in the centre of the hall.

'Ain't never seen an 'orse like that before,' he said. 'Is it painted?'

'It's not a horse,' Sherlock pointed out, 'it's a zebra. And no, it's not painted. That's what they look like in the wild.'

'I never heard of a "zebra",' Matty observed. 'What's one of them, then, when it's at home?'

'It's an animal that lives in Africa.'

'What's it look like?'

Sherlock hesitated. 'It looks like a horse,' he admitted. 'A horse with stripes.'

Matty gazed at him critically. 'Well in that case,' he said, 'I'll call it a striped 'orse until I see one of these "zebras" for myself.' He smiled. 'You ought to approve of that,' he added. 'I'm followin' the evidence, rather than takin' someone's word.'

'He's got you there, Sherlock,' Mycroft said as he crossed the hall towards the library.

'Why are zebras striped?' Matty asked.

'I read somewhere,' Sherlock replied, 'that it disguises them when they are in thick vegetation – the sun shining through the trees makes stripes of light and dark, and their stripes mean that they blend in and don't get seen by lions and other predators. That can't be right, though, because everyone says that zebras live out on the plains, not in the trees.'

'A good point,' Mycroft said. He was standing over by the door to the library. 'There must be some other explanation. See if you can work out what it is.' He paused. 'Sherlock, please join me as soon as you have freshened up.'

Sherlock followed the footmen with his cases up the stairs to the room that he remembered occupying in his youth. He was pleased to see that his books were still there, lined up on the windowsill – the Greek legends, the Roman histories, along with the plays of Shakespeare, Marlowe, Jonson and Webster. There was a layer of dust on them that he could see from the doorway, and their pages, facing the window, had been discoloured by the sun.

A washbowl sat on a pedestal near the bed. Beside it, on a chest of drawers, was a large jug.

'There's fresh water in the jug, sir,' one of the footmen said, standing in the doorway. 'Would you wish us to unpack your bags for you, sir?'

'No, thank you – I'll do it myself.'

'Very well, sir.' He turned and left.

Sherlock quickly opened his case and took out a fresh shirt. Stripping his old one off, he splashed water on his face, neck and chest, and dried himself off with a towel. He dressed again in the fresh shirt, then walked to the door.

He turned back to look again at the room. He wasn't sure how he was feeling. He wasn't sure how he *should* be feeling. He'd never lost a parent before.

*Hadn't he?* a voice asked from the back of his mind. Amyus Crowe had grown to become like a father to him, over the short time they had spent together. Crowe had taught him things, the way a father should, and had given him the mental tools he needed in order to start taking responsibility for his own life, holding his hand when necessary and letting him go when that was the best thing to do. Crowe had, in many ways, been a closer father than his real father.

Maybe that was why he was feeling so conflicted. This house was meant to be his family home, but Mycroft was the only member of the family to whom he felt any real connection now. If his real father ever came back from

India, then Sherlock wasn't sure what they would even talk about.

Sighing, he turned away and walked along the balcony towards the stairs. He passed one of the guest rooms, and noticed through the open doorway that Matty was standing in the centre, looking perplexed.

'What's the matter?' he asked.

Matty shook his head. 'I ain't often stayed in a place this big, or this comfortable,' he said. ''Cept when we was in America, before we took the ship 'ome again. I don't think I'll be comfortable 'ere.'

'Put the mattress on the floor,' Sherlock advised. 'That'll make it harder for you to sleep on. Either that or take a blanket and sleep in the stables with the horses, if that makes you feel better.'

'All right.' Matty grinned. 'Good ideas, both of them.'

Sherlock kept going, down the stairs. He assumed that Mycroft and the family solicitor would be in the library, but before he could turn in that direction a small figure appeared from the direction of the kitchens.

'Sherlock, dear? Is that you?'

It was Sherlock's Aunt Anna: small, almost birdlike in her movements.

'Aunt Anna?'

She smiled: a tremulous little smile of greeting. 'Sherlock! How lovely to see you!' She caught herself, and frowned. 'Oh, I didn't mean that, exactly, given the circumstances. What I meant to say was that under other circumstances it would be lovely to see you, but that I'm sorry that we had to meet again under these circumstances, involving as they do the sad passing of your dear mother.' Her face cleared, and then she frowned again. 'Except that, if the circumstances were not as they are, then I might not be here at all, and we would not be meeting.' A pause ensued, in which Sherlock opened his mouth to say something, but she continued: 'Of course, relations within our family had improved a great deal after . . . after that little problem we had with Mrs Eglantine . . . and who is to say that your dear mother, were she still alive, would not have invited me to visit here anyway, after the death of my own husband, dear Sherrinford – who, after all, was her brother-in-law?' She stared up at Sherlock, wide-eyed and suddenly panicky. 'You did hear that your uncle had died, didn't you? I presume that your brother informed you. I would have written, but –'

He took her small, frail hands in his left hand and raised his right hand to her face, putting a finger against her lips to shush her for a moment. 'Aunt Anna, I am very happy to see you again, despite the tragic circumstances, and yes, Mycroft did tell me about Uncle Sherrinford's death. Please accept my condolences. Are you still living at Holmes Manor?'

She nodded. 'The house is far too large for me, of course, but I cannot bring myself to leave it. There are so many memories there. I remember dear Sherrinford saying –'

'I am sorry that I couldn't be at the funeral,' Sherlock

interrupted, knowing that she could go on forever if not stopped. 'He and you were very good to me when I came to stay. I would have been there, but I was –'

'You were in China. I know – Mycroft wrote to tell me. He was very concerned that we knew that, when you didn't come back from London, it was not because we had done anything wrong, or because you did not like living with us.'

'Nothing could be further from the truth, Aunt Anna. You were both so kind to me at a time when I didn't really know what I was doing or what I wanted to be.'

'You seem so much older now,' she said, reaching up to touch his cheek gently. 'China has changed you. You have grown up into someone much stronger. You have the same strength that your brother has, but you have your mother's gentleness as well.' She hesitated. 'I can only hope that you have not inherited your father's unfortunate . . . disposition of the brain.'

'I suppose time will tell,' he said simply.

'Would you tell me more about China? It is a country I have heard much about, but I would be keen to learn more. I hear they have the most exquisite cups and saucers.'

'I would love to sit down with you over a cup of tea and tell you everything that happened to me, but that will have to wait. My brother wishes to see me in the library.'

'Then you must go, of course. I will see you later. There is plenty to keep me occupied here. All the arrangements for the wake, of course – the food, and the drink, and the flowers! The servants here are very good, but they do need a steadying hand, and I am glad to help. It keeps me busy, and stops me from thinking about . . .'

She wandered away, still talking. Sherlock watched her go, smiling. It had been almost a year since he had last seen her, but Aunt Anna was still exactly as he remembered.

He felt a moment's grief as he remembered his Uncle Sherrinford – a tall man with a big white beard who used to quote Scripture all the time. He had been a good man, a scholar, and Sherlock was sad that he had never had the chance to talk properly to him.

He turned and headed towards the library, where his brother was waiting.

His father's library was nothing like the extensive archive of history, theology, geography and other abstruse subjects that had lined the walls of his Uncle Sherrinford's library. Siger Holmes's tastes ran more to leather-bound volumes of various magazines such as *Punch*, along with histories of military campaigns, biographies of various famous military figures, and journals, travel books and ledgers concerning the Holmes family and estate dating back many generations. For a moment Sherlock felt a sickening wrench of nostalgia for those simple days when his father would be sitting at the desk, reading some military history, while Sherlock would lie on the floor with a book in front of him, randomly selected from the shelves. He had read about so many different things there, memorized so many facts by accident, all at his father's feet.

He took a deep breath and pulled his attention back to the present.

Mycroft Holmes was sitting at the large oak desk that Sherlock remembered his father sitting at so often during his formative years. Another man was standing off to one side, staring out of the French windows at the Holmes estate. He was portly, with a florid complexion and a fringe of white hair running around the back of his head. He turned as Sherlock entered, and walked towards the boy with his hand outstretched.

'You must be young Sherlock,' he said. 'I am pleased to meet you. I am –'

'Father's solicitor,' Sherlock said. 'The butler said that you were here.' He cast a quick glance at the man's clothes and hands. He was doing reasonably well, in financial terms, but he was frustrated with the Law and was, in his private life, a reasonably good watercolour artist, mainly of landscapes. He was unmarried, but he had been in a secret relationship with his secretary for many years now – a situation that he was happy with, but which she wished would become more formal. He also had a dog – a red setter, Sherlock thought.

The entire thought process only took a second or so. Sherlock glanced up and saw that his brother was looking at him, smiling. Mycroft knew exactly what thoughts had gone through his mind, and no doubt his brother would have spotted a couple of things that Sherlock had missed.

'A spaniel, not a red setter,' Mycroft said. Before the solicitor could say anything, he added, 'Sherlock, thank you for joining us. Mr Lydecker and I have just been discussing the issues concerning the family, and this house. Sadly, the estate has been allowed to fall into a state of disrepair over the past few years, since our father left for India. Mother was unable to keep on top of it, but she kept the true situation from me, and instructed the servants to do the same. There is much work that needs to be done, and very little money to do it with.' He shrugged. 'Father's Army pay is being paid to him directly, in India, and he appears to be spending it all. There is nothing coming back, and so the estate is forced to fall back on its own resources, like a body which is receiving no food and has to digest its own fat reserves. It is not a situation which can go on forever.'

'Longer for some of us than for others,' Sherlock murmured, glancing at his brother's expansive stomach, which was pressed up against the edge of the desk.

'Even those of us who have had the foresight to lay down substantial reserves cannot live forever on them,' Mycroft pointed out. 'The problem is, with Father in India it is difficult to do anything official. Any documents for signature would have to be sent to him, which means substantial delay and the risk that they might get lost somewhere along the way.'

'The solution,' Mr Lydecker said, 'is for your brother to be given temporary Power of Attorney, until such time as your father returns.'

Sherlock shrugged. 'You have my approval, if you need it,' he said. 'Do whatever needs to be done. I trust you to make the right decisions.'

'Thank you,' Mycroft said simply. He turned to Mr Lydecker. 'Please draw up the necessary documents for signature.'

Mr Lydecker nodded. He turned to go, then turned back. His gaze went from Mycroft to Sherlock, and back again. 'There is, of course, the difficult matter of your sister to consider,' he said cautiously. 'I understand that she is . . . courting. Should she marry, then her husband will arguably have a legal claim on whatever proportion of the estate devolves to her. You need to be sure that he is a decent, honourable man, and not the kind of person who would exploit the situation for profit. Forgive me for saying so, but your sister is not exactly the kind of catch that a handsome man with a job and good prospects would normally consider. She is attractive, I admit, but her character is . . .'

'Sometimes there and sometimes not,' Mycroft interrupted. 'You raise a difficult subject, Mr Lydecker, but you raise it with tact and at the right time, when it is not too late to do something about the situation.' He thought for a moment, then glanced over at Sherlock.

'I would welcome your opinions on this situation, Sherlock.'

'Me?' Sherlock was amazed. 'What can I possibly tell you about the future prospects of emotional relationships, or the suitability of suitors?'

'Firstly, I trust your fine mind, and secondly, you have had an emotional bond with a woman, which is more than I have done.' At Sherlock's obviously puzzled expression he added, 'Have you forgotten Virginia Crowe so soon? You were certainly strongly attracted to her, and she to you. And then there was Niamh Quintillan, in Galway. I thought I detected some mutual attraction there as well. Frankly – and this makes me rather sad – you have a better success rate with the opposite sex than I do.'

Sherlock could feel himself blushing. 'I wouldn't have put it quite like that . . .'

'Of course not, but the facts remain. I suggest that we talk to Emma ourselves, and then talk with this man, James Phillimore, whom she has apparently taken up with. We need to find out what kind of a man he is. In Father's absence, I need to determine Mr Phillimore's intentions with respect to our sister.'

'That will be . . . interesting,' Sherlock murmured.

Mr Lydecker nodded. 'Then it is settled. I will return tomorrow with the documents for signature.' He shook Mycroft's hand, then Sherlock's hand, and left.

'Welcome to the world of adult decisions,' Mycroft said.

# CHAPTER THREE

Leaving the library, Sherlock crossed the hall towards the stairs, intending to head upstairs and check that Matty was all right. He was halfway across the tiled floor when he noticed that the front door was open. It had been closed earlier on, and he knew that the servants wouldn't have left it like that, so Mr Lydecker must have failed to close it properly when he left. Sherlock walked over to the door to push it shut, but through the gap he saw a familiar dark-haired figure walking away from the house, towards the nearest trees. It was his sister, Emma.

On impulse, Sherlock started walking after her. As he walked he tried to analyse his motives. Obviously he wanted to say hello to her – he hadn't seen her in almost two years – but also he was intrigued to see what she was doing. His sister's mind had always seemed to flit from one thing to another like a butterfly moving from flower to flower, and Sherlock had often been intrigued by the strange leaps it made.

He thought about calling out to her, but he decided immediately not to. Emma had always been of a delicate disposition; sudden noises and shocks could panic her, and it took hours to calm her down. Instead he just followed – not secretly, but not noisily – hoping to find some place where he could make her aware of his presence calmly.

Emma headed into the woods that bounded Holmes Lodge on three sides. She stuck to a well-worn path that Sherlock remembered from his childhood. It led to a nearby river, to a point where the river diverted from its fairly straight line and wound through the trees in a near circle, following some depression or crease in the ground, before finding its way back to a point a few tens of feet from where it had wandered off its path. From there it went straight again, continuing on until it left the estate. There were fish in the stream, Sherlock remembered, and otters could sometimes been seen slipping into the water from the banks and hunting them. There was also a deep area just where the river diverted from its straight course, and Sherlock could recall his father, his mother and his brother all warning him, at various times, to keep an eye on Emma if she went near the water at that point. He had never been entirely sure whether they were worried that she might slip in by accident, distracted by the flittering of her thoughts from subject to subject, or that she might deliberately cast herself in while in the grip of some mental weakness. Perhaps both.

Emma kept to the path through the trees. She was carrying something – was it a book? Sherlock couldn't tell at that distance; the sun was blocked by the leaves, and everything was cast in shadow. Sherlock could hear small animals running away from them beneath the leaves and twigs on the ground, and birds falling silent as the two of them grew near, and then starting up their song again after they had passed.

How often had he walked or run through these woods? Sherlock wondered. How many generations of birds and animals had he outlasted? If his footprints could somehow be coloured and preserved for posterity, would there be a single piece of ground around there that was uncoloured?

Eventually the trees thinned out into a large clearing, and Emma emerged into the open air. The river was in front of her – coming in from the trees on the right and going out through the trees to the left, but making a big looping detour in the middle. She sat down on a fallen tree, tucking her dress carefully underneath her.

Sherlock stopped in the treeline and watched her for a while. The book that he thought she had been carrying turned out to be a pad of paper. She kept it open on her lap while she used a piece of charcoal from her pocket to sketch something that Sherlock couldn't see.

He wondered whether it was something *she* could see, or whether she was just sketching something from her imagination. Abruptly he dismissed the thought. He didn't know *what* she was sketching, and without evidence he wasn't going to let his thoughts be guided by the preconceptions of others.

He coughed deliberately, and started to walk towards where Emma was sitting, making no effort to hide the sound of his feet brushing through the grass or crushing twigs and pine cones underfoot. She didn't seem to be aware of his approach, focused as she was on her drawing. Even when he got to her shoulder she didn't react.

'Hello,' he said gently.

She looked up, smiling. Her face was older than he remembered: the puppy-fat of childhood gone now from her cheeks and jaw and replaced with an angular sharpness. Her eyebrows, he noticed, were thick and well-defined. She wasn't beautiful, by any stretch of the imagination, but she was striking.

'Sherlock! There you are! I've been looking for you!'

It was as if she had only seen him a few hours before, rather than years.

'Emma,' he said, and smiled back. 'It's good to see you again.'

'Where have you been?'

'I went away to school,' he said, trying to work out from her expression whether this was news to her, or whether she remembered. 'Then I went to stay with Uncle Sherrinford and Aunt Anna, and then I went to Oxford. Oh, and I went to France, America, Russia, China, and Japan as well.'

'Aunt Anna is in the house,' she said, still smiling.

'I know – I saw her.' He paused for a moment. 'Mycroft is there as well.'

Her smile widened. 'Mycroft! It seems like ages since I saw him.'

Sherlock wondered whether to mention Matty, but decided to keep that information to himself for a while longer. There was no point in overburdening her with new information. He remembered, from his childhood years, that Emma could only process so many new facts at any one time before getting confused. Instead he asked: 'What are you drawing?'

She turned the sketchbook so that he could see the picture. She had blocked out the sweep of the river with broad strokes of the charcoal and was filling in the trees on the other side. She had obviously inherited the artistic abilities of the Vernets – the French family that the Holmeses had married into a few generations back and which had produced several well-known painters.

'It's beautiful,' he said honestly. 'You have a real eye for art. I wish I did.'

'There are beavers,' she replied.

'Pardon?'

'Beavers – in the river. They're building a dam out of twigs and branches and earth so that they can catch fish. They're building it just here.' She indicated on the sketch the point where the river started to curve around in a loop. 'I think that when they've finished, the water of the river will rise over the banks and go across the ground to where the loop straightens out again. After a while, I think the river will go straight across, and this loop will become a circular lake. I don't know what the beavers will do then. Build another dam, perhaps. I try to draw them sometimes, when I am here, but they're quite shy. I think they're getting used to me, though.' She paused, looking past Sherlock and then back at him again. 'I wanted to draw the river the way it is now, so that I can remember it when it has changed.'

Sherlock stared at her, amazed. Her words indicated that she had a good grasp of what was going on. Perhaps she was getting better, getting over whatever it was that had been causing her to be so unfocused.

'What else have you been sketching?' he asked.

'All kinds of things. Butterfly wings, birds, deer . . . oh, and James!'

'James?' Sherlock asked, but she was already riffling through the pages of the sketchbook, looking for the right one. 'James! My fiancé!'

'Mycroft told me that you had a fiancé,' Sherlock said carefully. 'Where did you meet him?'

'I'm allowed to go into town sometimes, with Mother,' she said, still concentrating on the sketchbook. At the mention of their mother, Sherlock felt a sting of grief suddenly run through him. Did Emma know what had happened? Or had she been told, and then forgotten, the way she did sometimes?

'Do you know why Mycroft and I are here?' he asked.

She looked up for a moment. 'I think so,' she replied. A cloud seemed to pass across her features. 'Something happened to Mother, didn't it? She's gone away and she won't be coming back.'

'Mother died,' he said simply.

'That's what I meant. And Father went away, but he *will* be coming back.'

'That's right.'

'Ah – here it is!' She opened the sketchbook at a particular picture. It showed the head and shoulders of a thin-faced young man wearing a stiff collar, tie and bowler hat. He had an extravagantly large moustache and bushy sideburns. Sherlock wasn't sure whether his eyes were too close together or whether Emma's sketch of him was a little off in its proportions. 'He looks very . . . serious,' he said.

Emma nodded. 'He is. He has a job in . . . Arundel, I think.' She thought for a moment. 'He asked me something, but I can't remember what it was.' A moment, then: 'Oh yes! He wanted to know who to ask if we can get married, if Father isn't here. I told him that he should ask Mycroft.'

'That's right,' Sherlock said. 'Mycroft is looking after the family now.'

'That's good.' She nodded seriously. 'If Father is away, and Mother is . . . dead . . . then James will need to look after *me*.' She looked away, across the river. 'I don't think I'm very good at looking after myself,' she said quietly. 'Sometimes I forget to eat for a whole day.'

'Mycroft will want to meet him,' Sherlock pointed out. 'And I think I should as well.'

'Everyone should meet him, if he is going to become one of the family.'

'Indeed. What does he do?'

'Do?'

'How does he make his money?'

'Oh.' Her mind seemed to suddenly jump back to a previous point in the conversation. 'It was in the cathedral!' she said brightly. 'I was sketching some of the tombs, and he was there, looking at the stained-glass windows. He asked if he could see my drawings, and we got talking, and he asked Mother if he could take lunch with us!'

'That was very –'

'How did Mother die?' she asked suddenly, her face serious. 'Had she been ill?'

'Yes, she had. She was ill for a while.'

'I thought she was. She spent a lot of time in bed, and even when she wasn't in bed she was tired a lot of the time. I wondered whether the men had taken her away.'

'The men?' Sherlock asked.

'The faceless men. I see them outside the house sometimes, at night. They hide in the bushes, but I can see them. I wondered if they had come for her.'

Sherlock felt a strange feeling run through him. Emma was seeing things. Did that mean she was getting worse, or had she always seen faceless men, and other things, and just never talked about them?

'Did I tell you about the beavers?' she asked brightly, as if the subject of faceless men had never arisen.

'Yes, you did.'

'They're very industrious. It's like they've got a plan, and they have to stick to it. Did she . . . suffer?'

Sherlock felt a mental jolt as the conversation turned back on itself yet again. 'I don't know,' he said honestly. 'I wasn't here. But if Mother died of tuberculosis, then I don't think she was in much pain, until right at the end. She just got more and more tired until she just . . . gave up.'

'Oh.' The silence lengthened between them, then she continued in a small voice: 'Will there be a funeral, or has it already happened and I forgot about it?'

'The funeral is tomorrow.'

'Can I go?'

'Of course you can.'

'That's good.' She looked up at him, and for once her gaze intersected with his, and he could see his sister's personality in her eyes. 'I get confused,' she said. 'Sometimes days or weeks slip past without me realizing.'

'I know.' He put a hand on her shoulder. 'But you're still my sister, and I love you. Mycroft loves you too – he just won't ever say that. And the only thing that either of us want is for you to be happy.'

'I am happy,' she said, putting her free hand on top of his. 'I'm happy most of the time, and marrying James will make me even happier. Can I sketch you?'

Sherlock smiled. 'Really? Sketch me now?'

'The light here is very good.' She indicated a tree a little way away whose trunk diverted sideways after emerging from the ground before straightening up and heading for the sky. 'Sit on that tree trunk, and don't move.'

Sherlock sat there for a while, looking out across the river as the sun moved in the sky and the shadows lengthened on the ground. Emma applied her charcoal stick to the paper industriously, working with her head bent and her tongue sticking out from the corner of her mouth. She seemed so happy, so self-absorbed. Seeing her like that, it was entirely possible for Sherlock to believe she was absolutely fine, and that it was the rest of the world that was at fault.

Eventually she leaned back and looked at the paper critically, then at him, then back at the paper. 'I think that's it,' she said.

'May I see?'

'Of course.' She held the paper out. He crossed the ground between them and took it, not knowing what to expect.

The portrait was excellent. It caught him in profile, his hair pushed back by the breeze and the sunlight catching his forehead and cheeks. He seemed to be searching for something, looking out into an infinity of time and space. He looked older than he remembered the last time he had caught sight of himself in a mirror. It was as if he was looking at some future version of himself.

'This is amazing,' he said.

'Honestly?'

'Yes, honestly.'

'Then I shall have it framed and put it on the wall of the house that James and I live in, so that I can remember you when you aren't there. I already have drawings of Father before he went away and Mother before . . . before she went away as well.'

'You'll need to do a drawing of Mycroft as well,' he pointed out.

'I'll need a much larger piece of paper,' she said seriously.

'It's nearly dinner-time. Shall we go back?'

'I'll stay here for a little while longer. The beavers sometimes come out late in the afternoon, and I like watching them.'

'All right, but make sure you do come back before sunset.'

'I will.'

Sherlock walked back to the house, strangely reassured by his conversation with Emma, but determined to make the acquaintance of her suitor before too long.

He changed his clothes when he got back, then read for a while before dinner. Someone had found Matty a change of clothes, and he'd had a bath. Sherlock wasn't sure what to make of this new, sparkling clean and neat Matty. He also thought he recognized some of the clothes as having been his when he was younger – and smaller.

Dinner was a strange affair. Sherlock and Mycroft didn't feel like making much conversation, given the circumstances, but Emma seemed to take to Matty and chatted to him through all five courses, which were delivered by a set of servants who all had black bands tied around their arms as a mark of mourning. Sherlock thought that they were probably all wondering what was going to happen to them now, with Sherlock and Mycroft's father gone abroad, their mother dead and their sister apparently considering marriage. There was a fair chance, he realized with a sudden lurch in his stomach, that there might not be anybody left to actually *live* in the house, if Mycroft was working in London, and Sherlock was studying in Oxford. He couldn't let that happen, he thought. Their father needed somewhere to come home to.

'There will be a funeral service at the family chapel tomorrow morning,' Mycroft announced after coffee had been served. 'The servants will all be given time off to attend, of course. The vicar from the local church will come in to take the service, following which Mother's coffin will be interred in the crypt in the grounds of the house.' He glanced at Matty. 'It is the tradition of the Holmes family – several generations are already interred there, as will Sherlock and I be in our time.'

'Not too soon, I hope,' Sherlock murmured. He glanced around, suddenly becoming aware of something. 'Where's Rufus?'

'He elected to eat with the servants. He said –' and Mycroft raised an eyebrow – 'that the conversation would be more entertaining, and the food would be exactly the same, so there was no real choice in his mind.'

'Could James be at the funeral service?' Emma asked, suddenly looking up the table at the two brothers.

'I'm afraid not,' Mycroft said, quietly but firmly. 'It is for family and servants only. However, Sherlock and I will pay a visit to him tomorrow afternoon. I think we need to determine . . . his intentions towards you, and also his suitability as a husband.'

Emma raised her head, as if she was going to argue. Sherlock quickly interrupted to say: 'I'm sure he's *perfectly* suitable, Emma, but Mycroft and I need to talk with him, find out what his prospects are. Father would have done exactly the same.'

Emma didn't look mollified. She opened her mouth to say something, but it was Matty's voice that Sherlock heard next.

'There's some funny people around,' he said, looking at Emma. 'Sometimes they take advantage of people like you – people who see the world as a nice place where the sun is always shinin', even when it ain't. Your brothers are just lookin' out for you – you know that.'

'I do know that,' she said. 'And I am grateful.' She paused, then added, 'I'm still going to marry him, though.'

After dinner Mycroft excused himself to go back into the library. Sherlock decided to go to bed. It had seemed like a long day, even though nothing very much had happened, and he was tired. The strange thing was that although nothing had really happened, he felt like his life had changed since he had woken up. The situation he had been in first thing that morning was not the situation he was in now. He undressed, washed quickly in the fresh water that the maids had provided, and slipped between the sheets on the bed. Within moments he was asleep.

Sherlock was dreaming of his father when he was pulled abruptly from sleep.

All he could remember, as he struggled up into consciousness, was a landscape of bare earth with the occasional dry bush struggling to survive, and a heat-haze that made the distant hills waver like something seen reflected in water. He had been running for his life, and when he looked over his shoulder he could see sword-wielding warriors running behind him. They had turbans on their heads and their huge beards were being whipped back over their shoulders by the winds. The expressions on their faces were all the same: implacable hatred. He knew that they weren't chasing him – they were chasing his father, who was somewhere up ahead – but he had to get to his father and warn him before the warriors could get past. If they found his father first, they would cut Siger Holmes into pieces.

For a few seconds the dream melted into the reality of his bedroom, and he thought that the hand on his shoulder was one of the warriors trying to pull him back, but when he managed to rub the sleep from his eyes he saw that it was Emma, his sister, who had woken him.

'What is it?' he mumbled. 'What's wrong?'

'They're here,' she said simply. 'The men with no faces. They're here in the house again. I think they've come for *me* this time.'

'Emma, you've been dreaming again. Go back to sleep.'

He turned over and was about to pull the blankets back over his body when she said: 'No – I'm not dreaming. They're here! They've come for me!' She sounded scared.

Reluctantly he pushed the blankets away and climbed out of bed. 'All right – I'll go and take a look if it will make you feel better,' he said. 'But I promise you, there's nothing there.' Quickly he pulled on his trousers, a shirt and his shoes. 'Right – where do you think these faceless men are?'

'They were in my room,' she whispered. 'I didn't move, because I didn't want them to know that I was awake. They were very quiet but I felt them watching me. After a while they left to go downstairs. I got up to see if I could get a glimpse of them, but I saw one through the window. He was standing outside the house, looking up. I think he was watching my bedroom.'

'Well, let's take a look and see if we can see him,' Sherlock said, moving towards his own window. He pulled the curtain back and glanced out, not expecting to see anything. The moon was behind the house, and for a moment the contrast between the blackness of the shadow it cast and the bright illumination beyond dazzled him. Once his eyes adjusted, however, he could see the lawn outside, the gravel of the drive, and the corner of the portico that shielded the front door. Across the lawn was a clump of bushes that he remembered hiding in as a child while his father growled like a bear and pretended to hunt for him. The memory sent a pang of nostalgia and sadness through his heart.

He was just about to let the curtain fall back, and tell Emma that she had definitely dreamed about these strange, faceless men, when he noticed a shadow move beside the bushes. Someone was standing there. The moonlight was shining directly on them, but Sherlock couldn't see their face properly. It was as if they had no proper features.

Sherlock felt his skin crawl. Emma hadn't been dreaming after all!

As he watched, the figure stepped back into the shelter of the bushes.

It had to have been an optical illusion. There was someone there, although it couldn't have been a man without a face – that would be nonsensical. Emma's talk of faceless men had set his imagination running, and he had to suppress it. There was no such thing as faceless men. It had been a trick of the light.

He moved back from the window and let the curtain drop back. He wasn't sure if he had been seen or not. His thoughts were racing. Why was someone out there, watching the house? Had there been someone in Emma's bedroom, or had she imagined that but actually seen the person in the bushes and combined the two into a connected narrative? He wasn't sure, but he needed to find out – and quickly.

'You stay here,' he said quietly, 'and lock the door after I leave. I need to investigate further. I'll be back soon.'

'Be careful,' she said, and gave him a tremulous little smile. 'You're my little brother – I wouldn't want anything bad to happen to you.'

He slipped out of the door and closed it behind him. A moment later he heard the click of the lock engaging. The upstairs hall was in shadow. The balcony overlooking the downstairs hall was off to his right, and the other bedrooms to his left, with Mycroft's first. He could faintly hear his brother snoring: a deep, sonorous noise like the purring of some massive jungle cat. For a moment he wondered whether he ought to wake up his brother, but only for a moment. His brother was neither quiet nor fast when he moved around. If there was any chance of intruders being in Holmes Lodge then Mycroft was better off out of it until it was over.

What about Matty? The lad was Sherlock's best friend, and he was both quick-witted and surprisingly strong. His bedroom was on the other side of Mycroft's. Rufus Stone's was next along the corridor. He was perhaps a better choice than Matty – as an agent of Mycroft Holmes he was trained for this kind of thing, and Sherlock had seen him fight before. Aunt Anna's bedroom was on the other side of the corridor, and Sherlock hoped fervently that she would sleep through this – whatever 'this' was.

Instead of waking up either of them, Sherlock moved in the opposite direction: over to the balcony. He stood there for a while, looking down into the hall. The moonlight was shining through a window in the portico, and the tiles of the hall floor seemed to glow white. A leaf was lying on the floor, and Sherlock realized that either the front door was open, or it *had* been open, and the leaf had blown in.

Someone was in the house.

Listening, he could hear what sounded like quiet movements downstairs. His brother was fast asleep, judging by the snoring, and he didn't think it would be Rufus or Matty wandering around down there. The servants should all be sleeping as well – they worked long hours, and the moment they could get some rest they would grab it gratefully. He supposed it could be Aunt Anna, but there was the leaf on the floor to consider. The front door had been opened. That meant there was a good chance that whoever it was downstairs, was an intruder. Or intruders. Thieves, presumably. There was no other reason why someone would break in.

Unless it was something secretive and dangerous to do with Mycroft and his work for the Foreign Office . . . but Sherlock didn't think that was the case. At whatever time in the morning this was, any assassins targeting

Mycroft would have made straight for the upstairs bedroom, rather than hanging around downstairs and making noises that might disturb the house. No, they were searching for something – probably in Sherlock's father's study. Money, maybe, or jewellery.

But the intruders had been in Emma's room, if what she said could be believed. They had been moving around, and had woken her up. He frowned, thinking. If they were looking for jewellery or money, then why choose her room? Or had she dreamed about these faceless men at the same time someone was breaking into the house? Sherlock shook his head. That would have been a coincidence too far.

Whatever the truth, he would only find it out by catching the intruders and questioning them, and he couldn't do that by himself. He needed help.

He moved quietly along the corridor, past Mycroft's bedroom and on to Matty's. He opened the door as quietly as he could, but the slight squeak of the hinges had already woken up his friend. Matty was turning over, eyes wide and mouth opening to ask what was going on. Sherlock quickly moved across the room and put a finger against Matty's lips. He shook his head. Matty nodded, understanding that something was going on and he had to keep quiet.

Sherlock pointed towards the window and held up a finger, then pointed down towards the floor and raised the finger again, then another finger, and frowned. Matty nodded his understanding: there was one person outside and one or two people downstairs. He didn't seem unduly surprised. He threw the blankets off. Underneath he was dressed. He obviously saw Sherlock's expression and he smiled. He was used to sleeping on a barge, or out in the open, by himself, and he had lived the kind of life where he might have to make a run for it at any moment, chased by some stall-owner whose food he had stolen, or some thugs who thought it might be a laugh to pick him up and throw him in a canal. Sherlock should have guessed that he had no use for nightwear. That presumably also explained why Matty showed no surprise at being woken in the middle of the night and told there were intruders around. For him, it was business as usual.

Sherlock pointed at his own chest, then downstairs. Matty nodded. Sherlock then pointed at Matty, then to the wall separating Matty's room from Rufus Stone's, then downstairs. Matty nodded again. He understood: Sherlock was going downstairs and Matty was going to wake Rufus and join him.

They both headed towards the door, and separated – Sherlock moving in the direction of the stairs, and Matty sidling along the corridor wall towards Rufus's room. Sherlock turned to look as he reached the top step and saw that Matty had disappeared and Rufus's door was partially open. There was no noise from within.

He slipped down the stairs silently, back against the wall. Halfway down, he could see the door to the library through the banisters. It was half open, and Sherlock could hear soft sounds of movement from inside. He glanced towards the front door. It, too, was partially open, giving the intruders a means of escape if they were discovered, or giving the watcher outside a way of warning them if he saw anything.

*He?* Sherlock remembered the featureless face of the person outside, and shivered momentarily.

He moved across the hall towards the library, avoiding those tiles that he knew might shift beneath his foot and make a noise. He glanced back towards the stairs, but there was no sign of Rufus and Matty yet.

He got to the library door and edged his head around the frame, just far enough so that he could see inside.

The library was lit by an oil lantern on the desk. By its light Sherlock could see two figures. Their backs were towards him, and they were bending over the desk, seemingly examining papers that were scattered across it. Sherlock didn't remember the papers from earlier – it looked like the figures had taken them from the desk drawers. They were dressed in black coats that fell all the way to the carpet, hiding their feet. They had black leather gloves on their hands that came to points, like claws. Their heads were dipped low in front of them, staring at the desk. It almost looked from behind as if they didn't have any heads at all on their shoulders.

# CHAPTER FOUR

Sherlock glanced behind him, at the stairs again. Still nobody.

He turned back to the library, but his hand brushed against the library door. It swung further open with a squeak of hinges.

The two figures turned to look at the doorway.

Their faces – their entire heads, from where their necks vanished into the collars of their long coats upward – were wrapped in ribbons of material. The ribbons were like bandages, only they were black instead of white. Some of the ends of the ribbons hung loose, waving slightly with the sudden movement of the heads, like locks of hair, only thicker. They had no eyes, only dark holes in the material where their eyes should have been, and their mouths were just lipless black slashes.

Sherlock took a shocked step backwards, but then gloved hands grabbed him from behind, jerking him still further back. He wrestled himself forward, twisting his body. Behind him was the figure from outside – the one he had seen in the bushes. The front door was wide open. Its face was wrapped in black material as well, and its shadowed eyeholes stared pitilessly down at him. He was about to bring his arms up, knocking the figure's hands away, but the figure pushed him, sending him staggering back against the half-open library door. The door pushed fully open and he fell inside, falling at the feet of the two other black-clad intruders.

The three of them gathered around him, staring down blankly, making no noise. Their gloved hands reached down for him like claws.

It was like something from a nightmare.

Before any of the gloved hands could touch him, one of the figures was jerked backwards by something behind it. Sherlock caught a glimpse of Rufus Stone's concerned face, still puffy and flushed from sleep, and then his friend and mentor was wrestling with whatever or whoever it was that he had pulled away. Another of the figures suddenly stiffened, then fell sideways. Matty was standing behind it holding his father's cricket bat, rescued from the hall. The third figure jerked its head left and right, trying to work out what had happened. Sherlock lashed out with his feet, catching it beneath its chin – assuming it even had a chin beneath those black bandages. It staggered away, into the hall, then turned and ran towards the open front door. In the library the figure that Rufus Stone had been fighting suddenly backhanded Rufus across the face, sending him sprawling. It too ran for the front door. Sherlock turned to where the third figure had fallen after Matty had hit it, but it had vanished. Seconds later he heard wood and glass smash on to stone. His head jerked around towards the window that faced out on to the garden. The third creature was standing in front of the window. It had thrown Sherlock's father's chair through the glass, creating a means of escape. It turned its head towards Sherlock, fixing him with its blank, black stare, then jumped up to the windowsill like a vulture, and ran off, its long coat flapping around its body like wings.

In the hall the other two figures had got to the front door unimpeded, and were heading through it to the front drive, coats swirling like dense smoke caught in a draught.

'What the hell was that?' Rufus asked, climbing to his feet and holding his jaw gingerly.

'They were looking at stuff on the desk,' Sherlock said breathlessly. 'Emma saw them and woke me up. She said they were in her room.'

Matty was still holding the cricket bat as if he expected to have to use it again at any moment. 'They were lookin' for somethin'? What was it? An' who were they, wiv their coats and those bandages?'

'I don't know. I honestly don't know.' Sherlock looked at the front door, swinging on its hinges. 'I'm going after them,' he snapped, suddenly angry. 'They invaded this house and rifled through my dad's stuff as if they had every right to do it – but they didn't! It's wrong, and I want to find out what they were looking for!'

He sprinted towards the door.

'Sherlock!' Rufus shouted, but a red mist of fury had descended across Sherlock's vision. 'Matty!' he yelled over his shoulder. 'Check on Emma and tell Mycroft what's happened. Ask him to sort through the stuff on the desk to see if he can work out what they wanted. Rufus – can you secure the house and get the window boarded up? Otherwise they might come back and find a way in again.'

Both Matty and Rufus called out something after him, but he was already heading out of the door into the cold night air and he didn't hear what it was.

There was no sign of the black-clad figures on the drive or the lawn. They had probably managed to get to the entrance and out on to the road. He was about to run after them but his eyes scanned the lawn, noticing the undisturbed beads of moisture on the tips of the leaves of grass, and then looked across the gravel, undisturbed by any footprints. Maybe they hadn't gone that way after all.

He swerved, heading sideways towards the bushes where he had seen the figure earlier, watching the house. He glanced sideways, up at the house, as he ran, seeing the silhouetted figure of his sister in the upstairs bedroom window. He thought she waved to him, but he wasn't sure.

His feet pounded across the lawn, driving deep into the earth and sending divots of grass flying. He could feel the air burning in his lungs and whistling in his throat. He burst through a gap in the bushes into a clearing beyond, sprinting along a path that he remembered from his childhood towards the wall around the estate. There were boot-prints ahead of him on the path: three sets, deeper in the front than they were at the back, indicating that whoever or whatever had left them had been running as well.

The ground was muddy underfoot, and Sherlock found that he was using a lot of energy wrenching his shoes out at each step. It gave him a strange, lurching gait as he ran. His only consolation was that the same thing was probably happening to the people he was chasing.

*People?* A sudden shiver ran down his spine. The black bandages around their faces, the wrinkled leather gloves and the long black coats gave them an unearthly impression, as if they weren't human at all, but some bizarre visitations from another realm. He shook his head to dislodge the thought. It was stupid; whoever they were, they had to be humans – just wearing things that would help disguise them. Maybe they wanted to be mistaken for supernatural entities, or maybe it was just an accidental thing, but they *were* people. Spirits didn't steal from humans.

Branches lashed at his face as he ran. One nearly caught him across the eyes, and he flinched. He raised his hands to protect himself, but that made running even more clumsy, and the springy wood just whipped across his palms instead. For a second his mind flashed back to Deepdene Academy for Boys, where even the slightest disobedience resulted in five strokes of the cane across the open hand. He'd been caned several times over the years – he had a habit of telling teachers that they were wrong during lessons, or climbing over the school's wall during prep so he could get to the local town and visit the library. He was well out of that place. It had been a form of hell.

As this was, in a different way. His face and hands were bleeding, and mud was weighing down his shoes, making him run slower and slower. He suddenly had a vision of the faceless things he was chasing, managing to somehow skim across the wet ground without touching it, borne up by the flapping black wings that he had mistaken for coats. Again, he had to force the thought away. There was nothing supernatural about these thieves.

Really, there was nothing.

The moon kept coming into sight through the tangled branches of the trees and then vanishing again. He was running across a patchwork of brightly illuminated ground and deep shadow, like some crazy chessboard. The constant flickering of the light made him feel dizzy, and twice he had to stop himself from veering away from the path that he was following.

Fortunately he ran into a clearing before things got too bad. The moon shone down on to the space like a spotlight illuminating a stage. In the middle of the clearing was a stone folly: a little pyramid, about twice Sherlock's height, made of grey stone and built by some Holmes ancestor who had either travelled to Egypt or just read a book about it – the family stories were contradictory. Weathering and bad construction had led to some of the stones having cracked, or fallen from their positions to the stone podium on which the pyramid had been built.

The three things he was pursuing were standing in front of the pyramid, waiting for him. The moonlight seemed to sink into the blackness of their clothes and their bandaged heads, and vanish. Their coats hung down to the ground, hiding their bodies. Their shadows, cast by the moonlight, just seemed to be extensions of their coats, making them look even taller and more frightening.

They were holding curved silver knives that glowed in the moonlight.

Sherlock hesitated. It wasn't exactly a trap, but there were three of them, and one of him. Logically he ought to withdraw. The odds were against him.

But they had been in his house. They had been searching through his father's papers. He couldn't just let them go.

Torn between logic and anger, he just stood there on the edge of the clearing, hesitating. Retreat or advance? Fight or run?

The little voice of reason that he could sometimes hear in the back of his mind chose that moment to say something. It pointed out, quite calmly, that even if he could fight one of them for a few minutes, he might be able to tear off a part of their coat, or hear their voice as they taunted him. Any clue might allow him to track them all down later. Even better, if he confidently strode forward to fight one of them, then the others might take the opportunity to run. After all, they were men, not some kind of demon, and he could almost certainly deal with one of them, knife or no knife.

Heart beating fast, he walked forward into the clearing. A line of dead branches lay on the ground, fallen from the trees edging the space. He bent and picked two of them up. He hefted them: they felt good and heavy in his hands, not likely to break if he hit someone with them.

Ahead of him, the shadowy creatures to his left and right spread out, moving to either side and leaving the one in the centre to face him. That one just stood there, waiting. Who knew what was going through its mind?

Sherlock kept walking forward, deliberately not hesitating or showing any sign of fear. When he'd been in China, just a year ago, he had come across a book by a philosopher named Sun Tzu. The philosopher had said, about warfare, that most battles were won or lost before they were fought. Sherlock had assumed at the time he meant that the person with the largest army or the most strength would always win, but the more he had thought about it, the more he realized that it was all about confidence. Walk into a fight believing absolutely that you will win, and you will make your enemy hesitate, and an enemy that hesitates is at an immediate disadvantage.

That, at least, was the theory. Sherlock wasn't sure whether Sun Tzu had ever put it into practice.

Suppressing any nerves and any worry about being hurt or killed, Sherlock walked towards the dark figure. He stopped about ten feet away, hands partly raised to keep the branches up as protection. The holes in the figure's face that hid its eyes were just black against black, but Sherlock could still feel its gaze burning him.

'You broke into my house,' he said, and he was glad to hear that his voice was steady. 'I want to know what you were looking for.'

Silence. The figure just stood there, motionless, but Sherlock was aware that the ones on his left and right were moving to put him at the centre of a triangle.

'Was it something that belonged to my father?' he went on. 'Or were you just looking for money or jewellery, like common thieves?'

Still nothing.

'Do you know how ridiculous you look?' he asked. 'Where did you get the costumes from – a fancy-dress shop? The bandages just make you look like you've been in an accident.'

Sherlock had been in fights before, and he'd had instruction from both Amyus Crowe and Rufus Stone. The key thing, they had told him, was to watch your opponent's eyes. Don't get distracted by his weapon or what he does with his hands – those could be a feint, meant to fool you. Watch his eyes, and read in them when he is committing to an attack.

That was all well and good, but the dark figure's eyes were hidden in the darkness of the holes left by the way the bandages had been wrapped.

If it even had eyes.

Without warning, the dark figure stepped forward and slashed at Sherlock with its knife, bending slightly and bringing the blade slicing up from the level of its left knee to above its head. At least, that had been its intention. Sherlock had seen a tell-tale twitch in the material of its coat sleeve, however, and he had already predicted what move it might make. He twisted and brought his right arm down hard. The branch connected with the figure's right forearm. Its knife spun away, across the clearing. The figure made a stifled grunting noise as it reflexively grabbed its right arm with its left, and stepped backwards in pain.

With the middle figure momentarily disabled, Sherlock whirled around. As he had expected, the other two were closing in on him fast. He took two steps towards the one on his right and lashed out sideways at its head with the other branch. It brought its knife arm up to protect itself, but too late. Instead, it turned the movement into a clumsy stagger backwards, out of the way.

That left the third figure, but by the time Sherlock could turn, it was closing in on him, knife jerking forward. Sherlock tried to twist out of the way but the knife tore through his jacket and scraped along his ribs. He could feel blood, hot and quick, run down his skin. Rather than back away, he clamped his right arm downward, to trap the knife. The figure tried to pull back, and Sherlock went with it, forcing it to move backwards faster and trip over its own long coat. The figure fell back. Sherlock tried to release the knife, bringing his arm up so that he could use the branch against the creature as it went down, but the blade had tangled in his jacket and the figure wouldn't let go. Sherlock was pulled forward, off balance.

Something sliced the air above his head. He could feel its passage, like a cold breeze across his scalp. He turned, still off balance, to see the figure on his right coming at him again, fast, knife raised and aimed at his eye. He twisted, falling backwards on to the figure whose knife he had already trapped. He came down heavily on it, feeling the air whoosh out of its lungs. The thrusting knife just missed slicing through his forehead. He kicked out with both feet, catching the lunging figure in the stomach. It folded up and fell sideways.

The figure beneath him was struggling, and Sherlock brought his elbow back hard. It impacted in the figure's stomach, and Sherlock heard a cry of pain. He rolled sideways, over and over, feeling his elbows scrape on the ground. When he thought he was safe he pushed himself up to his knees, and then scrambled to his feet. Quickly he glanced around, evaluating the situation.

The figure that had started off in the middle was sitting

on the stone podium surrounding the pyramidal folly, still holding its arm. Maybe Sherlock had broken a bone. The figure that had started off to his right was climbing to its feet shakily. The knife that it had been holding was lying on the ground. The third figure was also curled up on the ground, but it was still holding its knife.

Sherlock realized that he had dropped his branches in the confusion of falling and rolling. He scanned the ground, looking for them, but realized they were too near the figure that was curled up. If he tried to retrieve them, it might come to its senses enough to lash out at him.

He glanced over to the figure that had been climbing to its feet. It was standing upright now, and it looked like it was going to come at him again, even without its knife. Desperately Sherlock looked around for some other weapon he could use. Nothing! He might have to fight hand-to-hand with this one.

Something pushed him hard from behind. He fell forward, twisting as he went down. One of the black-clad figures was behind him. As his back hit the ground, the impact pushing the breath from his lungs in a great *whoosh!*, he saw the man pick up the stone from the ground and move closer, ready to bring it down hard on his head. He tensed, ready to try and knock the stone away, but instead he heard shouting.

'Hey! Stop where you are!'

It was Rufus Stone's voice.

'Oy!'

That was Matty's: shorter but more emphatic.

The black-clad figure glanced sideways, then dropped the rock and ran.

Sherlock turned to watch him go, then started to climb to his feet.

'Are you all right?'

That was Rufus.

'I think so,' he muttered.

'What did you think you were doing, chasing after them?'

He shrugged. 'I don't know. It seemed like a logical thing to do at the time.'

'You might have got yourself killed!'

'I might,' he said, feeling the strength seeping back into his muscles. 'Then again, I might get hit and killed by a passing carriage in the street. I can't live my life avoiding *all* risk.'

'There's avoiding risk,' Matty said from beside him, 'and then there's actively seekin' it out.'

'Have they gone?' Sherlock asked.

'They ran the minute they heard us,' Matty confirmed. 'Strange coves, wiv those long coats and that stuff round their heads. They was too fast for us to catch up.'

'They'll be over the estate wall and gone,' Rufus said. 'What we need to do now is to get back and make sure that everyone else is all right.'

Within a few minutes he was back at Holmes Lodge, sitting in a comfortable chair in the library with a cup of tea at his side. His brother was sitting in a second chair, behind the desk, wearing a silk dressing gown that made him look like a circus tent. Rufus Stone was standing by the window, and Matty was sitting cross-legged on the carpet beside him.

'You,' Mycroft said, 'have been in the wars.'

'At least I'm alive,' Sherlock answered.

'Leaving aside the odds of that outcome,' Mycroft growled, 'let us move on to these intruders, and what they might have wanted. Our sister tells us that she has seen them outside the house at night before, but that this is the first time she knows of that they have been *in*side. What, in your estimation, did they want?'

Sherlock shrugged, feeling the muscles in his shoulder protesting. 'I wish I knew,' he said. 'They were searching the desk – that is all I know.'

'I have spent several hours going through every document here, and I can state with absolute assurance that, as far as I can see, there is nothing here in which anyone outside this family could have any interest. Perhaps they were opportunistic thieves, looking for some money or some bonds, or perhaps they thought there was something here but were mistaken. We may never actually know what they were truly after. I will put some of the footmen on watch, I will make sure all outside doors are locked and bolted, and I will inform the police tomorrow. Let us hope that this is the end of the matter, and that these ruffians will not return.'

He paused. 'Well, when I say *I*, what I mean is that Mr Stone will do all of that – if you would be so kind, Mr Stone.'

'My pleasure,' Rufus said.

'And for now, I suggest that we all go back to bed.' He paused. 'After all, we have a funeral to attend tomorrow.'

Sherlock nodded, and headed for the stairs alongside Matty and Rufus, but as he went he glanced back at Mycroft. His brother was still sitting behind the desk, his elbows on its leather surface and his head supported by his hands. He glanced briefly at Sherlock, and Sherlock could tell that he did not necessarily believe that this was the end of it.

Not at all.

The next morning dawned grey and blustery, with occasional squalls of cold rain. Sherlock woke to find that mourning clothes, sober and black, had been laid out for him. He put them on, feeling them scratch against his skin. Pulling off the bandages and the dressing, he found that the wound on his chest had stopped bleeding and was only tender to the touch. It had obviously seemed more impressive than it actually was.

He went downstairs to where a breakfast had been laid out. He wasn't hungry, but he helped himself to some toast and some kedgeree anyway. Emma was there, eating a slice of toast. She seemed to have completely forgotten about the events of the night before; Sherlock decided that he didn't want to remind her. Not today, anyway.

At the sound of a gong being rung, the family and servants assembled in the hall. Rufus Stone was there, standing with the butler and the housekeeper. Mycroft inspected them all, checking in particular that the servants were properly attired, and then he led the way out of the house and along a path that led to the family chapel.

The chapel was an old stone building, partly covered in moss, which looked like the smaller brother of a regular church. It was where the Holmes family had worshipped for many generations. Sherlock himself was finding that the older he got, the harder it was to believe in an all-knowing, all-powerful deity who still somehow needed angels to carry messages for him and praise him for all eternity, but he had to admit that the chapel itself seemed to radiate peacefulness in the same way that the stones of his father's church in India apparently radiated heat.

A coffin had been placed on trestles in front of the altar.

The vicar was a man that Sherlock recognized from his childhood. He never seemed to smile, and his unkempt white hair surrounded his head like a halo. He spoke, and the congregation sang, and then he spoke again, but Sherlock was only there in body. In spirit he was back in time, remembering listening while his mother played Bach sonatas on the piano, or watching while she embroidered a tapestry with a saying from the Bible, or telling her his theories about why dogs would answer to their names being called while cats never did. That was all he had of her now – memories.

He felt like he should be crying, but the tears wouldn't come. Somehow, as he had grown up, that reservoir of tears seemed to have dried up. He wasn't sure that he could cry about anything now – Virginia Crowe leaving him for another boy, his mother dying . . . nothing. The landscape inside his head was dry and barren. He seemed to be observing life as it passed him by now, rather than taking part in it.

Eventually the service came to a conclusion, and the congregation filed out into the sunlight. The vicar led the way along a path through the trees that led to another building. This one was smaller than the chapel, with a lower roof and no steeple, although its door was thick and impressive. This was the family mausoleum, where the bodies of the Holmes family were laid to rest.

*To rest.* Even as the coffin containing his mother's body was carried towards the mausoleum by four men that Sherlock didn't recognize – local parishioners, perhaps, or employees of the funeral director – his mind was mulling over that phrase, and others that people used at funerals, and rejecting them. There was no rest. There was no peace. Whatever was in that coffin wasn't his mother any more, it was just what had been left behind after whatever had made *her* had departed. What was that thing? The soul? The mind? The spirit? Whatever it was, it had left, dissolved like a melting ice cube in the sun. If Sherlock knew anything he knew that death was a one-way process. He was certain that there was no way back. And he was as sure as he could be that there was nothing on the other side. Despite what the vicar had said in the chapel, death was the final full stop on the story of someone's life.

Back at Holmes Lodge, small glasses of sherry and little snacks had been set out on silver trays on a sideboard in the morning room. While the servants headed back to the rear of the house to prepare lunch, Mycroft encouraged Sherlock, Emma and Matty to help themselves. Rufus Stone made as if to go with the servants, but Mycroft called him over.

'Your place is with us now,' he said. 'Help yourself to a glass of sherry. I have something I need to ask you, but for the moment Sherlock and I have something important to discuss.' As Rufus moved towards the sideboard, Mycroft pulled an envelope from his pocket. 'This arrived this morning,' he said. 'Please give me your initial impressions.'

Sherlock took the envelope from Mycroft. He glanced at it. 'The paper is not British, while the stamp and postmark are Indian,' he observed. 'However, the hand that wrote the address is different from Father's, and it is addressed to Mother, not to you.'

'It is from his Commanding Officer,' Mycroft said. 'It was sent on the same day as Father's last letter from India, but it obviously suffered slightly more of a delay in getting here.'

Sherlock pondered for a moment. 'Even if you have already written a letter telling Father's Commanding Officer about Mother, as you said you would, the letter would not have arrived in India yet, and of course given the circumstances any reply would not have been addressed to Mother unless its author was extremely careless or very distracted. Father's Commanding Officer must be writing separately from Father's last letter in order to tell us that something has happened. That means . . .' Sherlock felt a strange sensation, as if the floor was pitching beneath his feet like the deck of a ship. He put a hand out to the mantelpiece of the fireplace to steady himself. 'Father is dead, isn't he?' he said quietly. 'He has died in India, shortly after writing the last letter to us, and we are being informed.'

There was a buzzing in his ears that made it hard to hear what Mycroft said in response, but he thought he made out the words: 'No, Sherlock. Put that thought from your mind. Yes, the letter is from Father's Commanding Officer, but it is by no means a letter of condolence. It is more of an . . . informative letter, telling us about some mission that Father is involved in. Our father is fine, Sherlock. He is fine.'

The ground stabilized slowly, leaving Sherlock feeling

nauseous. The buzzing in his ears receded. He realized that Matty's hand was on his arm. He smiled at his friend in gratitude, and Matty took his hand away.

'Please, read the letter,' Mycroft said. 'Tell me what you think.'

Sherlock pulled the letter from the envelope. For a moment he thought he could smell very faintly some kind of spice, something local to India, perhaps, that had become impregnated in the paper. The scent lasted for a moment and then faded.

He began to read.

# CHAPTER FIVE

Dear Mrs Holmes,

Permit me first to introduce myself, and to apologize for the rudeness of my unexpected letter. My name is Colonel Cyrus Rossmore, and I have the pleasure of being your husband's Commanding Officer. Let me assure you immediately that your husband is in good health. No accidents have befallen him, and neither has any illness (apart from the usual health problems that India stores up for all of us, and surprises us with from time to time).

Major Holmes is a fine officer who has earned my respect, and the respect of the men he commands. He has a fine analytical mind, and a robust physique, which is why he has been chosen to carry out a special mission. This mission means that he will be away from the barracks here for a period of several weeks, if not months, and relying largely on his own resources. I cannot pretend that the mission he will be on is not dangerous, but everything here in India is dangerous to one degree or another – even putting on one's boots in the morning can be fatal if one has not checked first for scorpions that might have climbed in during the night. I say this not to worry you unduly, but to indicate that the risks that your husband is taking on this mission are no more severe than the risks he has been taking day to day.

I would not normally let members of an officer's family know about confidential missions, but this one is an exception for several reasons. One of those reasons is that I wish to warn you that the flow of letters to you and your family from Major Holmes is likely to be disrupted for a period of time. He will not, I am afraid, be in any position to put pen to paper, let alone to find a post box. I would not wish you to be alarmed by any such disruption. As soon as he has returned to us, I am sure that he will write enough letters to fill the gap.

In addition, I would ask two things of you, if I may. The first is that you do not attempt to discover, through any contacts or influences you may have, what mission it is upon which your husband has been sent. The very act of inquiring might trigger some unfortunate questions being asked, and his mission being discovered. The second is that, should anybody engage you in conversation or write to you asking what your husband might be doing in India, or elsewhere, then please tell them that as far as you know he is safe in his barracks, enduring the same conditions that we are all enduring here. Tell anybody who asks that, as far as you know, your husband's situation has not changed. Once his mission is finished, then, for all intents and purposes, this will be true.

*I thank you for your consideration, and I remain,*
*Your most obedient servant,*
*Cyrus Rossmore (Col.)*

Sherlock folded the letter up and placed it back in the envelope. He didn't say anything for a minute or so, letting the words written by Colonel Rossmore filter through his brain and looking for any hidden meanings or any unconscious clues. It was like filtering pond water through a fine sieve, and indeed there was a residue left behind that he inspected carefully.

'A secret mission,' he said finally. 'Something dangerous, presumably undercover. The first question is: why Father? Why not any of the more suitably qualified candidates there in India, or elsewhere? Father has not, as far as I know, been trained in secret work.'

'A good point, and one that had occurred to me immediately,' Mycroft said. 'Perhaps he has special knowledge that makes him an ideal candidate – a foreign language, perhaps, that he learned while out there.'

'The second question is: given the fact that Colonel Rossmore suspects someone might ask questions about Father's plans, does he therefore suspect that there are elements here in England who might be interested in his mission, and might try to stop it? It suggests that this mission goes beyond some tribal politics or a covert spying mission on some Indian dignitary.'

'That is a very pertinent point, and I am glad that you

spotted it as well. I had thought that perhaps I was being too sensitive. It is not, however, the most important point.'

Sherlock considered for a moment, bringing the words of the letter back to the forefront of his mind. 'Oh yes – the Colonel's thinly disguised plea for Mother not to contact anyone in a position of authority here in England – and I suspect he might be thinking of you here, Mycroft – seems to indicate that there might be people actually in the British Government, or the Army, who are, or might be, interested in the mission that Father has been sent on, and even that their finding out might compromise the success of that mission and perhaps even put Father's life in danger.'

Mycroft nodded. His expression was grim. 'I wondered if I was being unduly paranoid, but that is the implication I got from the letter as well. But this makes no sense – how can a mission that originates in India have some resonance that extends all the way back here?'

'What are you going to do?' Sherlock asked.

'I am going to burn this letter,' Mycroft replied, 'and I am going to forget that it ever arrived.'

Sherlock smiled at his brother. 'What you mean is: you are going to ask some very subtle questions in the corridors of power to discover whether something very secret is going on.'

'Yes, that is exactly what I am going to do. Leave it to me – if I discover anything, then –' he hesitated for a moment – 'well, to be honest, if I do discover anything, then I will have to think very carefully about whether or not I tell you, but the presumption is that I probably will. In the meantime, say nothing to anyone.' His gaze moved from Sherlock to Matty, and the boy quailed beneath the ferocity of his eye. 'That means both of you. I do you the favour, young Matthew, of assuming that whatever is safe with Sherlock is safe with you, and vice versa.'

'You can depend on me, Mr 'Olmes,' Matty said firmly.

'I know.' He gestured to Rufus Stone, who was standing over near Emma. 'Now to another matter.' As Rufus joined the three of them he glanced over to where Emma was staring out of the window, watching birds on the lawn. 'Tell me,' he went on, lowering his voice, 'have you made any progress in determining the facts of Mr James Phillimore's life?'

Sherlock stared at his brother in amazement. 'You've had Rufus looking into Emma's fiancé?' he asked.

Mycroft nodded. 'You know how delicate Emma is,' he said. 'Given her trusting nature and her difficulty in distinguishing between what is important and what is trivial, I felt that it was best we knew more about Mr Phillimore. While our mother was alive she could, to an extent, keep watch over Emma, but in her absence someone needs to have Emma's best interests at heart.' He glanced back at Rufus. 'So – what did you discover?'

Rufus checked to make sure that Emma couldn't overhear. 'James Westley Phillimore *is* his real name,' he said quietly, 'and there are records of his baptism in one of the local churches. His family appear to have been quite well respected, although they were considered to be quite stand-offish.'

'*Were* considered?' Sherlock asked.

'His parents are dead, both of an illness that carried them off some ten years ago now, and he has a younger brother to whom he rarely talks. He has few friends, and no hobbies that I can discover. He attends church every Sunday and puts a small amount of change on the collection plate, but I do not think that his Christian feelings go much beyond convention and habit.'

'What of employment?' Mycroft asked.

'He is an engineer by training, with a speciality in artesian wells.'

'What's one of them when it's at home?' Matty was frowning. 'I mean, I know what a well is, cos I drunk from them often enough, but an artistic well? That's a new one on me.'

'*Artesian*, not artistic,' Mycroft explained. 'Named after the Artois province of France, where many of these wells have been dug. The basic principle is simple: if there is a large depression or dip in the ground, covering several miles, then there is likely to be water percolating through the rocks around the rim of the depression that is considerably higher than the middle of the depression. That means, if a well is dug down to the water-bearing rock at the centre of the depression, then the pressure of all the higher water will cause it to bubble up to the surface naturally, rather than having to be pumped up or brought up by bucket. Locating the best place for these wells, and digging them, requires special knowledge and experience.'

'So,' Sherlock said, 'he is a man who has prospects. That's got to be good.'

'Perhaps. I am aware, however, of a number of men of good standing with excellent prospects in London whom I would not trust to look after a dog, let alone a vulnerable girl.' He made a *harrumph!* noise. 'Whatever facts we discover will not answer the key question. We cannot establish his character remotely, no matter how much evidence and how many facts we have at our disposal. We need to talk to the man, take his measure.' He turned to Rufus Stone. 'Have the butler get the carriage ready. We will be making a visit.'

It took half an hour for the carriage to be made ready and for Sherlock and Mycroft to extract themselves from the visitors' room without arousing Emma's suspicions. As the carriage clattered down the drive towards the road, Mycroft's expression was pensive.

'What's the matter?' Sherlock asked.

'I find myself in a curious quandary. On the one hand I want Emma to be happy, and I had also nearly given up hope that she would have any kind of normal life. On the other hand I want to ensure that she is not taken advantage of, that she is not made unhappy by a man who just sees her as being someone who can easily be controlled.'

'But there is more, isn't there?'

'There always is,' Mycroft confirmed. 'Life is never simple. I tend to think of problems in terms of the various levels or orders they present themselves as belonging to. The two things I have already mentioned are what I think of as being of the first order. There is a second order, lower and perhaps less important, but still worth consideration. On that level I would place my personal relief that, if Emma marries this man, then I would no longer be responsible for her – that duty would transfer to him. It is a rather base emotion, I know, but I cannot properly maintain a life and an office in London if I am always trying to make sure that Emma is all right. Set against that, also of this second order, I would place my concern that Mr James Phillimore is using marriage to a weak-willed and easily manipulated girl to gain access to the Holmes family fortune – which is not large, but it is tempting, especially to a man on an engineer's wages.'

'It's a complicated situation' Sherlock agreed. He frowned as a thought struck him. 'I wonder if Amyus Crowe ever wondered if I was a suitable match for Virginia.'

'I think,' Mycroft said carefully, 'that if Virginia had decided that you were a suitable match, then nothing her father said or did would affect her decision.' He glanced at Sherlock sympathetically. 'Have you heard from either of them?'

'Nothing,' Sherlock said. He felt a dull ache in his heart – the remnant of what had once been a sharp pain whenever he thought about Virginia Crowe. 'I think it is for the best. I cannot see myself ever settling down with a girl. There's something about me, Mycroft – I think too much about things.'

'Like Shakespeare's Cassius,' Mycroft said, nodding. 'In my darker moments I have wondered if the Holmes line will die out with this generation. If Emma can find happiness with this man, and if they have children, then at least the family will carry on, even though the name of Holmes will be lost.'

The conversation died out then, and the rest of the journey was concluded in silence.

The carriage stopped outside a detached house of modern construction on the outskirts of Arundel. The cathedral was visible above the trees, reminding Sherlock of the way that Edinburgh Castle had appeared to float above the town when he had visited a few years before.

Mycroft gave the front of the house a rapid examination. 'Hmmm, I see no evidence of female occupancy or visitation. That at least is something. What I do see is evidence of a stable income and a lack of imagination in the owner, along with a mind that takes pleasure in small things such as stamp collecting and ornithology. He is a lonely man, but he does not have a temper. That much is reassuring.'

'And he has the decorators in,' Sherlock observed, pointing to a cart half hidden around the side of the house. A painted sign on the side proclaimed: *Geo. Throop – Painter and Plasterer*.

'That,' Mycroft said, 'was so obvious that I didn't even think it worthy of mention.'

He stepped forward and rang the doorbell. A plump maid opened the door. An odour of fresh paint wafted out past her.

'Yes?' she inquired.

'Is your master in?'

'Who shall I say is calling?'

Mycroft handed her a visiting card. 'Please tell Mr Phillimore that Mycroft and Sherlock Holmes wish to talk with him.'

She disappeared into the darkness of the hall, leaving the door partially open. From inside, Sherlock could hear items of heavy furniture being dragged around. 'Do you think he's redecorating in anticipation of marriage to Emma?' he asked.

'If so, then he is being a little premature,' Mycroft growled.

The door opened wide, but instead of the maid inviting them to enter, as Sherlock had anticipated, a thin man in a rather old-fashioned suit stared at them. He had sideburns that were almost as luxurious as his moustache. His eyes were a very pale blue, and watery, and he held a top hat in his hands. There was dust on it, and Sherlock noticed that the ribbon around it was frayed.

'Mr Mycroft Holmes and Mr Sherlock Holmes,' he said in a high-pitched voice. 'You must be the brothers that Emma has told me so much about. A pleasure, gentlemen, an absolute pleasure.' He extended a thin hand towards Mycroft.

'Likewise,' Mycroft said, shaking the hand.

'I have been considering paying a visit to Holmes Lodge,' Phillimore went on, turning and holding his hand out towards Sherlock. 'But given your recent bereavement – for which I offer my sincere condolences – I thought it best to delay my plans.'

'That was very considerate of you,' Sherlock said. Phillimore's hand was cold and damp, and barely gripped Sherlock's at all – it was like holding on to a fish, Sherlock thought. If the man was an engineer then he was a theoretical one, not one who got to grips with things.

Phillimore half turned and indicated the shadowy hallway behind him. 'As you will have noticed, I have decorators in at the moment. They are making the most terrible mess. I would invite you in, but frankly I am embarrassed at the state of the place. If you will permit me to make a suggestion, perhaps we could take a brisk walk into town and find somewhere we could sit and have a cup of tea.'

'An excellent suggestion,' Mycroft responded. 'Especially if there is cake as well.'

Phillimore smiled. 'I know just the place.' He glanced up at the sky. 'I sense that there might be more rain later this afternoon – I shall just get an umbrella, and give the estimable Mr Throop some last-minute instructions, and then I shall be at your disposal.' He smiled, nodded, and stepped back inside the hallway.

Mycroft glanced at Sherlock. 'I detect no dissimulation,' he said quietly. 'The man seems quite stable and honest, if perhaps a little boring.'

'Perhaps that is what Emma needs,' Sherlock observed, 'a man who is as boring as she is interesting. On balance, that means that between them they would make a stable couple.'

'I am not sure that is how marriage works,' Mycroft observed. 'But then again, I am hardly an expert on the matter.'

As they waited for James Phillimore to reappear, Sherlock let his gaze wander across the face of the house, trying to see if he could replicate the observations that Mycroft had made. He managed all but one.

He turned when he heard Mycroft making a *harrumph!* noise under his breath. His brother was consulting the watch that hung from a chain on his bulging waistcoat. 'How long does it take to get an umbrella and give instructions to a workman?' he growled.

Sherlock wandered up to the corner of the house and looked along its length. He could see a garden at the back, surrounded by tall hedges. It was, all things considered, a nice house. Emma would, he thought, be happy there.

Glancing back at Mycroft, he saw that his brother was getting increasingly irritated. Not wanting to be the focus of an angry outburst, he started walking along the side of the house, past a row of closed and curtained windows. At the far end he looked into the garden. The lawn spread from the stone patio outside the French windows and the closed back door all the way to the tall hedge. Where the patio stopped, flowerbeds ran all the way along the rest of the back of the house. He noticed idly that the rain earlier had left puddles pooling all along the patio.

He wandered back to the front of the house. Mycroft's shoulders were hunched, and he seemed to be muttering to himself.

Sherlock walked past his brother, glancing into the shadowy hall as he did so. He couldn't see any movement. He thought he heard his brother say, 'Fifteen minutes – this is the height of bad manners!' When he got to the opposite corner of the house he looked along its length. It seemed no different from the side he had already looked at. Bored, he walked along this side as well, past more sealed and curtained windows, getting a view of the garden from the other side.

He couldn't hear anything from the front of the house, so he wandered along the back of the house. The flowerbeds, he noticed, were planted with a mixture of roses, rhododendrons and hydrangeas – bushes that had been allowed to grow out, rather than be pruned. He presumed that it was a practical measure against burglars – it would be difficult for anyone to force their way past the thick stems and thorns to get to a window.

The patio was covered in rainwater that hadn't drained away or evaporated. Unwilling to get his shoes wet, Sherlock diverted around the flagstones, walking on the damp and yielding grass, feeling the muddy earth sink beneath his feet, until he got to the side of the house where he'd been ten minutes before. He walked slowly to the front of the house, seeing his footsteps from before outlined in crushed grass and pearl-like drops of water.

At the front of the house he looked sideways again at his brother. Mycroft's hands were balled into fists, and he was muttering to himself.

'Why don't we just knock again?' Sherlock called. 'He's obviously got deep into discussion with his decorators.'

'More likely he's taken fright at the thought of talking to the brothers of his fiancée and he has run out of the back door, never to be seen again.'

Sherlock shook his head. 'There's a French window and a kitchen door at the back, but they are both closed. Based on the pools of water on the patio, the doors haven't even been opened, let alone anybody walking across the flagstones. And in case you thought that he might have climbed out of a window, they're all closed and the only footsteps in the soft earth are mine.'

'Then where *is* the man!' Mycroft cried.

The front door to the house opened wide. Mycroft

turned to face it, mouth opening to say something cutting, but the man standing there was not James Phillimore. It was a smaller man dressed in workman's clothes and a flat cap. He stared down at Mycroft and Sherlock.

'You blokes seen the owner?' he asked.

'We saw him earlier,' Mycroft answered, frowning. 'If you are George Throop then he went to speak to you.'

'Didn't make it,' the man said. 'Ain't seen him. Anyway, we're knocking off for the afternoon. Got to wait for the plaster to dry before we can do anything else.'

'Do you have any idea where Mr Phillimore has gone?' Mycroft demanded.

Mr Throop shrugged. 'Beats me.' He called back over his shoulder: 'Miss Winstanley, there's two gentlemen at the door waiting for Mr Phillimore.' He turned back to Mycroft and Sherlock. 'Best I can do,' he said. 'We've only got an hour for lunch, and this Mr Phillimore is very concerned about punctuality. Very concerned, he is.'

He walked out of the door and past Mycroft. From behind him, two other workmen emerged. Their faces were dusty and their clothes had streaks of paint on them. Sherlock paid particular attention to their heights and their faces as they passed, just in case Mr Phillimore was trying to sneak past them for some bizarre reason, but they were all bulkier than he had been, with rough, unshaven faces. They glanced at him suspiciously, wondering why he was examining them so closely. One of them was cradling his arm, as if it had been injured.

Perhaps something had fallen on it while they were decorating, or moving the furniture.

Mycroft looked to Sherlock as if he was going to burst with indignation. He was about to call out when the maid came to the door again. She looked puzzled.

'Did the master not come out this way?' she asked.

'We have not seen him since he went back inside to fetch an umbrella,' Mycroft said, 'and that was twenty minutes ago. Perhaps you would be so good as to see where he is and remind him that he has visitors waiting on him.'

The maid smiled uncertainly. 'I'll certainly go and see what has detained him,' she said. 'Please wait here.'

'As if we have any other option,' Mycroft growled.

'Perhaps he has a large number of umbrellas, and he can't choose which one to bring with him,' Sherlock said brightly. Mycroft just glanced darkly at him, then turned away.

The maid returned five minutes later. She looked flustered. 'I can't find the master,' she said. 'He's nowhere to be seen. Are you sure he didn't come out this way?'

'If he did, then he possesses the fabled umbrella of invisibility,' Mycroft said. The maid just looked at him, puzzled. 'Did you check every room?' Mycroft went on.

'I did, sir, yes.'

'Is there any other way out of the house?'

'There's the back door,' the maid said, frowning, 'but he'd have to go past cook, and she's been baking pies all morning. She says she hasn't seen him. Oh, and there's the French windows that lead out to the garden from the drawing room, but they're locked.'

'Could he have climbed out of a window?' Mycroft asked.

She looked at Mycroft strangely. 'Why would he do that?'

'We'll worry about the "why" later – could he have done so?'

'I suppose so,' she said, 'but I doubt he could have closed and locked the window behind him, and that's how they all are. There's no reason to have a window open in this weather.' She hesitated. 'I did find this,' she said, holding up a handkerchief. Sherlock could see a trace of blood on it, fresh and red. 'Maybe the master had an accident.'

'Maybe he did, but where is he?' Mycroft pursed his lips. 'Sherlock, you wait here,' he said. 'I shall make a perambulation of the house and look for evidence that Mr Phillimore has left in a hurry and in a manner that avoids passing us.'

'Remember the pools of water on the patio,' Sherlock said, remembering his own perambulation a few minutes before. 'They would have been disturbed if the French window had been opened and someone had walked across the patio, but they appear untouched. The patio is too wide to jump across, as well.' He thought for a moment, trying to recollect what he had seen. 'The windows all let out on to flowerbeds with bushes, and there is no sign that the bushes have been disturbed. Also, someone jumping down from a window would have left marks in the wet lawn, but there were no such marks. The same would be true if anybody had used a ladder to reach a window from the lawn.'

'I told you, gentlemen,' the maid said, 'all the windows are closed and locked, including the French ones.'

'It's not that I do not believe you, Sherlock,' Mycroft said, 'but evidence is best checked first hand.' He walked off, disappearing around the corner of the house. Sherlock stood there, staring at the outside of the house and trying to work out what was going on. The maid stood in the doorway, obviously unsure what to do.

Mycroft returned from the opposite direction a few minutes later. 'You are, of course, correct,' he said. 'There would have been indications in the puddled water, the lawn or the flowerbeds if someone had left the house other than through this door, but I see no such marks. Besides, I noticed rain on the window frames that would have drained away if the windows had been opened.' He shook his head. 'This really is a puzzle. I can only assume that Mr Phillimore is still in the house but is hiding in a cupboard or under a bed.'

'If he doesn't want to see us that badly,' Sherlock said, 'then perhaps we ought to leave him to his own devices.'

Mycroft raised an eyebrow. 'If he doesn't want to see us that badly, then perhaps we ought to determine the reason why.' He nodded decisively. 'We shall search the house,' he announced to the maid. Indicating the handkerchief which she still held, he added: 'Some harm does appear to have come to your master, and we need to determine what, and check whether he needs help.'

'Oh, I don't think the master would approve of people ransacking his house without his permission,' she said, raising a hand to her mouth.

'Then he can come out from hiding and tell us so himself,' Mycroft said. He would have pushed past her, but his bulky frame filled the doorway, and she retreated before him like a dinghy before a steamship.

Sherlock followed his brother into the house. The hallway was small and carpeted, with a coat stand, an umbrella stand and a table. Mr Phillimore's dusty top hat sat on the table, where he had probably set it down when he went back inside. Stairs on the left led upward, and there were several doors leading to various rooms. The smell of paint and plaster was stronger inside than out.

'You search upstairs first,' Mycroft said. 'I shall stay here so that he does not sneak past us. Check all wardrobes and cupboards. Check under beds. Look for trapdoors that lead up into the attic.'

Not without some misgivings, Sherlock went up the stairs. He felt edgy about searching another man's house without his permission, but something was obviously wrong.

There was only one floor upstairs. The hall had nothing in it but a roll of carpet and some furniture, which had obviously been moved out of one of the three bedrooms to allow the decorators access. Sherlock quickly but thoroughly searched the three bedrooms and the one bathroom.

Two of the bedrooms had dust sheets thrown across the beds, the chairs and the dressing tables. Each room was neat and tidy, free of dust and free of any human habitation. With some misgivings Sherlock opened the various wardrobes and cupboards that he found, but there was nothing in them but clothes of a rather old-fashioned cut. Mr Phillimore was not hiding behind the curtains either. The space under the beds was empty as well, apart from some slippers and a bedpan. He also looked under the dust sheets in case Mr Phillimore was sitting very quietly, hidden beneath one of them, but of course he was not. Sherlock also checked all of the windows, but they were shut and locked. Glancing down to the garden beneath, he could still see no trace of footprints or any other sign that someone had left the house that way.

Hands on his hips, he looked around in frustration. Where on earth could James Phillimore have gone?

# CHAPTER SIX

One of the bedrooms was empty of furniture. The carpet had also been removed, leaving bare floorboards, and the curtains had been taken down as well. Sherlock remembered seeing the carpet rolled up in the hall. Three of the bedroom walls had been freshly plastered and were still damp, while the fourth wall had been covered with floral wallpaper. The pattern wasn't to Sherlock's taste – it seemed old-fashioned, but then so did James Phillimore. A bucket of plaster, a bucket of wallpaper paste, several more rolls of wallpaper and some tools had been left in one corner. Sherlock took a quick look around, but there was nowhere there for a man to hide – even a man as thin as his sister's fiancé.

In the hallway, just outside the bathroom, a trapdoor gave access to the roof space. It was bolted shut. Sherlock was about to leave it, but then it occurred to him that perhaps James Phillimore had climbed up into the attic, and then someone – perhaps the maid – had bolted the trapdoor behind him and removed whatever he had used to climb up there. That would mean that there was some kind of conspiracy to hide Mr Phillimore, but Sherlock was beginning to run out of options as to where the man could have gone. He retrieved a footstool from one of the bedrooms and used it to gain access to the trapdoor. He threw the bolt and pushed it upward. Dust fell into his eyes. The space revealed was dark, but when he stuck his head up into the attic and waited for a few moments his eyes got used to the darkness and he began to see thin beams of light slanting across from gaps in the brickwork and the slates of the roof. They revealed that the attic was completely empty. There was no space, no area of shadow, where James Phillimore could hide.

Sherlock bolted the trapdoor again, climbed down and took the footstool back to the bedroom where he had found it. Slowly he went back downstairs to where Mycroft was waiting impatiently. The maid was still standing near him, obviously unwilling to leave a dangerous madman alone.

'Well?' his brother snapped.

'Nothing,' Sherlock said. 'I looked everywhere.'

Mycroft shook his head in frustration. 'He must be somewhere!' He turned to the maid. 'Is there a cellar in this house?'

'No, sir.'

He sighed. 'Sherlock – search the rooms down here as well. Check chimneys and sideboards. Leave the kitchen until last.'

Sherlock did as he was told, searching the front room, the drawing room and the dining room. Each was decorated with reasonably old furniture and engravings of buildings and bridges – obviously things that appealed to James Phillimore's engineering training. He checked any cupboard space that was large enough to hide a man, and most of the ones that weren't, but they were all empty apart from the usual detritus of brushes, brooms and stored Christmas decorations. He also checked the windows carefully, paying particular attention to the French windows that led out to the garden, but they were all locked and the space behind the curtains was empty. The puddles of water, the bushes and the lawn outside appeared as undisturbed from this direction as from outside, and there was sufficient dust on the frames to suggest firstly that Mr Phillimore had not left via any of them and secondly that his maid was skimping on her duties.

He returned to his brother in the hall. The maid had finally gone. 'Nothing,' he said. 'Absolutely nowhere that a man could hide, and yet no way he could have left.'

'There is only one remaining possibility,' Mycroft announced. 'He must have left via the back door, and the cook is lying when she says that she didn't see him.'

'Or the cook is Mr Phillimore in disguise,' Sherlock pointed out, 'and it is the maid who is lying.'

Mycroft led the way to the back of the house, squeezing through the narrow doorway into the kitchen. The cook – a large woman with forearms like a dock worker – was rolling pastry out on the kitchen table. The maid was standing on the other side of the table, and judging by the glower on the cook's face the two of them had been talking about Mycroft's invasion of the house. On the far side of the room was a doorway leading, he presumed, to a pantry, and then to the garden.

'What's all this about then?' she challenged him. 'Coming into a gentleman's house all unannounced and uninvited. We should call the police, that's what we should do!'

'Be my guest,' Mycroft said. 'There is something strange going on here, that much is obvious. Now, do you maintain that your master did not come into this kitchen and leave the house by that back door?'

'I do,' she said, squaring up to him, rolling pin raised in defiance. 'And any man that says otherwise is a liar!'

Sherlock glanced past her to the floor that lay between her and the pantry. 'There's flour on the floor,' he pointed out. 'Mr Phillimore couldn't have left that way without leaving footprints.'

'Unless this good lady here scattered the flour after he had passed,' Mycroft pointed out.

The cook seemed to swell up with anger. Sherlock pushed past her quickly, before she could explode, and went into the pantry. The shelves were stocked with food, and there was the door leading out into the back garden that he remembered seeing earlier. He glanced out through the glass. The door opened out directly on to the lawn, but there were still no marks to indicate that anybody had walked in the soft earth, and the droplets of water from the earlier rain still clung to the blades of grass. 'It's no good,' he said, returning to the kitchen. 'I can't see any trace of anyone going out this way.'

'Then where has the man gone?' Mycroft demanded, thudding his cane down on the tiles of the kitchen floor. 'Where can he possibly have gone?'

Sherlock closed his eyes and thought for a moment, trying to break through the puzzle that had been presented to them.

'Do you agree with me that none of the decorators who left the house could have been the man we saw on the doorstep?' he asked, eyes still closed.

'I do,' his brother answered. 'They were shorter, and wider at the shoulders, and the physiognomy of their faces was completely different to that of Mr Phillimore.'

'It occurs to me,' Sherlock said, 'that we don't actually know if the man we spoke with *was* Mr Phillimore. The maid went back into the house, and then he appeared, but we never saw the two of them together. The same with the cook here.'

'If you are suggesting that either of these ladies here is Mr Phillimore in some kind of disguise then I would suggest you rethink your theorizing. They are both far too short, and neither of them is thin enough.' He glanced critically at the maid and the cook. 'I suppose that there could be some padding involved, but the height of the gentleman who spoke to us outside would be impossible to disguise – and he was not wearing anything that would have made him look taller. I gave his shoes a thorough investigation, as I do with everyone I meet. Shoes can be very instructive, I find.' He paused for a moment. 'I grant that the man we spoke to might not have been Mr Phillimore, as we were never formally introduced, but whoever he was, he is now missing.'

Sherlock glanced at the maid. 'Do you have any photographs of Mr Phillimore around the house?' he asked.

'I believe there is one in the drawing room,' she said dubiously. After a long moment she added: 'Would you wish me to get it for you, sir?'

'If that wouldn't be too much trouble.'

The maid scurried off. The cook glanced at Mycroft and Sherlock, sniffed, and said: 'If you don't mind, gentlemen, I'll return to my duties. These pies won't make themselves.'

'Let us get out of your way,' Mycroft said. The two of them walked back to the hall just as the maid was emerging from the drawing room. She held a small photograph in her hand. 'This is the master,' she said, handing it across.

Sherlock and Mycroft both checked the photograph. It showed the man they had spoken to outside the house – the tall man with the sideburns, the moustache and the watery blue eyes – standing beside a seated woman. The woman was their sister, Emma.

'Evidently this relationship is important to Mr Phillimore,' Mycroft observed, 'if he went to the expense of having a photograph taken of the two of them together.'

Sherlock had noticed something else in the image. 'Emma looks happy,' he said quietly. 'More than that, she looks contented.'

'Does she?' Mycroft replied. 'I will take your word for it.'

'At least we know that the man we met was James Phillimore,' Sherlock observed.

'That would appear to be the case, but the question remains – where *is* the man?'

'And the other question,' Sherlock pointed out. 'Why has he disappeared so suddenly?'

Something was nagging at the back of Sherlock's mind. He took a moment to let it come to the forefront, where he could consider it. He had seen something – something upstairs.

'The roll of carpet!' he announced.

'There was a roll of carpet upstairs?' Mycroft nodded. 'I presume that there was carpet missing from one of the bedrooms?'

'There was!'

'Then Mr Phillimore must be inside the roll of carpet,' Mycroft announced. 'Once the impossible has been eliminated from your mind, then whatever remains must be the truth, however improbable it seems.'

The two of them rushed up the stairs to the hallway. Sherlock indicated the roll of carpet that had been left running alongside the skirting board. 'It doesn't look large enough to hold a man,' he pointed out.

'Perhaps not, but appearances can be deceptive. Remember that Mr Phillimore is tall and thin.'

'Not that thin.' Sherlock bent down and took hold of the roll. 'Only one way to find out,' he observed, and pulled. The carpet unrolled across the hallway.

There was nothing inside but dust.

'Well, the thought was good,' Mycroft observed as Sherlock rolled the carpet back up again.

Sherlock stayed crouched down for a moment, hand resting on the carpet. 'There is still something bothering me,' he said slowly. 'Something I saw up here.'

'I have sometimes observed that distracting the mind with a different subject can often allow it to make connections that one might otherwise have missed,' his brother observed. 'We do not understand the workings of the mind in the same way that we understand the workings of the body, which is a great shame. The man who could explain how the brain works would, I think, become famous. How is Charles Dodgson, by the way?'

The abrupt change of subject threw Sherlock for a moment. 'He is . . . as well as he ever is, I suppose,' he said. 'He still talks of beading rooks rather than reading books, which gives you an indication of how he plays with words, but he has a fine brain.' As he said the words it was as if a light suddenly illuminated his brain. 'Of course! The wallpaper!'

'It worked,' Mycroft said with a self-satisfied tone in his voice. 'What have you realized?'

Instead of explaining, Sherlock sprang to his feet and rushed into the bedroom that was in the process of being decorated. Mycroft followed him.

'Look around,' Sherlock said excitedly. 'What strikes you?'

'It strikes me that the plastering work is slapdash, and that the wallpaper is not straight,' Mycroft observed. He frowned. 'It also strikes me,' he went on slowly, 'that decorators usually let the plaster dry on a wall before putting the wallpaper on, but here they appear to have started papering the wall before the wall is ready.' He pointed. 'Look, the wallpaper has already started to peel back at the corners because the wall underneath is damp.'

The two of them looked at each other.

'Can we?' Sherlock asked in a hushed voice.

'Look at it this way,' Mycroft replied. 'Either we will be saving a man from a bizarre and unusual imprisonment, and possibly saving his life into the bargain, or we will be ruining his house and destroying our sister's chances of a happy marriage.'

'So – the stakes are pretty high then.' Sherlock glanced at his brother's face. Mycroft's expression was serious. 'How sure are we about this?'

'As I said – when the impossible has been eliminated from your mind, then whatever remains must be the truth, however improbable it seems. It is apparently impossible for James Phillimore to have left this house, therefore he is still inside. You have checked all the rooms and the attic, and not found him. He must, therefore, be *between* the rooms. It is the only option left.'

Sherlock nodded. Taking a deep breath, he leaned forward and took hold of a corner of the new wallpaper, then pulled.

The wallpaper peeled away from the wall easily. The plaster underneath was indeed still damp, like the plaster on the other three walls. Some of it came off on the back of the paper, revealing fresh horizontal wooden laths that had been nailed between vertical wooden beams.

'A decent decorator does not put wallpaper on wet plaster,' Mycroft said. 'Not unless he is trying to cover something up. Can you pull some of those laths off the beams?'

Sherlock grabbed the discarded hammer from the floorboards and inserted the chisel-like end of the head into the gap between two laths. He pulled hard. The lath pulled out from the wall with a squeal. Sherlock quickly pulled the next lath out.

The sun, shining through the glass of the bedroom window, illuminated the space between the laths of this wall and the wall of the next door bedroom.

And the frantic face of Mr James Phillimore.

He had been gagged with a dirty cloth that had been tied behind his head. Only his face was visible, but Sherlock assumed that his hands and legs had been tied as well. His eyes bulged and he was desperately jerking his chin: the only part of his body apart from his eyes that he could move.

'Get him out,' Mycroft said darkly.

Sherlock tore at the laths, flinging them to one side as each one came free. They revealed more and more of Mr Phillimore's dust- and plaster-covered suit. Ropes were tied around his chest, pinioning his arms, and around his legs.

As Sherlock removed more and more of the laths, James Phillimore fell forward. Sherlock and Mycroft caught him and pulled him out of the space in the wall where he had been hidden. They laid him on the floorboards and Sherlock pulled the gag from his mouth.

'Those men are *not* real decorators!' he cried.

'I believe we had already deduced that for ourselves,' Mycroft said drily. 'Can you tell us what happened?'

'I went to talk to Mr Throop, but he assaulted me, knocking me unconscious. When I woke up, a few moments later, he and his men had tied me up and were fastening the laths across the wall. I heard them quickly slapping some plaster across the laths, and then I think I passed out again. I really don't understand – what on earth is happening? I was not *that* unhappy with their work.'

'First let us get you downstairs and get some hot, sweet tea inside you,' Mycroft said. 'Once you have recovered from your ordeal we can talk about the reasons that Mr Throop – if that is even his name – might have for imprisoning you in such a bizarre way. Sherlock – please untie Mr Phillimore's arms and legs and help him downstairs.'

A few minutes later Mr Phillimore was slumped in a chair in his drawing room, and Sherlock had bullied the cook into making a pot of tea. Mycroft and Sherlock sat on either side of Mr Phillimore while he sipped gratefully at the tea. His jacket and trousers were covered in dust, and there were drips of plaster in his hair and down his face. His hair stuck up wildly.

'Now,' Mycroft said, settling back in a chair that was too small for him. The arms squeezed his bulky body around his hips, pushing his stomach up like a baking loaf that was spilling over the edge of its tin. 'Tell us everything. Leave nothing out: the smallest, most insignificant fact may prove to be vitally important.'

'Very well.' Phillimore raised a hand to his forehead. 'The two of you had arrived outside the house. I came out to talk to you. We arranged to go into town for a spot of afternoon tea. I went back into the house to retrieve an umbrella, as I was of the opinion that it might rain. As I was pulling the umbrella from its stand the decorator, Mr Throop, came down the stairs. I said that I was going out. He frowned – I remember that distinctly – and asked where I was going. I told him in no uncertain terms that it was none of his business where I was going. He insisted on knowing, and was very rude about it as well. I was of a mind to tell him that it was none of his business, and that he was employed to decorate my house with as much professionalism and as little fuss as possible rather than to ask impertinent questions, but in order to facilitate my leaving the house rapidly I decided to answer his question. Given that my affairs of the heart, and my integration into your family, are none of his business, I merely told him that I had a business meeting. The news seemed to disturb him. With the arrogance typical of the working class he presumed to ask me what kind of business meeting I had, with whom I was meeting and what I would be discussing. At that point I told him that *my* business was none of *his* business, and that I would be grateful if he could return to his decorating activities forthwith. At which point he descended the remaining stairs, walked up to me and punched me firmly on the chin.' Phillimore raised a hand to his chin and stroked it gently. 'I have never,' he said, offended, 'been punched before. Not at school, not in my apprenticeship, not on any of the engineering projects I have worked on. *Never*.'

'What happened after he punched you?' Mycroft asked.

'What happened was that I was knocked unconscious for a few minutes. I awoke to find myself tied up in the spare bedroom upstairs. I was lying on the floor, and they were standing over me, looking down.'

'Who exactly was there?' Mycroft asked, leaning forward.

'All of them! Every single decorator that I had employed to remodel my house was there in the room, and a fierce lot they looked too.'

'So the whole crew was in on it,' Mycroft said, glancing at Sherlock. 'It seems obvious, but it is worth checking.' He turned back to Phillimore. 'And then what?'

'Mr Throop kept asking me questions. "Where is the letter?" he said. "What have you done with the letter? Has the letter arrived yet?" I tried to tell him that I didn't know anything about any letter, and that no post had arrived for several days, but he didn't seem to believe me. "We've been waiting for days for it to turn up!" he said. "But it ain't!" He spoke in a very common manner. Very lower class. "Is there an office it could have gone to?" he asked, but I told him there was not. My office is here, in the house. He had the temerity to search me, would you believe – rummaging with his dirty hands through all my pockets, but he didn't find what he was looking for. Eventually he and his men decided that I didn't have this letter they were looking for, so they shoved me into a hole in my own wall! I tried to protest, but the brutes had gagged me as well! All I could do was to make noises like some kind of animal while they were manhandling me and then sealing the hole up with laths and plaster.' He closed his eyes and placed the back of his hand against the eyelids. 'I feared for my life, Mr Holmes. I do not mind telling you that I thought I was about to meet my Maker. I could hear the plaster being applied to the laths, sealing me in. I could smell it.' He took his hand away, opened his eyes and stared at Mycroft with an offended expression on his face. 'I have to say that the plastering they were doing was very shoddy work. They were just slapping it on willy-nilly. I employed them specifically because they assured me that they treated decoration as an art rather than a trade, but I did not get that impression from the way they were working earlier today.'

'If it's any consolation,' Sherlock said mildly, 'they were probably more concerned with hiding you away than doing a good job.'

'Yes,' Mycroft said, 'and the question *why* they wanted to hide Mr Phillimore here away is something we shall come back to, but for the moment – what happened next?'

Phillimore thought for a moment. 'It was dark. The laths and the plaster blocked out all the light. I tried to struggle, to break myself free, but the ropes had been tied too tight. I was having difficulty in breathing, as well. My mouth was obstructed, so I was breathing through my nose, but my sinuses are often inflamed and swollen due to various allergies, and often I have no choice other than to breathe through my mouth.' He glanced at Mycroft apologetically. 'I do snore terribly,' he said. 'I wake myself up sometimes with my snoring. Do you think Emma will mind, once we are married?'

'I do not know and I do not care,' Mycroft said with a tone of suppressed impatience at the way Phillimore's train of thought kept wandering. 'Please continue with your story!'

'I thought I was going to suffocate! I really did!' Phillimore said. 'I was concentrating on trying to get as much air through my nose as possible, but stress makes my nostrils close up, and –'

'The story!' Mycroft snarled.

Phillimore's head jerked back as if he had been slapped. 'Very well,' he said, offended. 'You don't have to be so unpleasant about it – I have had a most disagreeable experience.' He took a breath. 'Anyway – I was trying to take breaths through my nose, as I said, but I distinctly heard the sound of wallpaper paste being applied to the wall, and then wallpaper being hung. I could even hear the sound of the knife they used to cut the paper where it overlapped the skirting board at the bottom of the wall and the architrave at the top.' He shook his head. 'How Mr Throop can claim to be a reputable decorator when he hangs wallpaper on damp plaster I really do not know. If I see him again I shall have strong words with him.'

'Undoubtedly,' Mycroft said, with some restraint.

'I do not know how long I was there, in the dark,' Phillimore continued. 'Part of me was hoping that this was some jape, some joke that was being played on me. Perhaps some old colleagues of mine from the engineering profession had decided to trick me, and had paid these men to help. However, another part of me was of the opinion that I was being left there to die, and that part was definitely getting stronger the longer this went on. And then, just when I thought that I was doomed to be incarcerated in my own wall for eternity, you arrived.'

Mycroft leaned back, as much as he was able, in his chair, and glanced at Sherlock. 'What strikes you about this situation?' he asked.

Sherlock thought for a moment. 'There are several things,' he said eventually. 'Ignoring this mysterious letter for a moment, as we have no idea what it might be or why Mr Throop and his men might want it, I think there are five questions that I would want to have answers to. Firstly, and most importantly, why did they act *now*? They have been working here for several days without questioning Mr Phillimore. What set them off?'

'And your answer?' Mycroft asked.

'It was us, wasn't it?' Sherlock said, realizing. 'It must have been. We were the only new thing!'

'Indeed.' Mycroft glanced at Phillimore. 'Or, more precisely, it was probably the fact that Mr Phillimore told Mr Throop that he had a business meeting. Mr Throop made the assumption that this meeting had something to do with this important letter, that Mr Phillimore was going to discuss something with us that had to do with this letter, and so he decided to act.' He paused. 'What is the next thing that strikes you?'

'The fact that the gang wanted to keep Mr Phillimore alive, rather than kill him.'

Mycroft nodded. 'Very good. And your answer?'

Sherlock had already considered this, and had his answer ready. 'It was because they hadn't finished with him.'

'Correct. They wanted to be able to come back and question Mr Phillimore further, once we had left of our own accord. They obviously wanted this letter, and they were willing to go to extreme lengths to get it. Perhaps they thought that Mr Phillimore was lying to them, but they knew we were waiting outside and so they put him somewhere safe while they went away for a while and waited for us to go. Next?'

'Why did they pretend to be decorators in the first place?'

'Quite right. That one is obvious, however.'

Surprisingly, it was Phillimore who answered. He was watching the interplay between Sherlock and Mycroft like a cat watching a table-tennis match. 'I presume,' he said, 'that they wanted to have free and easy access to my house so that they could search for the letter if it had arrived, or intercept it when it *did* arrive.'

'Very good, Mr Phillimore. That tells us they knew that an important letter was due, and they placed themselves here at the right time.' He glanced at Sherlock. 'That allows us to make a significant deduction, by the way.'

Sherlock thought furiously. 'They couldn't guarantee that Mr Phillimore would take them on instantly,' he said slowly. 'That means they knew they had some time in hand. So – the letter wasn't sent from anywhere in

England, otherwise it would have arrived too quickly for them. It was sent from abroad, meaning that they had time to get in place to intercept it.'

'Very good.'

Sherlock looked over at where Phillimore was slumped on the sofa. 'How did you employ these men?' he asked.

'A pertinent question,' his brother rumbled.

Phillimore frowned. 'They turned up on the doorstep. They said that they were in the neighbourhood, and that another job had been cancelled suddenly. They offered me a discount if I had any work that needed to be done. They said they could turn their hands to anything – exterior building, gutter cleaning, chimney clearing, interior decoration, gardening . . . I had been thinking about having the house redecorated ready for . . .' He paused, and looked over at Mycroft apologetically. 'Ready for my dear Emma to move in as my wife, if you gave your blessing to our union. They turned up at just the right time, so I employed them on the spot.'

Mycroft looked at Sherlock, but didn't open his mouth; Sherlock, knowing what the question would have been, said: 'They took advantage of Mr Phillimore's good nature, and his desire for a bargain. Everyone has something about their house that they want correcting or improving. They knew if they offered a low enough price that he would agree to employ them.'

Mycroft nodded. 'There are certain rules in life that should be followed,' he said. 'Never take the first cab that turns up is one of them, never employ a workman who turns up unannounced at your door is another one.' He shrugged. 'Never mind. That leaves us with the most important question of all.' He turned towards Phillimore, and the man quailed under the intensity of his gaze. 'What is it that you do, or who do you know, that makes it so important that these men wanted to intercept a letter that they knew had been sent to you? You are not a diplomat, you have no position with the Government, and you are not rich. Why are you so interesting to these men – or, to be more precise, why are you so interesting to whoever has employed them?'

'I have no idea,' Phillimore said. 'Perhaps the letter might tell us.'

The following silence stretched until Sherlock thought it might snap.

'You have the letter?' Mycroft said. His tone of voice was calm, but Sherlock could hear the restraint in it. His brother was not a particularly patient man at the best of times, and this was not the best of times.

'I do,' Phillimore said.

'You had the letter all the time that Mr Throop and his thugs were questioning you, and all the time they were walling you up in your own house?'

'I did.'

'Why,' Mycroft said with incredible calmness, 'did you not give it to them and save yourself all this trouble?'

'I wasn't going to give in to their demands,' Phillimore

said, affronted. 'I mean, what kind of world would it be if every bully who came along could take what he wanted just by making threats of physical violence?'

'A very good question,' Mycroft replied. He glanced at Sherlock, and Sherlock could tell that his brother was reluctantly adjusting his opinion of their sister's fiancé. Perhaps he wasn't as much of a wet fish as he had seemed. 'Where *is* the letter, Mr Phillimore?'

'In my top hat, of course.'

Mycroft stared at him. 'Of course,' he repeated. 'In your top hat.' He paused, and Sherlock could sense that he was searching for the right words to continue. '*Why* is the letter in your top hat, Mr Phillimore?'

'Because I used to have a briefcase,' the man said simply.

Mycroft kept staring at him, not blinking. 'Of course you did.'

Sherlock decided to come to his brother's aid. 'I think,' he said gently, 'that Mr Phillimore is trying to tell us that he used to have a briefcase, but he lost it. He has probably lost several briefcases. In order not to lose important things like letters, bits of paper and pens, he now keeps them in his top hat. A man can lose a briefcase, but he doesn't often lose a top hat.' He smiled. 'I noticed that you have had your top hat for many years, Mr Phillimore. It is a treasured object.'

'Quite right,' Phillimore said, smiling at Sherlock. 'I see you have a brain like mine. Yes, I do keep leaving briefcases on trains, or in cabs, or in tea shops and restaurants. Very careless, I know. Sometimes I have retrieved them, but sometimes they have been lost – taken by some other person. In desperation, I decided that I would sew a series of little pockets inside my top hat where I could keep all the important things I was carrying around in safety.'

'Very . . . commendable,' Mycroft said. 'Sherlock, with Mr Phillimore's permission, would you care to retrieve his hat from the hall, where I remember seeing it when we entered, and bring it in here.' He glanced at Phillimore, who nodded his agreement.

The top hat was still sitting on the table in the hall. Sherlock picked it up. Resisting the urge to turn it upside down to see what was inside, he returned to the sitting room and handed it to Mr Phillimore, who delved inside it.

'Bill from the butcher,' he murmured, looking at something in the hat, 'note to myself to remind me to pay the bill from the butcher . . . ah, yes – the letter!'

He pulled it out of the hat and waved it. 'I knew it would be here!'

'If I may?' Mycroft held out a large hand, and Phillimore handed the letter across to him.

'It does not appear to have been opened,' Mycroft pointed out.

'I had not got around to it.' Phillimore shrugged. 'I have particular times when I feel like opening letters and particular times when I do not. I have been waiting until I felt like it.'

'May I?' Mycroft asked, holding the letter up. 'Or would you rather open it and read it yourself first? Having already pulled one of your walls apart, I do not feel as if I should presume any more on your good nature.'

Phillimore waved a hand. 'Oh, open the blessed thing. I have no secrets – certainly not from the brother of my intended bride. There will be nothing of a personal nature within.'

Mycroft gazed at the envelope for half a minute, turning it over in his hands, holding it up to the light and even sniffing it. Phillimore watched, entranced. Eventually Mycroft took a slim folded knife from his pocket. He noticed Sherlock looking at him with surprise as he unfolded it, and said, 'You may scoff, young man, but I take my personal security very carefully.' Instead of inserting the knife through a gap in the side of the envelope and then slicing along the top as Sherlock had expected, he carefully prised open the sealing wax that held it closed. Sherlock noticed that he didn't even break the wax.

Mycroft glanced at Phillimore. 'People do not pay enough attention to envelopes,' he said calmly. 'The paper from which each is made, the way it has been addressed, the way it has been sealed, the stamp, the postmark . . . each of these things can tell a story. For instance, I can tell you that this letter has been posted from Egypt. It was posted about two weeks ago, which would be about the time it would take a ship to make the journey from Cairo to London, and then for the letter to make its way here to Arundel. Its writer is a professional man, highly educated and trained, but he is currently living in rough surroundings and is not eating properly. He is disturbed by something that has happened, and he seeks your help.' He looked again at the envelope, and frowned. 'He posted this letter himself rather than let a servant do the job.'

A thought struck Sherlock. He frowned, leaning forward while it coagulated in his mind. A letter – a letter that was important enough for three men to pose as decorators, search a house and imprison the house's owner in search of it?

'Mycroft,' he said slowly; 'Is it possible that these are the same three men whom we found in father's library – the men who were searching *our* house?'

# CHAPTER SEVEN

'Hmmm.' Mycroft leaned back in his chair and frowned. 'An interesting supposition, but one not currently supported by the facts. The coincidence of numbers is interesting, yes, but here they were looking for something in particular – the letter addressed to Mr Phillimore. What could they have been looking for in *our* house?'

Sherlock opened his mouth to answer, but Mycroft's hand slammed down on the arm of the chair, interrupting him.

'I am a fool of the first water!' Mycroft yelled, surprising James Phillimore. 'Of course! The answer is obvious!'

'It is?' Phillimore asked.

'The letter was not obviously here,' Sherlock said. 'The three men searched for it extensively. Therefore it must have been somewhere else. It would have occurred to them – perhaps because you said something, or perhaps because of the photograph you have framed here – that you were engaged to be married. It is possible, they thought, that you had given the letter to your fiancée for safe-keeping. They found out where Emma lived and decided to break in and make a search.'

'They could hardly pretend to be decorators,' Mycroft pointed out. 'We did not need any decoration and besides, we had been bereaved. That was hardly the best time for them to turn up on the doorstep offering plastering and wallpapering services.'

'They had to hide their faces,' Sherlock pointed out. 'Obviously, if they were discovered in our house, the game would be up. Emma at the very least might have recognized them, if she had seen them here, at Mr Phillimore's house.' He glanced at Phillimore. 'Had she?'

'I believe she may have been here when they were working,' Phillimore said, frowning. His gaze flicked up to Mycroft, and then to Sherlock, and he blushed. 'We were chaperoned, of course,' he protested. 'Emma's aunt – *your* aunt – was here with us all the time.'

Mycroft shrugged. 'We have more important matters to worry about now than chivalry and morality. These men might well have killed my brother in their search for the letter, once he discovered them, and I fully believe that they would have been prepared to torture you until you gave them the letter. They are men without principles – dangerous men. Something needs to be done.'

'The key,' Sherlock pointed out, 'is probably in the letter. We need to find out what is in it. Did they want the letter because there was something in it that they wanted to know, or did they want to stop Mr Phillimore from receiving it?'

'Egypt?' Phillimore said suddenly, frowning. 'Did you say that the letter was from Egypt? I believe I was offered a job in Egypt. I was not offered it in the end, but I was not unduly upset – too hot, too far to go. I did not want to leave dear Emma for any length of time.'

'Indeed,' Mycroft said drily. 'I'm sure she would have pined terribly.' He pushed against the sides of the envelope, opening it up, then slipped the letter from inside. He glanced at Phillimore, eyebrow raised, checking that it was still all right to read the letter. Phillimore nodded.

'"Dear Brother,"' he read.

'Good Lord!' Phillimore exclaimed, 'it's from Jonathan – my younger brother!' He frowned. 'But why on earth would he be writing to me?'

'You and he have fallen out?' Mycroft asked.

'We did. I have not seen him for years. We both trained as engineers, but there was a great deal of competition between us, and we argued.'

Mycroft nodded. 'It happens in many families,' he said. 'I shall continue.'

*'I apologize for writing to you out of the blue like this. I know this letter will be a surprise to you, given our mutual history of either competing with each other or ignoring each other. When we were children together I recall that we were inseparable, and got up to all kinds of tricks. I regret the fact that things changed, and that some kind of invisible wall appeared between us.*

*'I am writing from Egypt because I know that*

*you had applied for the engineering job upon which I am currently employed. I hope that you can put any bad feeling over the way I have treated you behind you and find in yourself the ability to provide some assistance to a man who finds himself in a quandary. I have never been able to hold a candle to you when it comes to providing assistance to those in need.'*

'Ah!' Phillimore cried. 'I *knew* it! Whatever I had, he had to have, and whatever I wanted, he wanted as well. That is why I have no intention of telling him about my dear Emma!'

'You were interviewed for this post?' Mycroft asked.

'I was, but I received a letter telling me that my experience was not sufficient for their purposes. It is probably a good thing – the temperature and the disease in Egypt is not to my taste. I think I was going through some kind of romantic rebellion when I applied. I have got over it now.'

Mycroft raised an eyebrow. 'What was this work?' he asked.

'It was a French-led project to dig a canal between the Mediterranean Sea and the Red Sea,' Phillimore replied. 'They were hiring all kinds of engineering expertise, and I thought I might stand a chance. It is, as far as I can see, a very ambitious project.'

'I believe I have heard something about it,' Mycroft

sniffed. 'The project is nearly complete. The British Government is against such an overambitious and foolhardy venture. We are quite happy with the current situation in terms of shipping and international trade.' He continued to read.

*'You will, I am sure, already know that the project I am currently involved with is a very important one. Digging a channel 102 miles long and 26 feet deep between the Mediterranean and the Arabian Sea and filling it with water is, perhaps, the most difficult engineering job ever attempted. The rewards, however, are great – if it works, if we are successful, then ships will be able to use this channel in order to get to markets on the Western side of Africa, in India and in China. The project is not purely an economic one, however – the passage around the Horn of Africa is, as you must know, perilous, and many seamen from many countries lose their lives every year attempting it. If we can create this canal then the lives of many good Englishmen will be saved, and this is the reason why I am so enthusiastic about it.*

*'I do not know to what extent (if at all) you have been following the progress of this project in the newspapers. I do know that the British Press, reflecting the opinions of the British Government, is not in favour of the shift in economic power that is*

*likely to result when the canal is completed, and so does not report on it in favourable terms. There is, I believe, more emphasis on the fact that the workers on the project are effectively slave labourers (a situation that would not be tolerated in England, of course, but which has been common here since the construction of the pyramids) and the fact that many hundreds of them have unavoidably died – some of injuries received during the digging and some from diseases which are endemic to the area. These are tragedies, of course, but any project of any importance will result in deaths. Just think of how many men died during the construction of England's railways. Does anybody seriously think that the railways should not have been built just because people would and did die as a result? And at least those British workers were paid!*

*'Anyway, the canal, when it is finished, will probably be called the Suez Canal (or, in Arabic, Qanāt al-Sūwais). This is based on the fact that the southern terminus will be at Port Tewfik at the city of Suez. The northern terminus is at a place called Port Said. Neither is a location at which I would wish to spend any great length of time, I must admit. This entire country is too dirty, too hot and too chaotic for my liking, but I am being well paid to provide my engineering expertise and so I will just have to endure these privations for the*

*sake of future financial stability.*

*'It might interest you to know that the canal will be single-lane, unlike most of Britain's canals, with passing places at Ballah and the Great Bitter Lake. It will contain no locks; instead, seawater will flow freely through it. In general, the canal north of the Bitter Lakes will flow north in winter and south in summer, while the current south of the lakes will change as the tide changes at Suez.*

*'The man in charge of the entire construction project, and therefore my superior, is Ferdinand de Lesseps – a Frenchman, of course, but nevertheless very cordial and knowledgeable. He is working to plans developed by his countryman Linant de Bellefonds. I find it ironic that the French are so heavily involved in the construction of this canal, given that the Emperor Napoleon had previously contemplated the construction of a north–south canal to join the Mediterranean and Red Sea, but had to abandon the project when a preliminary survey erroneously concluded that the Red Sea was 33 feet higher than the Mediterranean, and would need locks that were too expensive and too time-consuming to construct. The error apparently came from the fact that the measurements on the land were mostly done during wartime, and on a number of separate occasions in separate places, which resulted in imprecise calculations.*

*'I realize, by the way, that this letter will strike you not just as a bolt from the blue, but also as a perhaps unwelcome communication from a family member with whom you have often been at odds (and that, I fear, is all my fault). Nevertheless, I am hoping that you can put any ill-will behind you and reciprocate the hand of friendship that I am extending from here in Cairo.*

*'I hope to hear from you soonest, but if I do not I remain,*

*'Yours sincerely,*

*'Your brother, Jonathan.'*

Sherlock and Mycroft stared at each other.

'This letter was apparently important enough for a burglary to occur at *our* house and for an assault to occur on Mr Phillimore here at *his* house,' Sherlock said, 'but it says virtually nothing.'

'On first examination,' Mycroft mused, 'there is indeed little here. The letter is merely a long-winded description of the project that Mr Jonathan Phillimore has been working on, and on which his brother James here failed to get a job.' He glanced inside the envelope. 'There is nothing else here – no other slips of paper or other enclosures. He sniffed, and frowned, but said nothing. 'These are deep waters, Sherlock,' he said, shaking his head. 'Deep waters indeed. I wish we had more information to go on.'

'Those workers will be coming back,' Sherlock pointed out. 'Why don't we just ask them?'

Mycroft raised an eyebrow. 'Please explain yourself.'

'*If* the three men who left this house earlier were the three men who broke into Holmes Lodge, then they would have recognized me from when they attacked me. They got a good enough view of my face. I didn't immediately recognize *them* and raise the alarm, so they believe their disguises of black coats and wrapped faces were enough to hide their identities. They left Mr Phillimore here, intending to come back later and question him further about the letter. They even told us that they were just going off for lunch, and they would return. They presumed that we would either leave when Mr Phillimore didn't return, or we would look for him in the house and not find him, and then leave anyway. There is no reason why they wouldn't come back. As far as they are aware, they haven't been identified, their secret is safe and Mr Phillimore is still here, plastered up inside the wall.'

'You suggest that we remain here until they return, render them helpless and then ask them what is so important about this letter?' Mycroft stared at Sherlock for a few moments. 'Just the three of us – an overweight Civil Servant, an underweight engineer and a boy who was recently stabbed? I admire your confidence, but I am unable to support your plan.'

Sherlock thought for a moment. 'The obvious thing to do would be to call the police,' he admitted.

'Most certainly,' Mr Phillimore interrupted.

'The problem is,' Sherlock continued, 'that the police would almost certainly see nothing to investigate. They might, at a stretch, believe that Mr Phillimore was the victim of some kind of prank, but all they would do would be to have a stiff word with the decorators. The decorators would either claim that nothing happened, or they would take the first opportunity to make a run for it. Either way, we would be left here not knowing what was happening.'

Mycroft nodded his huge head. 'You have a point, Sherlock, but I do not see any alternative. I can ask questions through my superiors in the Foreign Office about what might be happening in Egypt, but I doubt they will take any interest.'

Sherlock was silent for a moment. He was doing what Amyus Crowe had taught him: taking stock of all the resources that he had to hand – not just the obvious ones, but things that might be easily available to him if only he knew they were there.

Moments later a whole plan materialized in his mind, fully formed. It was risky, possibly even illegal, but it was the only way to find out what was going on.

'I presume,' he said, 'that Mother was on . . . medication in her final days.'

'She was on morphine to control the pain,' Mycroft said quietly. 'Our family doctor prescribed it.'

'And that morphine is still in her bedroom?'

'It is.' Mycroft closed his eyes. His face twisted as if a spasm of pain had passed through his head. 'I see what you are proposing. Correct me where I go wrong. We send someone back to the house to retrieve the morphine. Meanwhile, we – by which I mean you, me and Mr Phillimore – hide ourselves somewhere in this house. When the three decorator villains return, the maid makes them a cup of tea. Unbeknownst to them, the milk has been adulterated with morphine. They pass out, then we come out of hiding and tie them up. When they awake, we question them about what is going on.' He sighed. 'There are several stumbling blocks, Sherlock. Firstly, they might return before the morphine arrives from Holmes Lodge, and then what do we do? Secondly, neither of us is in a position to judge the dosage of the morphine. We might give them too much, and kill them. Thirdly, having just returned from lunch I would suggest that we can't guarantee that all of them will accept a cup of tea.'

'Oh.' Sherlock felt crestfallen. He had been so taken up with the grand sweep of his plan that he had failed to see the obvious flaws.

'Perhaps I might make a suggestion,' Mr Phillimore interrupted.

Sherlock and Mycroft turned to look at him.

'I have a sleeping draught upstairs in my bedroom.' He shrugged, and looked slightly embarrassed. 'I sleep badly at the best of times, and the powders, which my chemist gives me, sends me to sleep very quickly. I am very familiar with the dose needed. Secondly, there is some cider in a jug in the pantry. If the villains were offered cider rather than tea, I suspect they would leap at the opportunity.'

Mycroft smiled. 'Mr Phillimore, I underestimated you,' he said. 'You have improved Sherlock's plan to a point of workability. However, I would point out that you will, of course, need to explain to your maid what is going on, and she may not wish to be involved with something that skirts close to the edge of the law.'

Phillimore shook his head. 'I would suggest that we put enough sleeping draught for three large men into the jug, and merely tell cook that she should serve it to the decorators the moment they get back. She can say that I am not here, and that the cider needs to be used up before the end of the day, or some such story. I believe they will accept it.' He sniffed. 'They struck me as being men who would rarely pass up the chance of a drink.'

'I concur,' Mycroft said, 'although I suspect that you will need to find some explanation for your cook and your maid as to what has been going on in this house today. What with you disappearing, Sherlock and I searching the house and then you reappearing covered in plaster, I think they may be on the verge of handing in their notice.'

'Oh I shouldn't think so,' Phillimore said, frowning. 'They are used to my eccentricities.' He glanced at

Sherlock. 'At least, I am told by others that I am eccentric. I do not see it myself, I am afraid.'

'Take it from me,' Sherlock said. 'You are eccentric.'

'Emma finds it endearing,' Phillimore said, smiling shyly.

'She comes from an equally eccentric family,' Sherlock pointed out.

'In the meantime,' Mycroft continued, interrupting, 'I should send a telegram to my superiors, given that there may be an international dimension to this. They may wish to advise me, or make their own inquiries.' He checked his watch. 'We should move quickly, so that we are prepared for when these men reappear.'

The next few minutes were taken up with Mr Phillimore sprinting up the stairs and retrieving the sleeping powders, then heading for the pantry where he was to drug the cider and tell his cook to give it to the decorators when they arrived. Meanwhile Sherlock watched out of the window, ready to call out an alert if the men came back, and Mycroft wrote out a quick telegram on a sheet of paper. Once Mr Phillimore had returned to the room he called the maid in and told her to take the telegram straight to the Post Office and send it, then take the afternoon off to keep her out of the way.

Ten minutes after she left, Sherlock saw movement along the road. Three men were walking towards the house.

'I think they're here,' he said.

'Then we need to head upstairs,' Mycroft said. 'Mr Phillimore, are you sure your cook is up to this job?'

'She understands what to do,' Phillimore said. He raised an eyebrow. 'I believe she has taken a shine to Mr Throop. Giving him a glass of cider will not be a problem for her, I feel.'

'Did you tell her what you had added to the cider?' Mycroft asked.

'Certainly not! I felt it was better for her not to know. I did tell her to open the door when she hears the knocker and inform the men that I had gone out for a while. They will suppose that she just hadn't seen me, and made that assumption, when I was in fact still incarcerated in the wall of my own spare room.' He hesitated. 'I also told her,' he added, 'to leave the men there and head into town to get some vegetables, meat and fish. She was reluctant to leave the men alone, so I told her that the maid, Marie, would be returning soon, and that there was no need to worry.' He removed his glasses and started to polish them self-consciously. 'She is a good woman, and I would not want her to be frightened when the men all fall asleep together.'

'Good thinking.' Mycroft led the way out into the hall and up the stairs. Sherlock had to resist the temptation to push his brother, who laboured to move from tread to tread and had to use the banister to pull himself up. Mr Phillimore kept glancing over his shoulder nervously, expecting the decorators to come through the door any moment, but Sherlock knew that it would take them a good few minutes to cover the distance from where he had seen them to the house.

They got to the landing at the top of the stairs and were heading for one of the rooms that *wasn't* being decorated when they heard the front door knocker.

'It occurs to me,' Mycroft said quietly, 'that our plan comes to nothing if that is the postman instead of the decorators.'

'Just as long as the cook doesn't take it into her head to give *him* a glass of cider,' Sherlock murmured. 'It occurs to *me* that the men might just come straight upstairs to check that Mr Phillimore is still where they left him. If they do that they will see that he has been rescued.'

Mycroft shook his head. 'They have no reason to believe that he might have been found, and they will want to leave him inside the wall for a while in order to soften him up, render him more amenable to questioning. Besides which, I am sure they would not turn down the chance for some refreshments before recommencing their work. Interrogation is such thirsty business.'

From the safety of the spare room they heard the door being opened, and various voices – one female and several male. They listened closely for any sound of someone coming up the stairs, but instead the voices got quieter as the men followed the cook along the corridor towards the kitchen, and the cider.

'How long do we give it?' Sherlock asked.

'We should be able to hear the conversation slow

down as they feel sleepy, and then stop as they fall asleep,' Mycroft replied. 'That is when we shall act.'

They heard the cook's footsteps coming back into the hall, and then the sound of the front door opening and closing. Sherlock felt a shiver of anticipation as he realized that the three of them were now alone in the house with three dangerous thugs, and of the three of them he would only trust himself in a fight.

'How quickly do these powders work when you take them?' Mycroft asked James Phillimore.

'Usually within twenty minutes I am fast asleep,' he replied in a whisper. 'Even if I am reading, I fall asleep. I've often woken up in the morning with my spectacles still on my nose and a book in my lap.'

'So, quite quickly then,' Mycroft said. He looked at his watch. 'We will give them half an hour, just in case.'

As the three of them sat there silently, waiting for the criminals in the room below to fall asleep, Sherlock found himself remembering the various occasions when it was he who had been drugged, rather than someone else. A few years back the agents of the international criminal organization that called itself the Paradol Chamber had knocked him out with laudanum and transported him across the English Channel to France. A year or so after that they had done the same with a spray of some drug – probably morphine – directed into his face so that he breathed it in. He remembered on both occasions how soft and smooth his dreams had been, and how he hadn't been aware even that he had fallen into a drugged state. Waking up in France the first time and a lunatic asylum the second time had been a shock, however, but given the way that the drug had made him feel he could understand how some people could become addicted to it.

Mycroft checked his watch again, and said, 'That is half an hour, and I can hear no conversation from downstairs. Let us go down and check on your labourers, Mr Phillimore.'

The three of them went downstairs together and moved quietly across the hall and through a corridor to the kitchen. Three men – the same three that Sherlock had seen leaving Mr Phillimore's house earlier on – were sitting at the kitchen table. One of them had slumped forward with his head on his arms, while the other two were resting with their heads tilted backwards. All three were snoring. An empty copper jug and three empty glasses sat before them on the table.

Sherlock stared at them. If he was right, then these three men had tried to burgle his family home, and had attacked him when he tried to follow them. They had tried to kill him, and now here they were, completely at his mercy.

He tried to see in them some recognizable feature, something that would confirm that these were the same men. One of them had a bandage around his arm, he noticed. This might have been the man whose arm he had hit with a tree branch. Another had a purple bruise across the front of his neck, giving the appearance that he hadn't shaved.

In the end, he wouldn't know unless they actually confessed. Evidence could only take a person so far – it was indicative, but rarely definitive.

'Mercy me!'

The three of them turned. Standing in the doorway was Marie – Mr Phillimore's maid. She was holding several shopping bags, and she was staring at the three men asleep around the table in shock.

'Ah, Marie,' Mr Phillimore said. 'This is, ah . . .'

'Easily explained,' Mycroft interrupted smoothly. 'Mr Phillimore's decorators have been working very hard for a while, as you know. Unfortunately, the wallpaper paste they mixed up earlier contains a chemical which is meant to prevent mould and fungus from growing, but has also been proved to have a soporific effect on the human body. They have all fallen asleep. I suggest that you stay out of the kitchen, my girl, and let us tend to them.'

She looked at him as if he'd been speaking in Chinese. 'Shouldn't you call a doctor?' she asked. 'I mean . . .'

'We shall,' Phillimore said. 'I suggest you go and attend to your duties, Marie. I believe the upstairs needs tidying.'

'Yes, sir,' she said, and then, looking at Mycroft: 'Oh, sir – I went back to the Post Office to see if there'd been any reply to that telegram I sent, and there was. It must have come in awfully quick. I've got it here for you.'

She handed a sealed brown manila envelope across to Mycroft, then left, glancing dubiously backwards over her shoulder as she went.

'Wallpaper paste?' Sherlock said to Mycroft, smiling.

'It was the first thing that came to mind,' he said. He was using his pocket knife to slice open the envelope as he spoke. He removed a slip of paper and read it. His expression clouded over, a frown marring the normal unreadable expression.

'Bad news?' Sherlock asked.

'Rather a change of plan,' Mycroft said thoughtfully. He read the telegram again, then tore it into small pieces and slipped the pieces into a pocket of his jacket as if it was the most normal thing in the world. He glanced up to see Sherlock looking at him askance. 'If I screw the telegram up and throw it away, somebody might retrieve it and read it,' he explained. 'If I tear it up and throw it away then someone might reconstruct it from the pieces. If I keep the pieces and throw them away gradually, throughout the day, then it is much more difficult for someone to find out what it said.'

'Was it that important?' Sherlock asked, intrigued.

Mycroft looked at him for a few moments. 'I neither send, nor do I receive, trivial telegrams,' he said enigmatically.

'Do people really collect the pieces of a torn-up telegram and rebuild it so they can see what it says?' he asked. 'It sounds like something from a book!'

Mycroft drew himself up. 'I have,' he said huffily, 'gained significant diplomatic advantage by collecting the torn-up pieces of a message and reassembling it to reconstitute the original.' He paused for a moment. 'Well,' he added, 'when I say "I", I mean that agents of mine have done it. Searching waste-paper bins is beneath my dignity.' He turned to Phillimore. 'I have decided,' he said, abruptly changing the subject, 'that we should move these men from your house to ours. I presume you have no great attachment to them, and that you would rather see them gone?'

'Indeed,' Phillimore said, 'with the proviso that I will need to find a new team of decorators to repair the damage done by these men.' He paused, frowning. 'I hope you will tell me the results of any questioning,' he added. 'I would hate to be left in the dark.'

'I will tell you what I can,' Mycroft said mysteriously. He moved his gaze to Sherlock. 'I need you to convey a message to Rufus Stone. Get him here with a carriage. Bring young Matty – I think we will need all the help we can get.'

Sherlock was confused. 'You're not intending to take these men back to Holmes Lodge, are you?' he asked.

Mycroft nodded. 'They can better be controlled there,' he said decisively.

'But –' Sherlock started.

'No.' Mycroft slammed his hand on the kitchen table. 'There will be no discussion, Sherlock,' he said angrily. 'These men are coming back with us!'

# CHAPTER EIGHT

Sherlock stared at his brother in shock. He wasn't used to being told what to do by Mycroft, and he wasn't used to his brother shouting at him.

'Now go!' Mycroft snapped. 'Get Rufus Stone and a carriage here as soon as you can.'

'All right! I will!'

Sherlock backed out of the kitchen. The last thing that he heard was Mycroft saying to Phillimore: 'Now you will need to tie these men up. Do you have any strong rope around?'

'You want me to tie these men up!' Phillimore asked incredulously.

'Well I certainly can't do it,' Mycroft said, turning away.

Sherlock left them there, and walked out of the house. He was angry at Mycroft's peremptory giving of orders. Obviously Mycroft was his elder brother, and he was standing in for their father, but even so there were limits. After all, the two of them had grown up together!

Mycroft had sent the carriage home earlier, so Sherlock walked down to the town square and hailed a cab even though he wasn't sure he had the money to cover it.

'Can you put this on the account for Holmes Lodge?'

he asked the cabbie. The man nodded.

Well, that was settled then. Mycroft would eventually be paying for it.

The journey to Holmes Lodge took fifteen minutes or so. Sherlock ordered the cabbie to wait, then went and located Rufus Stone and Matty. Without telling them why, he told them that they had to get a cart and go to James Phillimore's house. As they set about organizing the cart Sherlock went back to where the cab was waiting. He knew that he should really have dismissed the cab and gone back in the cart, with Rufus and Matty, but he rebelled against the implicit instructions.

'Take me back to the town square,' he said to the cabbie. 'Put it on the same account.'

By the time he had walked from the town square back to James Phillimore's house, Rufus and Matty had arrived with the cart.

'What's the urgency?' Rufus called from the driver's seat.

'Ask my brother,' Sherlock called back darkly.

Rufus, Matty and Sherlock walked into the house together. Sherlock led the way to the kitchen, where the three decorators were still asleep. They were now tied up: hands behind their backs and ankles fastened together. Mycroft was sitting at the same table tucking into a pie, while James Phillimore was nowhere to be seen.

'Ah, Mr Stone,' Mycroft said, crumbs on his shirt front. 'Please take these gentlemen back to Holmes

Lodge. Secure them in the stables, please.'

Rufus Stone stared at the three men, paying particular attention, Sherlock noticed, to their various injuries. 'Are these the men who broke into your house?' he asked.

Mycroft shrugged. 'That has yet to be established,' he said, 'but rest assured that they are villains and they deserve to be tied up.'

'You drugged 'em,' Matty observed.

'Actually, the owner of this house and the cook jointly drugged them. It was merely my idea. Now, please, can we get them on the cart, covered up and taken back to the stables at Holmes Lodge?'

The journey took perhaps half an hour. The horses were slower than the one pulling the cab that Sherlock had taken, and Mycroft seemed anxious not to raise any suspicions. Sherlock, Rufus and Matty were forced to sit uncomfortably at the front of the cart while Rufus steered the horses. Mycroft sat hunched beside him like a black crow. Once they arrived, Mycroft supervised the moving of the three unconscious bodies into the stables.

'Well,' he said after it was all done, 'that was an interesting and unexpected coda to the day. I believe dinner will be served soon; I would suggest that we all go and clean ourselves up in readiness.'

'And the men in there?' Sherlock asked, indicating the stables.

'Oh, they won't be dining with us.'

'You know what I mean. What happens to them now?'

Mycroft stared at Sherlock. 'They will be questioned,' he said eventually. 'You need not worry about that any more.'

'But I do worry,' Sherlock said. He knew he was pushing his brother, but he had the distinct feeling that something was being hidden from him, that he was being excluded. 'They broke into our house. They attacked me. They attacked Mr Phillimore – Emma's fiancé. Do you just expect us to put all that aside and let you deal with it?'

'Yes,' Mycroft said simply, 'I do.'

'This has something to do with the telegram you got, doesn't it?'

Mycroft's face was as expressionless as a stone statue. 'You have an active imagination, Sherlock,' he said. 'You should try to curb that imagination.'

'Your superiors told you to take these men and segregate them,' Sherlock continued. 'What happens now – do you question them yourself, while nobody is around?'

'Sherlock, I am warning you . . .'

'Is this anything to do with Jonathan Phillimore's concerns about the canal they are building in Suez? It is, isn't it?'

'Please, desist.' Mycroft's face was still stony, but Sherlock detected a degree of distress beneath the mask. 'There are things I cannot talk about.'

'I've never known you to act like this before, Mycroft,' Sherlock said quietly.

'I have never had to act like this before,' Mycroft replied. 'My work life and my home life rarely overlap.'

Dinner was a quiet affair. Rufus Stone joined Sherlock, Mycroft, Matty, Emma and Aunt Anna. Given the presence of the rest of the family, Sherlock didn't feel comfortable raising the subject of what had transpired that afternoon, and nobody else raised the subject. Instead, Sherlock told Emma that they had seen her fiancé, and that he seemed like a pleasant enough man. She was pleased, but then a lot of things seemed to please Emma.

After dinner Sherlock caught Mycroft's arm as he was leaving the dining room.

'What are we going to do about questioning those men?' he asked. 'They'll probably have woken up by now. It's not that I have any great concern for their welfare, but we can't leave them there all night.'

'The matter is in hand,' Mycroft said, not looking at Sherlock. He attempted to leave, but Sherlock added: 'You're going to get Rufus Stone to question them, aren't you? You know that he would be prepared to hit them, or hurt them, to get them to talk, while I wouldn't. Mycroft, that's *wrong*.'

This time his brother turned to stare Sherlock in the eye. 'I have not asked Mr Stone to question them,' he said, 'but if I had, then that would be entirely appropriate behaviour. They broke into this house. More importantly, they tried to kill you, and they were in Emma's bedroom.

These things are unconscionable, and cannot be allowed to stand. I will take whatever action I deem necessary to discover what these men wanted.'

Sherlock gazed into his brother's eyes. He could usually tell what Mycroft was thinking, but his expression on this occasion was utterly unreadable.

'What was in the telegram, Mycroft?' he asked simply.

His brother stared at him for a long moment, then turned and walked away, towards their father's library.

Sherlock had wanted to spend a little time in the comfort of the library himself, but he had a feeling that Mycroft didn't want him around. Besides, with the two of them in the library the atmosphere would be tense. Instead, Sherlock went for a walk out in the darkness of the Holmes Lodge grounds. Intellectually he knew that the men had only broken in to find the letter from Jonathan Phillimore – which wasn't there – but part of him still wanted to patrol the grounds to check that the family was safe.

The moon shone down upon the house, illuminating the front in bright light but casting a dark shadow from the back. As Sherlock walked, an owl left its hidden perch on one of the trees and swooped down towards him, passing like an unquiet spirit only a few feet above his head before flapping its wings and gaining altitude. He turned to watch it go, but lost sight of it when it entered the shadow of the house.

Eventually, as he knew he would, he turned and

walked towards the stables at the back of the house.

He wasn't sure what he was going to do when he got there. Part of him wanted to ask the men who were tied up there some questions, even though he knew they probably wouldn't answer him, but part of him just wanted to make sure they were still there, and hadn't either escaped or choked on their gags and died.

He had the sense that something was going on that he didn't know about: something monolithic and uncaring. He didn't like it.

He got to the corner of the house and was about to pass into the shadow cast by the moon when he heard quiet voices. He stopped, pressed himself against the stone of the house and peered around the corner.

The stables were a hundred yards or so beyond the house. In front of them, a carriage stood. Two men stood by the horses, holding their heads to make sure they didn't make any noise. These weren't Holmes family horses, this wasn't a Holmes family carriage and these weren't Holmes family servants. Someone had quietly come on to their property and was doing something underhand.

As Sherlock watched, another two men carried a struggling bundle from the stables and threw it into the carriage. The carriage's springs rocked as the bundle hit the floor, and Sherlock heard a muffled groan. It was one of the three men that they had drugged and removed from James Phillimore's house earlier. Someone was rescuing them!

No, that didn't make sense. If they were being rescued then the ropes tying them would have been cut, and their gags removed. This wasn't a rescue – this was a removal . . .

His brain raced, trying to work out what to do. He could start shouting, raise the alarm and mobilize the servants, or he could sneak back into the house and get Rufus Stone.

He had just decided to start shouting for help when a figure walked out of the stables and stood in the moonlight, watching as a second bound figure was carried to the carriage.

It was Mycroft.

Sherlock moved further back, feeling his heart sink. What on earth did Mycroft want with these men so late at night, and why hadn't he told Sherlock anything about it?

Another figure moved out of the stables. This time it was Rufus Stone.

'Are you ready to go?' Rufus asked Mycroft.

'I think so. The journey back to London will be uncomfortable, I fear.'

Rufus glanced into the carriage. 'It certainly will,' he said. 'They're stacked up like logs in there.'

'I didn't mean uncomfortable for *them*,' Mycroft snapped, 'I meant uncomfortable for *me*.'

'What are you going to tell Sherlock?'

Mycroft sighed. 'I shall tell him nothing. I will need

you to write a note to Sherlock as if from me, telling him that I was urgently recalled to London due to some diplomatic emergency or other. You have, I know, an amazing ability to forge other people's handwriting – you have seen enough of mine to do a decent job. Suggest to him that he returns to Oxford as soon as possible rather than stay here at Holmes Lodge. Once you have done that, leave some rope lying around here, and make sure that the ends are cut through. He will assume that the men have been rescued by their friends. He will want to search for them, of course. You can let him do that safely – he will not find them, but it will keep him occupied for a while and stop him from thinking too deeply about what might have occurred. He will probably write to me, or send me a telegram. I shall delay in replying. If fortune is on our side then other things will catch his attention and he will forget about this mystery. The wonderful thing about Sherlock is that he is so easily distracted.'

Sherlock felt a slow burn of anger within his chest. His brother was not only keeping things from him, but was actively intending to lie to him! What was going on? There must have been something in the telegram from Mycroft's superiors that had prompted him to take this action, but why? What was it about the seemingly innocent letter from James Phillimore's brother that had provoked such an immediate reaction?

'And me?' Rufus asked. 'Once I have written the letter and arranged the scene here, what do you want me to do?'

'Follow me back to London. I will need your assistance in questioning these men further.'

Mycroft nodded to Rufus Stone, and started clambering into the carriage. 'Look after Sherlock,' he said as he disappeared. Two of the men – the ones who had been holding the horses' heads – climbed up to the driver's board. One of them took up the reins while the other two men walked away, keeping to the shadows but heading for the gates to the road outside. Rufus Stone watched as the carriage pulled away. He didn't seem happy.

The carriage slewed around and headed for the corner of the building where Sherlock was hidden. He sprinted back to the porch, and hid himself inside just as the carriage quietly came past, heading for the gates. Within a few seconds it had vanished.

Sherlock felt betrayed. He felt . . . abandoned. His own brother was keeping things from him.

For a few minutes, as silence fell again across the house and its grounds, he stood there. He didn't know what to do. In a situation like that he would normally seek out either his brother or Rufus Stone for advice, but that wasn't going to work now. He was on his own.

No, he wasn't. He had Matty.

He slipped up the stairs and along the corridor to Matty's room. For the second night in a row he woke his friend up with a finger against his lips to keep him quiet. For the next half-hour he told an incredulous

Matty what had happened at James Phillimore's house, and then more recently outside Holmes Lodge.

'I always said your brother was a dark 'orse.' Matty scratched his head. 'What do you think we can do?' he asked. 'What *can* we do?'

As always, Sherlock was grateful for his friend's immediate and wholehearted desire to help, and to do something.

'I've been thinking,' he whispered. 'That letter is the key to the whole thing. There wasn't any information in the letter itself that could have provoked this kind of reaction from Mycroft's superiors, and I couldn't see any sign of a code in what Mr Phillimore's brother had said. I've seen codes hidden in messages before, and usually there's something strange about the message itself that gives it away – something clumsy or unusual because particular words have been chosen so that every fifth word, for instance, spells out a secret message, or because sentences have been made to start with certain letters so that if you take all of these initial letters then *they* spell out a secret message. There was nothing in the message that made me think there was something hidden there, though.'

'Are there any other ways of hiding messages?' Matty asked.

Sherlock thought. 'I suppose there might have been something hidden under the stamp, but it would have had to be a very small message. Or –' He slapped his forehead. 'Of course!'

'What?' Matty asked.

'Invisible ink! I've been so stupid! You can use lemon juice, or various other things, to write messages on paper. They fade to invisibility when they dry, but if you hold them over a candle then the message appears.' A thought struck him. 'It was staring us in the face all along – Mr Phillimore's brother actually *said*: "I have never been able to hold a candle to you when it comes to providing assistance to those in need." *That* was a message to Mr Phillimore to hold a candle to the letter and look for invisible ink.' Sherlock strained to remember the contents of the message. 'He also said: "When we were children together I recall that we were inseparable, and got up to all kinds of tricks." I bet he and his brother used to send messages to each other using invisible ink when they were children. What else did he say? "I regret the fact that things changed, and that some kind of invisible wall appeared between us." So, he actually mentioned "invisible", "candle" and "tricks". It was all there!'

'And this Mr Phillimore didn't work it out 'imself?' Matty sniffed. ''E needs to pull 'is socks up if 'e wants to marry into *this* family.'

'More to the point, I'm surprised that Mycroft didn't work it out. He must be slipping.' As he said the words, Sherlock remembered how Mycroft had sniffed at the envelope. Had his sensitive nose detected a trace of lemon juice? Had he worked out from the mere *odour* of lemons that there was a secret message in the letter?

Sherlock shook his head. 'We need to take another look at that letter,' he said. 'We need to check for invisible ink so we can find out what the message is, because Mycroft isn't going to tell us.'

'Shall we go now?' Matty asked. 'Or after breakfast?'

They ended up waiting for breakfast for the simple reason that they didn't want to wake Mr Phillimore up before sunrise to ask if they could take another look at his letter. There was also the fact that Matty didn't want to travel on an empty stomach to take into account.

Emma was there at breakfast. That stopped Sherlock and Matty talking about what they were going to do, because Emma would almost certainly have asked if she could accompany them to Mr Phillimore's house. Instead they made innocuous conversation, bursting to say something more important but unable to.

Rufus Stone wasn't present, fortunately. That way Sherlock didn't have to pretend to be surprised at Mycroft's absence and to try and look like he believed any lies that Rufus was telling him.

As quickly as they could after breakfast, Sherlock and Matty saddled up a couple of horses from the stables and set off for Mr Phillimore's house.

As they prepared the horses, Sherlock noticed the cut lengths of rope that had been left lying around in the straw. The sight sent a pang of anguish through his heart. He hated being lied to – especially by family.

They got to James Phillimore's house shortly after

nine o'clock. Sherlock rang the bell, and Marie – the maid – answered it. When she saw Sherlock she winced. Obviously she had troubling memories of the day before.

'Can I help you, sir?'

'Is Mr Phillimore in?' Sherlock asked.

'I'll see if he is available,' she replied, and vanished back into the house. This time she actually shut the door on him. Sherlock found himself wondering if she had just vanished back to the kitchen, or wherever she spent her time when she wasn't opening the front door, and had left him and Matty to stew on the doorstep until they decided to give up and go home. He was just about to knock on the door again when it reopened.

'The master will see you,' Marie said. It was clear from her tone of voice that she disapproved.

Phillimore was waiting in the drawing room. 'Mr Holmes!' he exclaimed, 'I was hoping that you would return and tell me what has transpired with those three thugs.' He glanced at Matty. 'And you've brought a friend with you – how wonderful.'

'This is Matty – Matthew Arnatt,' Sherlock said. 'I'm afraid I can't tell you very much about what we found out from those men, but I was hoping that we could take another look at that letter. I think we may have missed something.'

Phillimore frowned. 'Did your brother not tell you?'

Sherlock felt a sinking sensation in his stomach. 'Tell us what?'

'That the same thought had occurred to him. He came here late last night. *Very* late last night, in fact. I was just preparing for bed when he rang the doorbell. He was, I have to say, very short with me. He said that he needed to take the letter from my brother for testing. I was most reluctant to let him have it, but he was *very* insistent.'

'He took the letter?' Sherlock asked.

'He did.' Phillimore frowned. 'Did he not tell you when he got back to Holmes Lodge?'

'No – he must have forgotten.' Sherlock forced a smile. 'I apologize for wasting your time, Mr Phillimore.'

'Please tell your brother that I *would* like to have that letter back,' Phillimore said as he escorted them to the door. '*My* brother and I have had our differences over the years, but I welcome his attempt to repair our relationship. That letter is very dear to me.'

'I promise to raise the matter with Mycroft at the first opportunity,' Sherlock said.

'And . . .' Phillimore hesitated. 'Please convey my deepest regards to my dearest Emma. Tell her that I have been staying away, in deference to her bereavement, but that I hope to see her again soon.'

'I will do that,' Sherlock replied. Privately he couldn't help thinking that, given Emma's perilous mental state, she might well have forgotten about Phillimore by the time Sherlock returned.

'Oh, one more thing,' Sherlock called as Mr Phillimore began to close the door.

'Yes?'

'Years ago, when your brother and you were on good terms, did you play a lot together?'

He smiled in remembrance. 'Yes, we did.'

'And did you play lots of tricks on your parents and your teachers?'

'We did indeed. I recall that we made up our own language, which we used to speak whenever we didn't want the adults to know what we were saying. Oh, and we used invisible ink to write notes to each other. It used to infuriate our teachers when they would find us passing notes back and forth but there was nothing on the notes. It was such fun.'

'Thank you,' Sherlock said. 'You've been a great help – more than you know.'

As the door closed behind them, he slammed his hand into his leg in frustration. 'Mycroft got here first!' he exclaimed. 'He has the letter!'

''E's almost certainly taken the message to London with him,' Matty pointed out. 'Along wiv those blokes. What do we do now?'

The answer was clear in Sherlock's mind. Having started on this journey, he had to keep going. 'We're going to go to London and get the letter back,' he said firmly.

'Ain't that goin' to be a problem?' Matty asked, frowning. 'I mean, we don't know where 'e's goin' to 'ide it.'

'Brother Mycroft spends his whole life in only three separate places in London,' Sherlock pointed out. 'His rooms in Whitehall, the Diogenes Club, also in Whitehall, and his office in the Government Buildings.'

'Which I'm guessin' are in Whitehall.' Matty smiled. 'Your bruvver don't like movin' around too much, does 'e?'

Sherlock couldn't help smiling as well, despite the gravity of the situation. 'If he could sleep and eat in his office then he'd stay there all the time. Alternatively, if he could sleep and work in the Diogenes Club then he would do that instead. Eventually, of course, he would lose the use of his legs entirely, but it might take him a while to notice. Or care.' He thought for a moment. 'I doubt that he would take the risk of allowing the letter to lie around in his rooms or in the Diogenes Club. There have already been two attempts to retrieve it, and both the club and his rooms are vulnerable. No, for safety's sake, and because the letter concerns matters to do with the Foreign Office, he will probably take it to his office and leave it there.' He glanced at Matty. 'How do you feel about breaking into the Foreign Office and stealing a letter?' he asked.

Matty shrugged. 'I done worse in my life.' He caught Sherlock's expression, and added: 'I ain't goin' to tell you what, though.'

A depressing thought struck Sherlock. 'I suppose it's possible Mycroft might put the letter into a safe, rather than leave it on his desk. That will cause us problems.'

Matty shrugged. 'Depends what kind of safe,' he said. 'Anythin' over five years old I can prob'ly get into. It's just a case of listenin' to the tumblers click as you turn the knob. I got good 'earing.'

'You'll have to teach me how to do that,' Sherlock said, staring at Matty in wonder.

'If I teach you how to do it,' Matty pointed out, 'then you won't need *me* any more.'

'I'll always need you,' Sherlock said simply.

Rather than respond to that, Matty just nodded gratefully, and looked away. 'When are we goin' to head for London?' he asked. Sherlock thought he could hear a catch in Matty's voice.

'There's no point waiting,' Sherlock replied. 'We need to get there and get the letter before Mycroft has a chance to analyse it and put it safely away somewhere. We're going straight to the station now, and we're going to catch a train.'

They got to Arundel Station with plenty of time to spare before the next train, and left the horses at the nearest stables with enough money having been passed to the stable boys that the horses would be looked after until they returned. They looked around cautiously in case Rufus Stone was travelling at the same time they were, but they didn't see him. Half an hour later they were on the train heading for London.

It was only after they had passed through the outskirts

of London that Matty suddenly said, ''Ang on – who's in charge of your 'ouse now? Your bruvver's left, an' so 'ave you. Who does that leave – your sister?'

'I suppose Aunt Anna is in charge now,' Sherlock said dubiously. In fact, it hadn't even occurred to him to leave a note for her telling her what was going on, or send any instructions to the servants to carry on until he got back. In the same way, it probably hadn't occurred to Mycroft to do anything similar when he left so abruptly. The Holmes family did have an issue with thinking things through properly, Sherlock had to admit. He wasn't sure that he would have agreed with Mycroft that he was easily distracted, but once he was focused on a particular thing, then he did have a habit of letting everything else slide.

'Maybe I'll send a telegram,' he said weakly.

The train arrived eventually at Victoria Station. Sherlock and Matty headed east on foot.

''Ow are we goin' to get in?' Matty asked as they walked past the grim frontage of the Tothill Fields Bridewell Prison.

'I'm still working on that,' Sherlock said. In fact, he had no idea.

They passed Westminster Abbey, and kept walking. Eventually they got to Whitehall: a wide thoroughfare with Trafalgar Square at its top and the Houses of Parliament at its base. Sherlock had been there several times over the years, and he knew his way around. The Foreign Office was two-thirds of the way down, on the right: a very grand building of brown stone with an ornate roof and high windows. The faces of some of the stones had been carved with little decorative peaks and troughs, like miniature stone hills.

'What now?' Matty asked as they came within sight of the building. 'I was thinking we might say we was chimney sweeps come to clear soot out of the chimneys.'

'That won't work,' Sherlock replied. 'We're too clean, and too well fed. Nobody would believe we were chimney sweeps. And besides, there's usually an adult with them to make sure they don't run off.'

'All right then – what do *you* suggest?'

'We wait, and observe,' Sherlock said.

They spent several hours in various positions around the front and the back of the Foreign Office, watching as important-looking men in frock coats, striped trousers and top hats entered and left via a door that was guarded by doormen in formal uniforms. The men who came and went all had impressive moustaches, sideburns or beards. After a while they seemed to blend together in Sherlock's tired mind, so that it seemed the same man was entering and leaving time and time again. Once or twice carriages drew up and diplomats in exotic robes and strange hats or headdresses got out and went inside with plenty of ceremony and handshaking from the diplomats who had come outside to greet them.

Twice while they watched, newsboys with piles of

newspapers entered the building, waved through by the uniformed doormen.

'Look at that,' Sherlock said the second time it happened. 'The newspaper boys have free rein to enter the building. The people who work there must read the newspapers for reports of foreign news that hasn't made it through diplomatic channels yet. The boys probably wander through the corridors, selling the newspapers to whoever wants them. That gives us a way in. We just need to get a pile of whatever newspaper edition comes out next, and walk past them as if we have every right to be there. I think there's three or four editions of some of the newspapers every day.'

'So we steal them?' Matty asked.

'We buy them,' Sherlock countered. 'Buy the whole pile from the next boy who comes along.'

'Or we could just steal them,' Matty murmured.

It was half an hour later that a boy wearing a cloth cap came past them carrying a pile of newspapers. Sherlock was going to approach him, but Matty held him back. 'Look, just give me a couple of shillings,' he said quietly. 'I think 'e an' I speak the same language. 'E certainly looks more like me than 'e does you.'

Matty caught up with the boy and walked beside him for a few minutes, chatting. Eventually the boy stopped. Matty handed a coin across, and the boy handed him the pile of newspapers. He ran off, and Sherlock walked up to join Matty.

'Easy as fallin' off an 'orse,' Matty said.

Sherlock grinned. 'Give me half the newspapers, then walk beside me up to the Foreign Office doors. Look as if you've got every right to be there. Actually, look as if you don't *want* to be there.'

'Hey, I've snuck into places before,' Matty replied, sounding slightly offended.

Together they walked towards the impressively big building. Sherlock was expecting to have to say something, or explain why they weren't the usual delivery boys, but the doorman on duty just waved them through. Maybe the faces of the boys who delivered the newspapers kept changing, or maybe he just didn't look at them after so many years of working there. Whatever the reason, Sherlock and Matty just walked right past him.

Inside the building, they found themselves in a foyer whose floor was tiled in white and black marble. Ahead of them an enormous white stone staircase rose up like a cascade of frozen water. Its banisters were wide enough that Matty could have slid down them on a tea tray. The air was cool, and the echoes of distant footsteps mixed with the clatter of typewriters.

'Where now?' Matty hissed.

'Keep moving,' Sherlock said. 'Mycroft told me his room number once, just in case I ever needed to send him an urgent telegram while he was at work. I can still remember it. All we need to do is to keep walking along the corridors until we find it.'

'Sounds like a plan,' Matty said.

They walked along the first corridor they came to, with Sherlock checking the room numbers as they passed. Several times men in the offices saw them and called out, wanting to buy a newspaper off them. In fact, they were so successful at selling newspapers that Sherlock worried they might run out before they got to Mycroft's office, and have no obvious reason for wandering the corridors. For that reason he made sure that he and Matty moved fast, and didn't linger in doorways.

The numbering system, if there was one, wasn't intuitively obvious, and so Sherlock and Matty had to keep looking for the right room instead of working out where it was. They discovered eventually that Mycroft's office wasn't on the ground floor. Instead of going back to the main hall, and the white marble staircase, Sherlock found a door at the end of a corridor that led on to a metal spiral staircase. They went up to the next floor and started again.

After ten minutes on the first floor of the building, Sherlock saw the right number by the side of a half-closed office door. He indicated to Matty that they were in the right place. He was just about to put his newspapers down and move towards the door, ready to listen for anybody inside, when it opened and the large bulk of his brother's body emerged.

# CHAPTER NINE

Sherlock grabbed Matty's arms and shoved him sideways, through an open door and into the next office. Matty started to say something, but Sherlock grabbed his jaw and stopped his mouth from moving.

'Ah – the newspaper boys,' a voice said. 'Is that the late afternoon edition?'

'Yes, sir,' Sherlock said automatically. He turned his head. The man sitting at the desk was as thin as Mycroft was fat. His top hat and frock coat were hanging on a coat stand, and Sherlock could see springy metal bands around his upper arms, presumably keeping his cuffs from falling on to his hands. He had a green visor held to his forehead by a band around the back of his neck, shielding his eyes from the light from the tall window.

'Give me a copy,' he said. 'I'm expecting news from Constantinople.'

Sherlock handed a newspaper across and the man threw a coin at him. 'Bring the evening issue as soon as it arrives. Bring it straight here first, then you can do the rest of the building after. There's a half-shilling in it for you if I get the newspaper first.'

'Yes, sir.'

There was a pause as the man opened the newspaper,

then realized Sherlock and Matty were still there and glanced at them, waiting for them to leave. Sherlock for his part was worried that Mycroft was still out in the corridor, maybe talking to someone, but he didn't want to raise suspicions here. He pushed Matty out of the office, making sure their backs were towards Mycroft's office.

In fact, his brother's recognizable figure was striding down the corridor away from them.

'Lookin' for the lady wiv the tea trolley,' Matty guessed.

'We've got a few minutes,' Sherlock said. 'Let's get in there and look for that letter.'

They moved quickly along the corridor and into Mycroft's office. Sherlock was half afraid that his brother might have been sharing it with someone else, but if he was, then Sherlock supposed he and Matty could just pull the newspaper trick again. In fact, there was only one desk, and the office was empty of anyone else.

Sherlock put his pile of newspapers down and glanced around. Everything was neatly filed away. The maroon leather surface of the desk was almost bare, apart from a green blotter, a fountain-pen stand, an inkwell and a photograph in a frame. Sherlock couldn't help himself: he reached out and took the photograph, expecting it to be either of their parents or possibly of him and Emma.

In fact, it was a picture of a woman in a white dress. From her freckles Sherlock judged that she was probably a redhead. Her hair was curled, and her smile was so vivid and genuine that Sherlock found himself smiling as well.

'I said it before – 'e's a dark 'orse,' Matty observed. He had put his newspapers by the door.

Sherlock put the picture down. 'He probably doesn't even know who she is,' he said dismissively. 'He keeps it here just so everyone else thinks that he has a woman in his life.'

Matty just stared at him. 'Give 'im some credit,' he said eventually. 'I know 'e's 'urt you, but he's doin' whatever 'e is doin' for a reason. That telegram you said 'e got – it was prob'ly givin' 'im orders. Don't assume that 'e's lyin' about *everythin'*.'

Sherlock sighed. 'You're right, of course,' he said

The top of the desk was clear, so Sherlock checked the desk drawers. There were fountain pens, propelling pencils, rulers and pencil sharpeners in the top drawer, envelopes in the second draw, blank paper and notebooks in the third drawer, and a revolver in the bottom drawer. Sherlock stared at it in amazement.

'Dark 'orse,' Matty murmured when he saw what Sherlock was looking at.

Having exhausted the desk drawers, Sherlock stared around the room, frustrated. There was a cabinet against the wall by the door, but it was locked. A chunky metal safe was set into the wall opposite the desk, but that was shut and locked too. Matty had assured Sherlock that he could break into a safe, and so a locked cabinet would presumably present few problems, but Sherlock was worried about the time it would take. Assuming Mycroft had popped out for a cup of tea and a currant bun, instead of heading for a meeting, he would be back in a few minutes. As good as Matty might be, Sherlock was pretty sure it would take him longer than that to get into the cabinet, let alone the safe.

Frustrated, he put his hands on the desk and just leaned forward, head hanging down, trying to work out the best course of action.

'Can I ask somethin'?' Matty said. He had his hands in his pockets and he was staring out of the window.

'What?' Sherlock snapped.

'Those three blokes – the ones who broke into your house while they were pretendin' to be decorators at Mr Phillimore's place . . .'

'What about them?' Sherlock was only giving a small part of his attention to what Matty was asking. The rest was focused on trying to work out where his brother had put the letter. Surely it was here, and not at the Diogenes Club or his flat.

'Where do you think they are?' Matty asked.

'I don't know. Why?'

'Well, your brother took 'em away under orders, far as we can tell. They must be bein' kept somewhere, an' questioned.'

'They committed a crime,' Sherlock pointed out. 'They've probably been arrested and are currently sitting in cells in a police station.'

'Let's hope,' Matty said bleakly. 'It's not like I've got any great love for the Peelers, but I'd 'ate to think of those guys held somewhere secret where nobody can get in to see 'em, wiv no legal brief able to get to 'em.'

'I'm sure that's not the case,' Sherlock said reassuringly, but he was concentrating on the desk, and the way his hands rested on it. There was something about the pad of green blotting paper that his hands were resting on that bothered him. It bowed slightly, as if there was something underneath it, pushing up the middle while he was holding the sides down.

He picked the blotter up and put it to one side. There, on the desk in front of him, was the letter from Jonathan Phillimore to his brother James. Sherlock scooped it up and waved it triumphantly. 'Got it!'

'Brilliant,' Matty exclaimed. 'Let's get out of 'ere.'

'Not so fast.' Sherlock thought quickly. He didn't want Mycroft to realize the letter was gone, not for a while anyway, but he didn't think they had enough time to test it for secret writing here.

For a moment he thought about slipping the letter out of the envelope, putting it into his jacket pocket and leaving the envelope behind, perhaps with a sheet of blank paper inside, but something stopped him from doing that. Instead he reached down and pulled out the second drawer of the desk. Quickly he riffled through the empty envelopes, looking for one the same size as the letter from Jonathan Phillimore. Once he found one he pushed the drawer closed, grabbed a fountain pen with the right colour ink in it and copied James Phillimore's address from the front of his brother's letter to the blank envelope, imitating Jonathan Phillimore's writing as closely as possible. He held the two envelopes up towards Matty. 'Do they look the same?'

'I dunno – I can't read, remember.'

'I don't care if you can read or not, I want to know if they *look* the same.'

Matty squinted. 'I suppose so.'

'That's all right then.' Sherlock slid the fake envelope beneath the blotter and adjusted the green pad until it was exactly as he had found it. He suspected that if it was even slightly crooked or slightly misaligned with the edges of the desk, then Mycroft would spot that something was wrong. He certainly would have done.

'Time to leave,' he said.

Matty poked his head around the edge of the door and glanced in both directions along the corridor. 'We're clear,' he said. 'I see blokes in expensive clothes, but your bruvver ain't one of 'em.'

They left rapidly. Sherlock waved a hand as they went through the doorway, giving the impression that they were saying goodbye to someone inside. After all, they didn't want it to look as if they had been in an empty office.

Five steps along the corridor, Sherlock realized they had left their newspapers behind.

'Quick!' he hissed. 'We need to go back!'

They grabbed their newspapers and left in the same way they had a few moments before. It wasn't that Sherlock thought they needed the newspapers any more – it was that he knew his brother would want to know where the two piles had come from if he saw them, and he wouldn't rest until he got an answer.

They moved in the direction opposite to the one that Mycroft had gone in, and as soon as they came to a stairway Sherlock led the way downstairs. They managed to get rid of five more newspapers before they got to the marbled entrance hall.

Once outside, in the cold afternoon air, they walked as fast as they could away from the Foreign Office building, leaving the remaining newspapers in the care of a surprised blind man with a barrel organ and a monkey on a rope.

'Where now?' Matty asked. 'And will there be food? Me stomach thinks me throat's been cut!'

'We need somewhere with a candle,' Sherlock said.

'Tavern?' Matty offered.

'Tea room,' Sherlock countered. 'There's an Aerated Bread Company tea room opposite Charing Cross Station. Let's get something to eat and drink there.'

Charing Cross Station was only a short walk away, and within ten minutes they were sitting at a table that had a candle conveniently flickering in its centre. Sherlock waited until the waitress had taken their order for a pot of tea and some scones with jam and cream before pulling the envelope from his jacket.

'Right,' he said. 'Time to find out what's really going on.'

'Just don't set fire to it by accident,' Matty replied. 'At least, not until we've 'ad our tea and scones. After that you can do what you want, as far as I'm concerned.'

Sherlock slipped the single-paged letter out of the envelope and sniffed it cautiously. There was indeed a slight lemony smell to it. That gave him the confidence to hold the letter over the candle flame – sufficiently far away that it would get warm but not catch fire.

'I can't see nothin',' Matty said eventually.

'Give it time.'

He kept the letter over the flame of the candle until his fingers were almost too hot to bear, but as far as he could see no extra writing had appeared on the sheet – either between the lines that were already there or around the edge. He huffed in frustration. He couldn't be wrong. The thought process that had led him to this point was unarguable. There had to be a secret message, because the three thugs had been after the letter, and it had to be secret writing because of the words 'invisible', 'candle' and 'trick', and because he hadn't been able to identify any code in the words themselves. He huffed again. What was he missing? Did it need something else apart from heat to reveal whatever secret message was there? If so, what was it? A chemical spray of some kind? The only way to check that would be to go all the way back to Arundel and talk to James Phillimore again to see what technique he and his brother had actually used.

No – there had to be something else. Something simple.

His gaze moved around the table as he thought, not really looking at anything in particular but simply drifting as his mind whirred away. He ended up looking at the envelope, and the fact that it took him several seconds to get to the simple and obvious solution annoyed him so much that he shouted 'I am a *fool*!' so loudly that people at the next tables turned to stare.

'What is it?' Matty asked.

'The secret message isn't in the letter at all,' he exclaimed. 'It's in the envelope!'

Quickly but carefully he took the envelope and pulled it apart, flattening it so that it was as close to a sheet of paper as possible. He held it over the candle with the address downward, and waited impatiently. This time he *knew* he was right.

Brown writing slowly appeared on the inside face of the envelope. Sherlock twisted it so that he could read the words.

*James – I'm sorry but I badly need your help. Are you acquainted with a man named George Clarke? He has some official position on the construction project, although I have never been able to work out what exactly it is, and I have major concerns that he is keeping something from me – something important.*

He seems to have his own agenda, over and above the digging of this canal. He has men who report to him, men who are not on the payroll of the project, and he often sends them off to do work which has nothing to do with digging the canal itself. I have also often found him in my office, when he expected me to be out surveying the ground, examining the maps and various engineering blueprints and comparing them with documents which he put into a briefcase the moment he saw me. Something is going on here, and I do not like it.

I have, of course, attempted to make my concerns known to my superiors, indeed to Monsieur de Lesseps himself in Port Said, but I strongly suspect that Mr Clarke is actually intercepting my letters to them. I don't dare arrange to travel to see Monsieur de Lesseps in case someone here decides to arrange an accident for me. I have attempted to get in touch with the Suez Canal Company at its headquarters in Paris, but I suspect that Mr Clarke is preventing those letters from even leaving the country. I hope that the apparently innocent nature of this particular letter will lull him into a false sense of security, and he will let it go. If this letter reaches you, then please, if you do nothing else, reply to it with a secret message in the same way so that I know my message to you has got through. Please let me know what you can determine about George Clarke, and please talk *to the Government if you can. It would help me as I decide what to do about his presence, and as I further investigate what exactly it is that he is doing on this project. I fear that it is something appalling.*

*Your brother,*

*Jonathan*

'That's it!' Sherlock exclaimed. 'We have it! There is some secret plot afoot to take over, or compromise, or destroy this new canal in Egypt. Jonathan Phillimore found evidence pointing to it and tried to alert his superiors, but his letters of warning were intercepted.'

''Ow do you know it's somethin' like a take-over or sabotage? The message don't say that.'

Sherlock nodded. 'You're right, but think about it. There are only so many things you can do on a big international building site. If you were involved in a financial crime – siphoning funds away from the project, for instance – you'd do it at head office, not where the actual digging work is going on. No, if this George Clarke is actually doing something illegal or undercover at the building site itself, then it has to be something to do with the engineering – and that means he has almost certainly been hired to sabotage it. That's why he's been looking at Jonathan Phillimore's blueprints – he's been looking for weaknesses, places he could do something that would break the canal, or prevent it being finished.'

'You're sure about that?'

'I'm very sure. So Jonathan wrote in secret to his older brother, overcoming whatever family issues were between them, but whoever is behind this plot in Egypt discovered that he had sneaked a letter past them, and organized agents in England to track the letter down.' He shook his head. 'Incredible that a plot so far away could be uncovered here in England, in a tea shop.'

'So what do we do?' Matty asked. 'Tell *your* bruvver?'

Sherlock sighed. 'No,' he said. 'Mycroft already knows.'

'You mean 'e worked out the invisible writin' stuff like you did?'

'No.' Sherlock shook his head sadly. 'Mycroft already knew. Or maybe he didn't, but his superiors knew. Remember what he said when he first read the letter – he mentioned that the British Government is against the digging of the canal, and that they are happy with the current situation concerning shipping and trade.' He stopped to think for a moment, and a horrible thought struck him. 'If the British Government is truly against the project,' be breathed, 'then would they actually go so far as to *destroy* it? Could the British Government have *hired* this George Clarke?'

Matty frowned. 'Why would they?' he asked.

'I've spent long enough with Mycroft, and I've been present at enough discussions that he's held with other diplomats, to know that the British Government is obsessed with keeping itself on top of the pile when it comes to power and influence – especially when it comes to France, Germany and Russia. Anything that could affect that balance, that could give another country more influence, has to be stopped. Jonathan Phillimore said that the project to build this canal from Suez to Port Said is being financed and run by the French. That means when the canal is completed, and ships are able to avoid the dangerous voyage around Africa, that the French will benefit. Either they will charge captains money to use the canal, thus providing funds to the French Government directly or indirectly, or they will preferentially let their own ships use the canal.' He raised his eyebrows as the full implications struck him. 'If French ships can bring cargoes from China and India back quickly, while British ships have to use the long route, then the balance of economic power will immediately shift! France will become the most powerful economic entity!'

'Don't they deserve to?' Matty asked. 'I mean, they are payin' for this canal. Presumably we could've paid for it, if we'd wanted to. If someone else stumps up the money, then good for them.'

Sherlock stared at him for a moment. 'Don't ever enter the Diplomatic Service,' he said finally. 'I don't think it could survive your honesty.'

'Not much chance of that,' Matty replied.

'It's got nothing to do with fairness and everything to do with gaining maximum power and influence for minimum effort. If it's cheaper and easier to destroy a French canal than it is to build a British canal, then that's what they'll do.'

Matty shook his head sorrowfully. 'An' your bruvver knows all about this?'

'He *didn't*.' Sherlock thought for a moment. 'I'm sure he didn't. When he first read the letter at James Phillimore's house he didn't have any reaction to the mention of the canal, apart from some disdain at the idea. It was only after he had sent a telegram to his superiors – presumably mentioning the letter and Jonathan Phillimore in passing – that a telegram came back giving him instructions to get all the evidence out of there and take it to London. He knows *now*, I'm sure, but he didn't *then*.'

'And he don't think it's wrong?' Matty shook his head. 'That's 'arsh.'

'Look, it doesn't matter whether he thinks it's wrong or not. He's got instructions. He's got *orders*.'

'*That's* why I wouldn't ever become a diplomat,' Matty said. 'I just don't like followin' orders.' He paused. 'And I ain't got the qualifications.' Another pause. 'An' I don't 'ave a nice suit an' 'at, like they do.'

Sherlock glanced at the envelope. The writing was fading away as the paper cooled down, leaving the surface blank once more.

'What do we do?' Matty asked.

'Do?' Sherlock stared at him. 'What *can* we do? This is an international thing! We haven't got any power or influence in this!'

Matty frowned. 'Weren't you the one who stopped the American Army from bombin' a bunch of rebels cos you thought killin' 'em was wrong? Weren't you the one who stopped the Paradol Chamber from blowin' up an American boat in China cos it would've started some kind of war? And now you're worried about alertin' people to an attempt to blow up a canal?'

'It's not –' Sherlock stopped. 'It's just that –' He stopped again, and took a deep breath. 'It's *Mycroft*,' he blurted finally. 'I can't go against my *brother*!'

'Bruvvers, fathers, sisters – if somethin's wrong then it's *wrong*.'

It was just at that moment that the waitress returned with their tea and scones. Sherlock was silent while the two of them cut the scones and spread jam and cream on them. He took a bite, hardly tasting it.

'All right,' he sighed. 'What *can* we do?'

'Mr Phillimore's bruvver was tryin' to tell 'is bosses what was goin' on, but 'is letters didn't get through. We could write to them ourselves.'

Sherlock shook his head. 'They wouldn't believe us. They don't know who we are, and we have no real evidence apart from a secret message hidden in a letter.'

'We could send 'em the secret message.'

Sherlock tried to imagine a group of French industrialists and financiers in frock coats and top hats intently waving an envelope above a candle flame. 'They'd just throw the thing away. They'd think it was a practical joke – or worse, some clumsy attempt to pause or stop the digging of the canal. They would probably think that we had faked it.'

'Then we've got to go out there,' Matty said.

'I suppose we do,' Sherlock said, still thinking about ways of getting a warning out to Egypt. His brain took a few moments to catch up with what Matty had said. 'Go *out there*?'

'Yep.'

'To *Egypt*?'

'Yep.'

'Just the two of us?'

Matty nodded. 'Yep.'

'Are you *mad*?'

He considered for a moment. 'Yep. Prob'ly am. Like I said: if somethin's wrong then it's wrong. If only you an' I can stop it, then we 'ave to stop it.'

Sherlock gazed at him, smiled, and shook his head. 'You are an amazing person, Matty.' He felt a sense of purpose, even of *happiness*, welling up inside him. 'Rufus Stone can't come with us, you know – he's working for Mycroft. We'll be completely on our own.'

'What about Mr Phillimore?' Matty asked. 'If 'e's worried 'bout 'is bruvver then maybe 'e'd 'elp us. 'E might want to come wiv us. At the very least 'e might get the tickets for us.'

'That's a very good point.' Sherlock took another bite of scone, and a sip of tea. 'Finish your food – we've got a journey to make.'

They walked back to Victoria Station after they had finished their food, and somehow, despite the enormous undertaking that they were about to engage upon, the sun seemed warmer and the breeze coming down The Mall fresher than it had been before.

It was late afternoon when they got back to Arundel. They retrieved their horses from the stables at the station and rode to James Phillimore's house.

The maid answered straight away, and didn't seem to recognize them. Her eyes were watery, and she kept dabbing at them with a handkerchief. 'The master . . . he can't see anyone right now, I'm afraid.'

'It is quite important,' Sherlock insisted.

'Even so – maybe you gentlemen could come back tomorrow.'

'It's about 'is bruvver,' Matty said, stepping forward.

The maid stared at him strangely. 'Perhaps you'd better come in then,' she said.

She escorted them into the visitors' room and left them there. From elsewhere in the house Sherlock could hear voices. Eventually James Phillimore appeared in the doorway.

'Mr Holmes, Mr Arnatt. You catch me at a bad time.'

'How so?' Sherlock asked.

'I have had a telegram from France, from the company that my brother has been employed by. They, in turn, have had a telegram from Egypt. Apparently my brother has gone missing.'

Sherlock and Matty exchanged glances. 'Then there is something we need to talk to you about,' Sherlock said.

# CHAPTER TEN

It took until the afternoon of the next day for proper arrangements to be made. Sherlock had to return to Holmes Lodge and tell his aunt, and his sister, that he would be away for a while. Fortunately Rufus had already left for London by the time they returned, so they didn't have to worry about telling *him*. Sherlock also had to pack. James Phillimore – who had surprised them both by telling them that he would be heading for Egypt as well, and would happily travel with them – had to organize his business arrangements and leave numerous sets of written instructions for his servants, as well as writing a long letter to Emma Holmes which he asked Sherlock to carry back to Holmes Lodge for him.

Sherlock had asked him, at one stage while they were making plans, why he was so set on going to Egypt.

'You tell me that my brother has asked me for help,' he said seriously, 'and so I shall help as much as I can.' He glanced around, and shivered. 'Besides, after my awful experiences in this house I feel I need some kind of break. I need to get away from here for a while. I have been unable to sleep in my own bedroom, knowing that at any moment someone might grab me, tie me up and hide me in a wall again.'

There was a travel agency in Arundel that specialized in foreign travel. After some research they recommended a direct route from Southampton to Egypt. The company who would organize it was called the Peninsular and Oriental Company, and their steamships left Southampton frequently and called in at Gibraltar and Malta before continuing on to the port of Alexandria. The entire journey would take shortly over a week to accomplish. James Phillimore quite happily paid the £27 ticket cost for each of them, in cash. He seemed to have access to a great deal of money that he had earned during his career and never spent on anything, and he was beginning to see this journey as something between an adventure and an expedition to help repair his family. Sherlock was beginning to like the man – he might be officious, nit-picking and highly strung, but he was also honest and open.

Fortunately there was also a tailor in Arundel who had some lightweight shoes, clothing and hats that would be suitable for a hot and sunny climate. Matty seemed to take this all in his stride. The only thing he had to say about it was: 'At least this time I'll be able to see the ocean. Last time I was tied up in a cabin most of the time.' Again, it was Mr Phillimore who paid. Sherlock offered to access the resources of the Holmes family but Phillimore said: 'No need, no need. Jonathan is *my* brother, after all.'

They had two days until the ship left Southampton.

The journey from Arundel to Southampton Docks would only take an hour or so on the train, and so there wasn't much to do after they had all packed. Sherlock had to spend his time at Holmes Lodge talking to his sister and to his aunt. He tried to make sure that they could run things in his absence, but he realized after a while that the butler, the cook, the maids and the footmen had been effectively running the house themselves since his father had gone to India. His mother, after all, hadn't been in any condition to take more than a slight interest in things. The staff ran the place like a well-oiled machine, only one that had no purpose apart from to keep going. It was a house without a proper family.

The letter supposedly from Mycroft but actually written by Rufus Stone was waiting in the hall for Sherlock to read. He just left it there. He already knew what was in it, so apart from the intellectual interest of seeing how well Rufus could mimic Mycroft's handwriting there was nothing there for him.

He did, however, write a letter back to Mycroft, telling him that the prisoners had escaped – knowing full well that Mycroft had set the scene to look that way – and that he was returning to Oxford. That, he hoped, would assuage Mycroft's suspicions for a while, and prevent him from finding out that Sherlock had actually gone to Egypt.

Emma took the news of James Phillimore's planned trip to Egypt better than Sherlock had expected. It seemed to him that she liked the *idea* of having a fiancé more than the reality. He thought that she could quite happily go on for years talking about the planned wedding without actually getting any closer to it. Perhaps James Phillimore was the same.

It was Aunt Anna who nailed Sherlock's feelings precisely. 'It is better to travel hopefully than to arrive,' she told him. 'That is an old saying, but it is a true one.'

'You are sure you will stay, while I am gone?' he asked her.

'Of course I will. Emma and I have fun together – sewing, gardening and playing the piano. We will be fine, Sherlock. You go off and do whatever it is that you are going to do.'

Sherlock's big fear was that either Mycroft or Rufus would turn up at the house again, and that he would have to pretend that he *wasn't* going to head off to Egypt to stop some kind of huge conspiracy. Either that or he would have to try and explain himself, and he was fairly sure that his brother would have done whatever he could to stop Sherlock from interfering. Knowing about the disappearance of the three burglars, Sherlock was worried that Mycroft might take it into his head to spirit Sherlock away to the same place. Fortunately Mycroft himself wrote, explaining that he was tied up in London with official business, and would not be able to visit Holmes Lodge until the coming weekend – several days away. By then, Sherlock hoped, they would all be well on their way.

On the evening before the journey started, Sherlock found himself outside Holmes Lodge, wandering around the grounds aimlessly. Thoughts kept flickering through his head. Were they doing the right thing? Was he putting Matty's life at risk? Did they have any reasonable chance of making a difference? After a while he found himself sitting on the plinth around the small pyramidal folly near which he had fought the three burglars a few days before. He rested his head in his hands, worries flitting around his mind like moths around a flame. What did he think he was *doing*?

After a while he realized that there were two separate issues here that he was muddling together – the disappearance of Jonathan Phillimore and the possible threat directed against the canal. They were linked, but he needed to separate them, if only for his own peace of mind. If he and Matty accompanied Mr Phillimore to Egypt with the express intention of finding Mr Phillimore's brother, and while they were there spent some time trying to get to see someone in authority in the Suez Canal Company, that was something he could accept, and his heart stopped racing so fast. If, when they found Jonathan Phillimore, they could help *him* to blow the whistle on the suspected sabotage: well, that was something else. Thinking about it this way, he found, made him feel a lot better.

It struck him, as he was walking, that perhaps one

of the reasons he was so set on going straight to Egypt to try and find Jonathan Phillimore was that Sherlock's own father was somewhere unknown and out of touch in India, and he had been informed in much the same way as James Phillimore had – by a message arriving from abroad. Perhaps his decision to help find Jonathan Phillimore was at least in part because he couldn't go and find his own father.

Back inside the house, he raided his father's library for books about Egypt. There were a few – a couple of histories of the country and a few books written by travellers – and he took them away and put them in his baggage. He would have time to read them on the voyage, familiarizing himself with what was ahead.

He slept well, and the next day a carriage containing James Phillimore turned up just after breakfast. The footmen loaded their suitcases on top, and they set off – into the unknown.

Sherlock had been to Southampton before. A couple of years ago, he and Amyus Crowe and Virginia had sailed from there to America. The process of getting on to the ship bound for Alexandria was straightforward: merely a process of presenting their tickets and their passports to the officials on the dockside. Their bags were taken away, to be carried to their cabins, and they were free to climb the gangplank to the impressively large steam ship – the SS *Princess Helena*, according to the sign on her bows – that would carry them all the way.

Two hours later, after all the passengers were aboard, the ship's steam whistle sounded, the gangplank was removed, and the *Princess Helena* was slowly towed by three tugs away from the dock. The sea was blue, dappled with light and dark shadows cast by the clouds overhead. Gradually they built up speed, and eventually, as they passed the Isle of Wight, the tugs abandoned them, the ship's engines built up steam, and the great wheels on either side of the ship started to turn, churning the water. They were on their way.

Watching as the Isle of Wight receded into the distance until it was lost in the haze, Sherlock found his emotions were mixed. On the one hand he loved travelling, and seeing new lands. On the other hand he remembered how much his life, and he, had changed between leaving England on his last journey, to China, and returning. How much might change this time?

Would Mycroft even acknowledge his existence when he returned?

For the rest of that first day, Sherlock spent some time on deck in a deckchair, reading the books about Egypt that he had found in his father's library, and also talking to other travellers who had been to the country in order to extract their impressions and knowledge. Mr Phillimore turned out to be allergic to the sun, and so spent a lot of time in his cabin where, he claimed, he was writing to Emma every day, telling her what had been happening to him. As Matty pointed out, *nothing* was happening to him, not in his cabin, so what was he writing so much about? Matty himself had fallen in with a group of other boys the same age as him, and was busy teaching them the skills of pickpocketing and general thievery that he had picked up in his life. They seemed entranced, and in turn they were teaching Matty about how to hold a knife and fork properly when eating, how to speak without attracting attention because of his accent, and the difference between the ways one addressed a Duchess or a Countess.

Sherlock remembered all too well the way that shipboard life could fall into sheer boredom, if one wasn't careful. He had his father's books about Egypt to read, of course, but there was only so much reading that a person could do every day without going mad or wanting to throw the book overboard. He could pace the decks, watching the horizon for the faint sign of another ship, or land, but he'd seen too many people on his last trip walking round and round obsessively like lions in a cage. Some passengers spent the majority of their time in the *Princess Helena*'s restaurant or the ship's bar, but that didn't remotely appeal to Sherlock. As far as he was concerned, eating and drinking were just ways of providing the body with fuel. One could choose how good the fuel was, of course – just like some kinds of coal burned better and produced less smoke, some kinds of food were tastier than others – but there was as little point in overloading oneself with food as there was overloading a fireplace with coal. And then there were the games – the upper rear deck of the ship had been painted green, and could be used as a croquet pitch, while there were several rooms set aside for card games such as bridge and baccarat. Croquet didn't appeal to Sherlock in the slightest – when a person had knocked a ball through a hoop successfully once, what was the challenge in doing it again? Card games he did find appealing, given that they involved using logic and memory to take advantage of the hand that had been dealt by luck. He had also learned quite a few ways of manipulating and marking cards a few months before by Ambrose Albano in Cloon Ard Castle, in Galway, and so he was pretty sure he could make a decent profit if he played for long enough. The trouble was that the card rooms were so filled with cigar smoke that every time one of their doors opened it was impossible to see anything inside apart from a misty white wall, and he hated smoking with a passion.

Despite his misgivings about obsessive behaviour, he spent quite a lot of the second day at sea alone at the railings, staring out into the deep blueness of the Atlantic Ocean, hoping to see a whale, or a dolphin, or something, and trying not to think about Virginia Crowe. After a few hours he gave up and decided to return to his cabin to research Egypt some more. Turning away from the railings he made his way to where a narrow walkway between two bulkheads would take him back to where he was staying. The walkway was blocked off with ropes, however – some minor repair that had to be made by the crew, he presumed – so he diverted along the deck and down a walkway that he had never had to use before.

He was halfway down when noises from an open doorway attracted his attention. He could hear feet scuffing on the wooden deck, and the sounds of physical exertion. It almost seemed as if a fight was going on, except that he couldn't hear any expressions of pain.

He moved quietly up to the open door and peered around the doorframe.

A man was inside, dressed in a white shirt, open at the neck, white trousers and rope-soled espadrilles. He was middle-aged, quite stocky, with salt-and-pepper hair cropped quite close to his scalp. He was standing on a padded cotton mat which nearly, but not quite, fitted the size of the room.

He was also holding a sabre, with which he was chopping and cutting at the air.

Sherlock glanced further into the room. There was nobody else there. The man was fighting with himself, it appeared.

Sherlock was about to move on, leaving the swordsman to his solitary exercise, when the man made a final lunge at nothing, held it for a few seconds, and then straightened up. He glanced at the door without any surprise, as if he had already registered the fact that Sherlock was there.

'Good morning,' he said. His voice was cultured,

with the faintest trace of a Hampshire accent.

'Good morning,' Sherlock responded.

'No doubt you are wondering what I am doing,' the man said. His eyes were pale green, and keen, like those of a cat.

'You appear to be practising sword-fighting moves in the absence of an opponent,' Sherlock observed. 'I presume you are on a journey and wish to keep your expertise up, but you have nobody to practise with.'

'Indeed,' the man said. 'The Captain had very kindly given me the use of this room for my exercises. K. James Marius Reilly at your service, formerly of the Service Corps, but recently retired Fencing Master to Her Majesty's Naval Officer Cadets at Portsmouth.' He almost, but not quite, saluted.

'Sherlock Holmes,' Sherlock responded.

Reilly glanced at him shrewdly. 'Have you ever fenced, Mr Holmes?'

Sherlock found himself remembering his desperate fight with Baron Maupertuis in his French chateau, a few years ago now. Sherlock's clumsiness with a blade would have killed him if it hadn't been matched by Maupertuis's own problems in manipulating his.

'Once or twice,' he answered. 'I've never been trained, though.'

'Would you care to have some training here? No charge – I'm tired of fighting against my own shadow, and I could do with a decent sparring partner, even if I have to train him up myself. Are you going all the way to Alexandria?'

'I am,' Sherlock said, intrigued. 'Have you taught before?'

Reilly nodded. 'In the Army. I use the Angelo system, but with references back to Diego de Valera's fifteenth-century work, *The Treatise on Arms*. You'll pick it up in no time.'

'I'm not sure I'm suitably dressed . . .' Sherlock protested.

'As long as you have something reasonably loose-fitting, you'll be all right.' He raised an eyebrow. 'What do you say? It will not only pass the time entertainingly for us both, but it will also provide you with some skills that may come in useful one day.'

'Do you have any spare blades?'

'I'm going to Egypt to set myself up as a *Maestro di Scherma*. The creation of the Suez Canal will make Alexandria and Port Said very cosmopolitan places. I want to be one of the first people to set up a fighting school there. I shall make a fortune!' He smiled self-consciously. 'I apologize – I am desperately trying to convince myself that I have made the right move in uprooting myself and moving to another country to teach something that they might not want to know. But yes – I have numerous blades with me, on the basis that I was unsure of the quality of the weapons I will find in Alexandria and its environs.'

'I think you'll find they have been making swords for longer than we have,' Sherlock observed. He found himself smiling at Reilly's naive enthusiasm. 'Very well,' he said. 'I shall take you up on your kind offer. Please – teach me to sword-fight.'

The rest of the day and the whole of the next passed in a whirl. Sherlock had expected to at least have been allowed to hold a sword fairly quickly, but after he had changed into appropriate clothing, Reilly took him through a series of exercises designed to expand his chest, raise his head, throw his shoulders back and strengthen his back. For several hours, with breaks for water, he found himself conducting various repeated exercises: holding his hands straight in front of himself, fingertips touching, and then raising them above his head in a circular motion; holding his hands straight in front of himself and then bringing them back so that they were held out to either side; and bending to touch his toes while keeping his back perfectly straight. He didn't mind: he could see the point of having his muscles stretched and his joints made more flexible. After those initial exercises he was encouraged to spend time holding his arms behind his back, with his left hand grasping his right arm just above the elbow and turning his body left, and then right, until it wouldn't go any further. There were also balancing exercises: taking his weight on the toes of his left and right feet, and holding himself straight for as long as possible. At each stage, while he was holding positions, Reilly would move close and, holding his shoulders, or his arms, or his wrists, attempt to force him further back so that his muscles stretched and protested.

Eventually they moved on to precise footwork exercises. Reilly concentrated on the advantages of varying the speed of moving backwards and forwards, constantly ensuring that Sherlock's torso was half twisted around, which allowed Sherlock to show only a third of his body target. Sherlock stood with his front foot forward, but his back foot pointing away at a right angle. He felt the pressure on his thigh as he lowered his body weight to maintain balance. It proved awkward at first, especially as he tried to maintain his imaginary sword in a position of *en garde*, poised to block any potential blows.

Matty sometimes came in to watch them, but often left within a few minutes saying he was bored. He seemed to be enjoying being the centre of attention of the kids he had fallen in with.

In between training sessions Sherlock ate ravenously in the *Princess Helena*'s galley, and at night he slept like a solid lump of wood: unmoving and completely unaware of the passage of time.

A few days after they had left Southampton, Sherlock caught up with James Phillimore and Matty over lunch – one of the few times Phillimore had come out of his cabin.

'I don't mean to pry,' he said, 'but could I take a look at the message that you got concerning your brother?

Things moved so fast over the past few days that I forgot about it, but I have some questions.'

Phillimore nodded, and reached into an inside pocket of his jacket. He pulled out an envelope and handed it across the table.

Inside the envelope was a slip of paper. Strips of white tape with typewritten characters on were glued in parallel lines across the paper. The message said:

> REGRET TO INFORM THAT YOUR
> BROTHER HAS DISAPPEARED FROM
> POSITION IN EGYPT STOP IF IN
> CONTACT PLEASE TELL HIM TO
> RETURN IMMEDIATELY STOP SUEZ
> CANAL COMPANY

'Hmm.' Sherlock leaned back in his chair, and let his gaze roam around the galley. It was half full: white-jacketed stewards were moving among the tables, delivering full plates and taking empty ones away.

'What's the matter?' Matty asked. 'You look like you're suckin' on a thistle.'

'I was wondering . . .' Sherlock glanced back at Phillimore. 'How did whoever sent this telegram know that you and Jonathan Phillimore are brothers? How did they know where even to send you a telegram?'

Phillimore frowned. 'I presume,' he said slowly, 'that my brother had listed me as his next of kin, even though we weren't on speaking terms for so many years. Our parents are dead, and he never married. There is nobody else – the fact that he reached out to me recently in his hour of need is . . . incidental.'

Sherlock nodded. 'That makes sense. I hope it's the truth.'

The SS *Princess Helena* docked at Gibraltar early on a warm and sunny day. Mr Reilly had said that Sherlock could take time out from sword practice to see the port, so Sherlock and Matty both disembarked to look around, impressed by the massive bulk of the Rock of Gibraltar as it loomed over everything else. Looking at the small town and the limited resources there, Sherlock wondered if the place was ready for what would happen when the Suez Canal opened – *if* it opened. He suspected that Gibraltar would suddenly find itself in a strategically important position and would probably not be ready for it.

Matty was particularly taken with the street vendors and the market traders who seemed to inhabit every main road. He was also taken with the small monkeys who prowled everywhere, stealing food and even money whenever they could.

'Can I take one wiv me?' he asked as the *Princess Helena*'s steam whistle blew, alerting all the passengers ashore that it was about to leave.

'No,' Sherlock said. 'Come on – we've got to get back.'

'But I could slip one in me pocket. Nobody'd notice!'

'What's it going to eat?' Sherlock asked.

'Whatever I eat.'

'Where's it going to sleep?'

'Wherever I sleep.'

Sherlock sighed. Obviously Matty was serious about this. 'Well, how's your horse going to feel about having a monkey around all the time?'

Matty's face fell. ''Adn't thought of that. 'Arold gets really jealous. Don't like cats nor dogs. Don't think 'e'd like monkeys.' He nodded resignedly. 'You're right – it was never goin' to work.'

They got back to the SS *Princess Helena* well before it cast off and started the next leg of its journey. Some passengers had left the ship at Gibraltar and others had joined, meaning that the mood onboard shifted slightly compared to previous days. The weather was different as well, after they had passed through the Pillars of Hercules and into the noticeably calmer Mediterranean – hotter, and more humid – and that affected the way people acted as well. Top buttons were undone on shirts, ties were loosened, and there was a general air of gaiety about the ship. The ship's bar, which had until now been a scene of perfect propriety, suddenly seemed to be hosting a party every night.

By this time Sherlock had worked out the professions, hobbies and other interests of everyone on board, based only on their clothes and their hands. It was a trick that Amyus Crowe had taught him, and one that his brother Mycroft also demonstrated on a regular basis. Sherlock had got to the stage now where he didn't even realize he was doing it, most of the time. He did check his deductions by engaging people in conversation once or twice, and asking them what they did back in England, but once he had established that he was correct sufficient times he didn't bother checking any further.

Eventually content that Sherlock had mastered the technique of good footwork, Reilly permitted his protégé to move on to blade work. And so, for the next few days, Sherlock found himself slashing and cutting at the empty air, just as he had found Reilly doing when he first met him. Reilly would shout out the number of a particular cut and Sherlock would launch himself on a lunge, stretching his body to move on to his opponent in a lightning fashion. He would be expected to immediately execute each attack with a level of accuracy. He soon found himself varying the guard poses for seconds on end, on instruction from Reilly: keeping his feet solidly on the ground and his muscles relaxed, allowing the sword to absorb the force of an attack.

The whole process fascinated him. He wished he had known all this when he had fought Baron Maupertuis in France. He could also see the point of the stretching exercises Reilly had put him through for the first few days: without them, his body would have rebelled against the strange positions it was being forced to adopt.

As well as the seven 'cuts' and the seven 'guards', Reilly introduced Sherlock to three several other important movements: the 'thrust', the 'parry' and the 'riposte'. The thrust, was pretty much as it sounded – a pushing forward of the blade while the right foot shot forward as the left foot remained to provide a solid base. The parries were blocking actions made with the blade, designed to stop an opponent's attack, which were aimed not only at the body but also the head. This move was often followed by an immediate counter-attack, which Reilly called the 'riposte'.

After a few days of this, Sherlock felt as if his muscles had been literally stretched. Strangely, he felt taller, with a longer reach. His body was changing, evolving thanks to the exercises. He also found himself dreaming about the exercises. Each night his brain would put him through the same set of movements that Reilly had put him through during the day.

And so it was three days into their voyage, in the middle of a calm blue sea, that the Paradol Chamber made their move.

# CHAPTER ELEVEN

They were heading across the ocean towards Malta. The sea was calm and the sun was high in a cloudless blue sky. Sherlock had started wearing the pale linen suit and the hat that James Phillimore had bought for him in Arundel. He was taking a break from sword-fighting, standing at the rail of the *Princess Helena*, with the outside wall of the ship's lounge behind him, staring out at the translucent waters, when he became aware that something around him had changed. He had for a while been aware of the noise of a group of men and women playing croquet on the ship's deck, just a little way away on his left, but the click of mallet hitting ball, and the chattering of the players, had suddenly stopped. The croquet pitch had been occupied pretty much every daylight hour since they had left Southampton, and Sherlock couldn't think of any reason why they would stop now. Glancing along the deck to the corner of the lounge, he could see the edge of the pitch: a flat green carpet with little metal hoops set up on it. Nobody was there. Intrigued, he left his position at the rail and walked along to see what had happened. So little of interest ever happened on a ship that perhaps their attention had been caught by something and they had all gone to look. If so, Sherlock wanted to know what it was.

The pitch was deserted, and there was no sign of the players anywhere nearby. In fact, there was no sign of anyone – passengers or crew. That wasn't the strangest thing, however. In the centre of the croquet pitch a table had been set up and covered with a white tablecloth. Two chairs were drawn up to the table. In the centre of the table was a pitcher of something that looked very much like cloudy lemonade with ice floating in it, and two glasses.

Sherlock looked around. He was the only person in sight.

He walked slowly towards the table. In front of the two chairs, on the pristine white linen of the tablecloth, there were two pieces of white cardboard, folded so that they stood up in the shape of a triangle. A name was written on the card nearest Sherlock.

It was his name. He could see that clearly, even though he was a good ten feet away. It was handwritten, but in a large and clear style that, he thought idly, probably belonged to a woman rather than a man. That thought was eclipsed, however, by the much bigger question that occupied his mind: who would consider setting out a table for him in the middle of the *Princess Helena*'s croquet pitch? Neither James Phillimore nor Matty would have bothered to do something that formal – besides, he saw them every day for breakfast, lunch and dinner. Perhaps if it was his birthday they might have arranged some sort of celebration, but it wasn't. The strangeness and formality of it might have appealed to Mycroft, but how would he even know that Sherlock was on the ship?

The name on the other card might well give him an answer, but he felt strangely reluctant to look.

In the end, of course, there was only one thing he could do. He walked over, pulled the chair out and sat down in front of the card with his name on it.

Nothing happened. He looked around, but nobody was approaching him, nobody was watching him. The deck was entirely deserted, which, thinking about it, was very unusual for that time of day. Usually it was crowded with sightseers.

He looked at the jug of lemonade, but he made no move to pour himself a glass. The ice made little *chink* noises as the ship shifted.

He suspected he knew what he had to do in order to move events on, but despite the fact that he wanted to know what this was all about, he didn't want to be too predictable. He wanted whoever was watching him secretly – and he knew there had to be someone – to start wondering whether he was ever going to pick up the other card and look at it. He wanted them to wonder whether he was just going to sip lemonade for a while and then get up and walk away.

In the end, of course, he reached out and picked up the other folded card. He had to know.

*Mrs Loran*

The words were in the same large, clear handwriting.

He knew the name instantly. It hadn't been far from his thoughts ever since he had met the woman for the first and only time a few years before. At the time she had been pretending to be an actress in a small theatrical company, but when they were together in Moscow Sherlock had discovered that she was actually a high-level member of the Paradol Chamber – the secret group that spanned countries and used criminal activities to achieve political ends. Actually, Sherlock corrected himself, he *hadn't* discovered that she was a member of the Paradol Chamber. He had been completely taken in by her portrayal of a middle-aged, matronly lady. She had told him herself, in a cafe, and even then, for a while, he had found it hard to take in. He had come to realize later that she actually *was* an actress, amongst other things, and a much better one than he had given her credit for.

The question was, what was she doing here on a ship heading for Alexandria?

No, that was just one of the questions. There was also, among others: why did she want to talk to him, and what connection did she and the Paradol Chamber have with what was happening at the Suez Canal construction site?

Having picked up the card and seen the name, Sherlock knew what would happen next, and it did. He looked around. Mrs Loran was standing a few feet away, looking for all the world like somebody's grandmother who had put her knitting down and forgotten where it was. She was wearing a long white dress with a short jacket and a large hat. She was carrying a parasol, which Sherlock thought was ironic.

'May I join you, young man?' she asked.

'Do I have a choice?' he replied. Memories of that cafe came flooding back, causing his heart to speed up and his breathing to become tight: the threats that had been made, the fire that Rufus Stone had started to get him out, and most especially two of the other people who had been there – Mr Kyte and Mr Wormersley. Kyte was dead, having run full-tilt into a halberd that Sherlock had set as a trap in an underground cave in Ireland. The last time he had seen Mr Wormersley the man's face was being attacked by a falcon, but he had later heard that Wormersley had been arrested by the Moscow police. As far as he knew, the man was still languishing in a Russian jail cell somewhere. He was sure Mycroft would have told him if Wormersley had got out.

Mycroft *would* have told him, wouldn't he?

'Thank you,' Mrs Loran said, stepping forward and pulling the chair away from the table. 'I do find that the older I get, the more my bones creak. The sea breeze doesn't really help, and as for the pitching and yawing of the ship in the waves – well, one doesn't know from one second to the next *where* one is going!'

She sat down and smiled at Sherlock, her hands carefully folded in her lap. For a moment, sitting there, Sherlock found himself thinking of his Aunt Anna. He was sure that she and Mrs Loran would have become fast friends. They could meet up in tea shops and talk about knitting, and embroidery, and murder.

'I wasn't expecting to see you here,' he said, breaking the silence.

'You weren't supposed to,' she replied. She tilted her head to one side, examining him. He wondered if she was going to tell him to fasten his top button, tighten up his loose tie or make sure he wore a hat to avoid sunburn. 'Your intelligence is sharp – the sharpest I've ever seen, with the exception of your brother – but if you have no evidence to analyse, then how can you come to a conclusion? There is no evidence that we have an interest in this matter.'

'Those three burglars – the ones who broke into Holmes Lodge and who imprisoned Mr Phillimore in his own wall: they don't report to the Paradol Chamber, do they?'

She shook her head. 'Certainly not!' She seemed affronted at the very idea.

'They were clumsy,' Sherlock went on. 'They made mistakes. That isn't what I expect of your organization.'

'Not *my* organization,' she corrected mildly. 'The Paradol Chamber has been in existence since before I was born, and will live on after I die. I am merely a replaceable cog in the machine. Eventually *all* the cogs will be replaced, but the machine will keep on working.'

'To what end?' Sherlock asked.

'Power. Money. Influence. They are all the same thing, in the end.' She paused for a moment. 'I doubt that I am giving away any secrets if I say that what we aim for is to be the power behind the scenes in every major government in the world. It may take a long time, but I think we will get there.'

'And in the meantime,' Sherlock observed, 'what do you get out of it?'

'Why does anybody do a job of work? For the money, of course, and for something to do, something to occupy the time.' She smiled again. 'Working for the Paradol Chamber is certainly lucrative, and it is far more interesting than running a post office in a small town somewhere. And I get to travel, which is nice.'

'I presume,' he said mildly, 'that the money is compensation for the risk. Is it worth it?'

'The risk?' She thought for a moment. 'I suppose there *is* a degree of risk involved. Certainly more than running a post office. Poor Mr Wormersely is still in a prison in Moscow – we could get him out, of course, but he deserves some punishment for his failure. His face looks like someone has tried to assemble it from a pile of jigsaw pieces, and he has had the most terrible infections. And then there's Mr Kyte and Baron Maupertuis. Even the power of the Paradol Chamber can't get *them* back from the place where they have gone – or, rather, the place where you sent them. But life is risk, young man. This ship might hit a rock or a reef and sink tomorrow. I might be run over by a runaway horse the moment I step off the gangplank when we make port.'

'Are you here to kill me?' he said simply.

She shook her head in a kindly fashion. 'Certainly not. You have interfered with our plans on several occasions, but we bear you no ill-will. What has happened has happened. There's no point crying over spilt milk, as my mother used to say.' She glanced at the lemonade and an expression of concern crossed her plump face. 'Oh dear – is that why you hadn't poured yourself any lemonade? Did you think it was poisoned? Here – let me pour some for you!'

She leaned forward, picked up the jug and poured lemonade into Sherlock's glass, and then into her own. Putting the jug down she took her own glass and sipped from it.

'Just to show you that it *isn't* poisoned,' she said reassuringly.

Sherlock reached out and took his own glass. It was cold against his fingers, and the ice cubes inside chinked together. He drank. The lemonade was tart and sweet at the same time.

'Lovely,' he said. 'Did you make it yourself?'

'No – I have people for that sort of thing.' She gazed at him, and he suddenly saw a glimpse of the steel behind the cosy façade. 'Of course, if we *had* wanted to poison you, we would have coated the inside of your glass with the poison and let it dry before setting the table.'

'I swapped the glasses around when I sat down,' he said calmly.

Mrs Loran laughed. 'Very good! No – you didn't swap them around. We were watching, of course. But I do admire your calmness under pressure, young man. I really do.'

'Why am I here?' Sherlock asked, putting his glass back on the table. 'Why are *you* here?'

'It's very simple. We need your help.'

In the following silence, Sherlock looked around. The deck where they were sitting was still completely deserted apart from the two of them. Whatever power the Paradol Chamber had, it was enough to create this buffer zone on an otherwise crowded ship. Were there chains across the deck, further down where he couldn't see them? Were there signs saying something like *Closed Due to Vital Maintenance*?

'What *is* the Paradol Chamber?' he asked suddenly.

'You know what it is. We are an organization of –'

'No,' he interrupted, 'the chamber itself. What is it? *Where* is it?'

'Ah.' She nodded. 'The Paradol Chamber is the room where the Council who run its activities meet. It is a room whose walls are made from sheets of pure amber, illuminated from outside. All those entering the room are masked in the Venetian style so that nobody knows who they are. In that chamber, history is not just made, but *planned*.'

'Where *is* the Chamber? Where do you meet?'

'The Chamber is wherever we want it to be. It can be

disassembled, moved and reassembled to look exactly the same. We never meet twice in the same place.'

He thought for a moment. 'This thing that is going on with the canal in Egypt, the thing that Jonathan Phillimore uncovered – you don't want it to happen, do you?'

Mrs Loran was silent for a while. She gazed out at the white-topped waves surrounding the ship. She seemed to be trying to decide what to say, how much to give away. 'It does not agree with our plans,' she agreed eventually. 'Creation of that canal across Egypt will cause a shift in political and economic power that will benefit the Paradol Chamber. It will reduce the influence of Great Britain, and it will give our agents a faster means of travel and of conveying messages. No, we *don't* want the canal to be sabotaged. We want it to be built.'

'And that is what these people are trying to do, isn't it – to sabotage it?' he pressed.

She nodded. 'Even *we* are not sure who is behind this rather clumsy plan. Our suspicion is that it is an ad hoc group of industrialists and politicians who see their own fortunes waning if the canal is completed. They believe that if they can prevent the canal being built *now*, then nobody for the next century or so will be able to finance it, or will be willing to take the risk. Things will settle back to the status quo that they are comfortable with.'

'Is my brother one of them?' This was the question that had been weighing down Sherlock's mind.

She shook her head. 'No, but the men he works for – the men in charge of the Foreign Office, and the men who run the Government – some of *them* are involved. Your brother is merely following orders. I doubt that he wants to, but he has to if he wants to keep his post and his pension.'

'I presume,' Sherlock said carefully, 'that you are telling me all this not just for fun, but because you want me to help you.'

'Yes,' Mrs Loran said. 'We do. Ironic, isn't it?' she continued. She reached out and took another sip of her lemonade. 'You have interfered with our plans before, but this time round our interests appear to coincide.'

'Don't you have your own agents in place?' Sherlock asked.

Mrs Loran shrugged. 'We did, but they were discovered and disposed of by the agents of these clumsy saboteurs. It was unfortunate – because of circumstances we didn't have our best people in the country, and so had to rely on recruiting locals. That was a mistake.'

'Jonathan Phillimore – was he one of your men?'

'Oh, please!' She raised her eyes in scorn. 'Lemon juice as an invisible ink? Do us the honour of giving us more credit than that, young man.'

'And if I do help you – what do I get out of it?'

She stared at him. 'Surely you are not suggesting that we *pay* you?'

'It's not a bad idea,' he admitted. 'But no – I wouldn't

accept your money. It just occurred to me that you seem to be expecting me to offer my services for free.'

'You and your friends are heading to Egypt to try and find Jonathan Phillimore and to try and stop the sabotage of the Suez Canal anyway,' Mrs Loran pointed out. 'You can do it with our resources and assistance, or you can do it by yourselves. Which do you think gives you the best chance of success?'

Sherlock paused just long enough that Mrs Loran began to look uncomfortable. 'I was hoping for more than just that,' he said.

'Such as?'

'I'm not sure yet. A favour, perhaps. You will owe me something.'

She laughed again. She had a girlish laugh, much younger than her face. 'Sherlock, we are a criminal conspiracy that spans the globe! We lie, cheat, blackmail and kill! What makes you think that we would honour any promise that we make to you?'

'Because,' he said, 'the only way that an organization such as yours can keep control over such distances and timescales is if you *do* keep your promises. Bizarrely, your people and your contacts must trust you to deliver on what you say. It's not as if you can draw up and sign legal agreements, is it? Your people trust you to pay them if they do a good job, and to rescue them if something goes wrong that isn't their fault. Your whole *enterprise* is built on trust, isn't it? Not trust as a moral, ethical thing, but trust as something you have demonstrated in everything you do.'

She gazed at him for a long time, as if re-evaluating him. 'I think you may even be cleverer than your brother,' she said quietly. 'Or at least, you have that potential.' Her voice became more formal, like a schoolteacher. 'Very well – we will owe you a favour, if you help us, that favour to be repaid at some time of your choosing, in a manner of your choosing, and said favour to be of a value roughly commensurate with the size of the favour that you are doing for us.' Her voice returned to its normal warmth and friendliness. 'After all, we won't give you Luxembourg in return for helping us out. Not the *whole* of Luxembourg, anyway. Does that satisfy you?'

He nodded. 'It does. So – what can you tell me that will help?'

'If you try to contact the Suez Canal Company and warn them that someone is trying to sabotage their work they will just fob you off. Your best option is to go directly to the man in charge – Monsieur Ferdinand de Lesseps. He is the main architect of the canal, and the man running all the works. If anyone will listen to you, it is him. He has a villa in Ishmaili, but you may need to use subterfuge to get in.' She looked out across the sea. 'If that fails, then look for Jonathan Phillimore. If you find out where he is, then you will find the conspiracy.'

Sherlock nodded. 'How will I get in touch with you, if I need you?'

'There will always be someone watching. There is a red handkerchief in your bag. Keep it in your pocket. If you need us, take it out and hold it up. We will be there.' She picked up her glass of lemonade and drank it. 'And now,' she said, 'we should conclude our meeting. I believe there is a croquet tournament scheduled, and I wouldn't like to delay it for too long.'

'I didn't bring a red handkerchief with me,' he pointed out.

'I know. If you had, there would have been no need for us to put one in your luggage while you were sitting here.' She stood up. 'I don't know whether we will meet again or not, but rest assured that we will be watching you with interest, whatever you choose to do in the future.'

'And I will be watching you,' he said. He raised his lemonade it salute. 'Be assured of *that.*'

She gazed at him fondly, like a grandmother trying to work out what present to give to her grandson. 'Just because we owe you a favour, young man, it doesn't mean that we won't kill you if you get in our way.'

'As I told Mr Kyte, just after he ran into the halberd I had left for him as a trap in Galway, and just before he breathed his last breath: only *I* choose when I die. Nobody else.'

He turned his head to gaze out across the ocean, not willing to engage in a staring contest, or a battle of words. They had both said their piece. When he turned back, Mrs Loran had gone.

# CHAPTER TWELVE

Sherlock didn't see Mrs Loran again during the trip. He managed to get a copy of the passenger list from the *Princess Helena*'s purser, but of course she wasn't listed – at least, not under the name 'Loran'. On the assumption that she was travelling under a different name he spent some time gradually identifying every woman on the ship and ticking their names off on the passenger list. After three days he had to stop – he could account for every single woman on board, and Mrs Loran wasn't any of them. He even went as far as sneaking into those areas of the ship where passengers weren't supposed to go – the engine room, the storerooms and so on – on the assumption that she had a base of operations down there somewhere, but there was no sign of her.

Putting the meeting, and Mrs Loran, behind him, Sherlock continued to work with Mr Reilly. This time the emphasis was on accuracy, and he was given a curved cutlass with a basket guard around the hilt to protect his fingers in case his opponent slid their blade along his to cut his hand.

Reilly had drawn a target diagram in ink on a large sheet that he seemed to have taken from the *Princess Helena*'s laundry. The target was in the shape of a person.

It was attached to a wall about ten feet away from where Sherlock had to stand. Inside the circle were several straight lines crossing from one side to another.

'These are "cuts",' Reilly announced. 'You will notice that each cut has a number written against it on the target. The intention is that, with the sword in your right hand, you cut the air as if you were trying to cut the sheet along that very line.'

The target also had dotted lines drawn in ink on it, and they were also numbered. These, Reilly said, were 'guards'. They worked in a similar way to the cuts, except that rather than attempt to *slice* these lines, Sherlock had to hold his sword so that it blocked the likely counter-attack of his opponent. There were markings on the diagram for the cuts telling him where to start and where to finish, and for the guards telling him where the point of his blade should be and where the hand should be.

'The reason why we are doing this,' Reilly explained, 'is that I want these movements to become second nature to you. I don't want you to have to think about them. In a sword fight, thinking means losing. You need to be able to react instinctively, without consideration. The way the human body works, if you exhaustively rehearse a movement, like a cut or a guard, then your muscles and your mind will remember it. You won't have to think about it when the time comes to use it: if someone comes at you from a particular direction then your body will *know* how to respond. If you *don't* exhaustively rehearse a movement then your mind will hesitate, when confronted with an attacking move, while it works out what it should do for best effect. That hesitation will cost you your life, if the fight is real. If it isn't, it will merely cost you victory.

In his sword-fighting tutorials, Mr Reilly now spent some time taking Sherlock through the actual anatomy of a sword: not just the blade, the hilt and the guard, but the different parts of the blade. In particular, he made Sherlock aware of the difference between the half of the blade closest to the hilt, which he called the 'forte', and the half closest to the point, which he called the 'foible'.

'The intention,' Reilly announced, 'is that when you engage your blade against your enemy's blade, you should see to engage his foible with your forte. This is the strongest part of the blade, whereas the foible is the weakest. It will absorb the blows through your whole body. The same holds true for your enemy.

They spent a good hour just on the process of withdrawing a sword from a scabbard. It wasn't just a case of pulling it out, Sherlock found. There was a proper way of doing it that stopped the blade from catching and fouling the scabbard. Unsurprisingly, just lifting the blade from the scabbard immediately placed him in a guard: that of 'prime' or 'number one' guard, which left it, and him, in a proper position from which to defend or to launch an attack. Following that, Reilly also took him through the various positions to adopt when facing an enemy: 'recover swords', 'slope swords' and 'return swords', as well as 'front prove distance' and 'right prove distance'.

After that, Reilly made Sherlock combine the various cuts and guards, so that they weren't just separate, distinct elements but were combined into a flowing motion, covering – it seemed to Sherlock – all of the possible combinations and permutations in strings, like 'cut 1', 'guard 3', 'cut 2', 'guard 2', 'guard 5', 'cut 4' . . . and so on, in seemingly endless combination.

Sometimes he would look up to see Matty watching him from the side of the room, and sometimes the two of them were alone. Matty seemed to be happy to do his own thing while he was on board the ship, and stay out of Sherlock's way. He certainly didn't seem to be interested in learning to fight with swords, and Reilly didn't seem interested in teaching him.

Over the next two days they passed the islands of Ibiza, Palma and Mahon in relatively quick succession, then later on Sardinia and Sicily, before they docked at the much smaller island of Malta. The other islands were under the control of France, Spain and Italy, of course, whereas Malta, like their previous stop of Gibraltar, was defiantly part of the British Empire.

As the *Princess Helena* slowed for its approach into the Valletta waterfront area Sherlock was struck by the clean lines of the windows, the bright stonework of the walls, and the coloured doors that ran all the way along the wharf – blue signifying that fish were stored there, green for vegetables, yellow for wheat, and red for wine, according to one of the ship's crew with whom Sherlock had talked.

When the *Princess Helena* docked, Sherlock watched the gangplank in case Mrs Loran disembarked, but he didn't see her. He had to admit that she was a much better actress than he had expected, if she had managed to disguise herself in such a way that he couldn't identify her. The other possibility was that she had disembarked secretly on to another ship that had come alongside them without anybody noticing, but that would have implicated everyone from the Captain down in covering up such a rendezvous, and surely some of the passengers would have noticed and said something? In the end it was abundantly clear that the Paradol Chamber had resources he could only guess at.

Malta seemed to be filled with palaces, churches and other beautiful buildings dating back hundreds of years. Sherlock only had time to visit one place during the little time they spent docked, so he chose the massive baroque Co-Cathedral of St John, and he barely had time to see half of it before he had to get back to the ship.

From Malta the SS *Princess Helena* kept heading east, past Crete, then bent its path southward towards the port of Alexandria in Egypt – its final destination. The weather had grown progressively warmer during the latter stages of the voyage to the point where it was uncomfortable to be out on deck during the hours around noon, when the sun was directly overhead in a pure blue sky. Hats were definitely required for the men, and parasols for the women, to prevent sunburn or heatstroke, and virtually everyone had started to take naps during the afternoon.

During the last leg of the voyage, from Malta to Alexandria, Mr Reilly and Sherlock actually sparred: blades clashing together in mock-fights. After so many days in which he had been practising movements and stances until they became second nature, Sherlock now discovered that whenever Mr Reilly lunged or cut at him, his body instinctively responded with the correct parry or guard. Previously, Sherlock had assumed that thought and logic could counter anything, and that fighting was merely the process of having a longer reach and a quicker response, and logically anticipating his opponent's moves. This was a revelation! His body – and potentially *any* body – could be trained to respond *without* thought: a machine driven by pure instinct. Thought wasn't enough.

Mr Reilly also impressed upon Sherlock the fact that any attack – thrust or cut – should *increase* in force and velocity as it was conducted, not *decrease*. Sherlock realized with shock that when he was attacking, his tendency was to put the emphasis on the initial motion, not the follow-through. Mr Reilly quickly disabused him of this notion.

From that point, their exercises became actual fights, with no quarter given or taken. Reilly was older than Sherlock, but he was more skilled. The whole thing balanced out, meaning that they were pretty evenly matched. Their fights could go on for ten, perhaps twenty minutes, with them moving forwards and backwards in the practice room, before one of them perceived a slight advantage and instinctively took it, swords clashing, sending impacts repeatedly up Sherlock's arm. He found himself lost, not even knowing what time it was.

On the last day of the voyage, as they began to approach Egypt, and the port of Alexandria, Mr Reilly stepped back during their regular sparring and lowered his sword. Sensing that this was more than just a ploy – and Reilly had warned him about opponents who lowered their weapons as a deception only to raise them again a few seconds later – Sherlock lowered his own sword, but kept it ready just in case he needed it again.

'I have to say,' Reilly said, breathing slightly heavily, 'that you have been a most excellent student. It has been my absolute pleasure to teach you over this past week.'

Sherlock smiled. 'I have learned a lot on this voyage,' he replied. 'More than I ever thought I would.'

'You have several characteristics that make you a most excellent swordsman,' Reilly continued. 'You are not afraid, for a start, your reflexes are admirably fast, and you can submerge your intellect and allow your instincts to take over.' He smiled. 'If you ever find yourself in a situation where your life depends on your swordsmanship, I am sure you will prevail.'

'Assuming that my opponent hasn't been trained by you,' Sherlock pointed out.

Reilly lowered his sword further and stepped forward

with his left hand extended. 'These past few days have been the most excellent fun. I wish you good luck, Mr Holmes, in whatever you choose to do with your life, but I would say that if you wished to make a living giving lessons in swordsmanship, then the world would willingly accept you. You have taken to these lessons as a duck takes to water. I have been fighting professionally for more years than I care to remember, and I cannot recall a better student.'

'You flatter me, Maestro,' Sherlock replied, using the highest honorific he could to acknowledge the respect he had gained for his fencing master. Lowering his own sword he shook Reilly's hand firmly. 'You are a most excellent teacher. I bless the fortune that brought me to this ship at the same time as you.'

Knowing that Egypt was nearer the equator than England, and that the Suez Canal was being dug mainly through desert and rock, Sherlock had expected Alexandria to be hot but dry. He was wrong. It was a port on the Mediterranean Sea, which meant that it was hot but also very humid. The sunlight was blindingly strong, making everything look faded, and Sherlock could feel its heat as a physical pressure on his forehead and scalp. Walking around was like moving through invisible clouds of steam, and there was a strong smell in the air of marshy, stagnant water. James Phillimore took immediate fright.

'I can actually *see* the particles of disease floating in the air!' he cried as they came down the gangplank from the ship. 'This place must be the first circle of hell!'

He pulled a handkerchief from his pocket and clamped it over his mouth and nose.

The Alexandria docks were a strange mixture of old stone buildings that looked like they had been there forever and could last just as long, and temporary shacks and huts that looked like they had been built yesterday and would fall down tomorrow. The locals were either dressed in loose robes and had material like scarves protecting their heads and necks or they were dressed in dark suits and had strange little brimless red hats on their heads. The Europeans, by contrast, were easily identifiable in their linen suits, shirts and ties, and white hats. Once or twice, as they disembarked and walked across the quayside, Sherlock caught sight of tall men dressed in black robes, with black scarves wound around not only their heads but their faces as well, leaving only a slit for their eyes. They made him uneasy. He knew it was unfair, but they reminded him of the men who had broken into Holmes Lodge and attacked him.

There were animals as well – lots of them. Not just the underfed dogs and scrawny cats that one might expect at any port in the world, but donkeys, horses and even camels. Sherlock had never seen a camel before, and was amazed by how strange they looked. Matty just looked at them, looked at Sherlock and said, 'You know that game where you draw a head on a piece of paper, then fold it over so that only the neck can be seen, and you give it to someone else? They draw a body, then fold it over and give it to someone else who draws the legs?'

'Yes. Why?'

He pointed to the nearest camel, which was gazing at them with what looked like contempt on its face. 'That's what you get if you do it for real,' he said.

Once the *Princess Helena* had docked, the crew started to take the baggage down to the quayside while the passengers disembarked and queued up in a massive and high-ceilinged hall to present their passports and their paperwork to a series of uniformed and frankly bored civil servants. From there Sherlock, Matty and James Phillimore, who spent most of his time mopping the back of his neck with a handkerchief, made their way via carriage to the hotel into which the Arundel travel agent had booked them.

'What's our first move?' Matty asked as they stood in the marbled lobby of the hotel. The space was kept cool by having small windows, and by large sheets of woven bamboo that hung from the ceiling and were pulled back and forth by ropes leading through small holes in the walls. Outside, in the heat of the day, small native boys pulled on the ends of the ropes for hours on end for just a few coins.

Sherlock thought back to his discussion with Mrs Loran on board the *Princess Helena*.

'We need to get to a town called Ishmaili,' he said.

'That's where Monsieur de Lesseps is living while he oversees the construction of the canal.

'How do you know that?' Matty asked.

'I . . . picked the information up somewhere,' Sherlock said, not looking at Matty.

Sherlock interrogated the hotel's desk clerk as to the best way to get to Ishmaili. It turned out that there was a railway line between the town and Alexandria, and there were several trains a day. Sherlock made a quick decision, and after they had eaten a quick European-style lunch in the hotel restaurant he ushered the other two out into the sunshine again, where they secured a carriage to Alexandria Station.

Buying tickets was an exhausting process, involving a great deal of hand-waving and the payment of what looked to Sherlock like an exorbitant amount of money, but eventually they were waiting on the platform. The other passengers were a cross-section of humanity, from people like them in linen suits and hats, carrying carpet bags or black leather Gladstone bags, to natives carrying wickerwork baskets filled with squawking chickens. Within half an hour a massive steam train of elderly design pulled itself along the tracks and hissed to a halt like some labouring beast.

They had First Class tickets, which meant that their carriage at least had wooden seats to sit on, and they weren't sharing it with the natives or the chickens. The men sitting around them – and they were exclusively men – seemed to be either people working on the canal or, Sherlock suspected, journalists wanting to write stories about its construction.

The journey was scheduled to take two hours, and it took them through a landscape of baked earth, scrubby bushes and a horizon that wavered uncertainly in the heat-haze. The carriage was ventilated only by whatever meagre breeze managed to find its way through the open windows, and since the air outside was roasted by the sun, all the breeze did was substitute moving hot air for still hot air. Despite the fact that they had First Class tickets – or perhaps because of that – there was a constant stream of native Egyptians coming through the carriage with trays of hot and cold snacks, fruit and drinks.

'Do not drink the water, and do not eat any food that hasn't been cooked, except for the fruit,' Phillimore warned them. 'I have read about this. The water here is infested with disease. Cooking kills the particles of the disease, and the skin of the fruits prevents those same particles from getting in.'

It was exactly an hour into the journey that the attack happened.

Phillimore and Matty were dozing. Sherlock was staring through the window at the unchanging picture outside, comparing it with the equivalent English countryside which would have kept flashing up new things to look at.

The window by his head suddenly cracked. Splinters of glass rained down on him.

# CHAPTER THIRTEEN

Sherlock glanced up in shock. There was a small hole in the window, surrounded by cracks running all the way to the frame.

In their seats, Phillimore and Matty jerked awake.

Something appeared outside the window. Sherlock's head snapped around in shock.

Several men riding camels were racing alongside the train, parallel with the track. They were holding rifles in one hand and the reins of the camels in the other, and they were wearing black robes which billowed out behind them and black cloth wrapped around their heads. Their camels didn't gallop the way that horses did: they had a strange lolloping gait, and part of Sherlock's mind – the part that wasn't incredulously trying to work out why someone was shooting at them – noticed that their right legs, front and back, moved in unison, and so did their left legs. It looked so clumsy, but they were keeping up with the train.

Looking around, Sherlock noticed that the other passengers had ducked beneath the level of the windows.

He looked out again. One of the men in black was jabbing his rifle in Sherlock's direction, trying to get the attention of the other two who kept glancing into the windows they passed as if they were looking at something.

The man who had noticed Sherlock looked directly into his eyes, pointed his rifle one-handed at Sherlock's face, and pulled the trigger again.

Sherlock ducked just as the bullet smashed the entire window. He was sure that he could feel the bullet drawing a blazing hot line through the air, just above his scalp.

This is deliberate, he thought wildly. They're looking for us!

He looked around desperately, trying to work out what to do, but apart from keeping down, he couldn't think of anything. It wasn't as if they could get off the train. They were trapped. He threw himself off the bench and into the space down by the floor.

The other two riders had finally noticed their companion's gesticulations, and had slowed their camels down to keep pace with Sherlock's window. All three of them were pointing their rifles at where Sherlock and his friends were sitting. They were aiming down, trying to get their bullets into the space where Sherlock, Matty and Phillimore were all squashed together.

Over the rushing of air past the window Sherlock heard several flat *cracks*. Across the other side of the carriage, wood splintered.

Sherlock poked his head above the window ledge. One of the camel riders was dropping back, but the other two were still keeping up, and still trying to take aim over the juddering ride of their camels.

Sherlock glanced backwards. He thought that the third rider was trying to jump from the back of his mount to the platform where Sherlock and the others had climbed on. He was trying to get on the train to kill them!

Sherlock ducked back just as more bullets sprayed the carriage, shattering windows across the far side. Sherlock wondered briefly what the driver and engineer were making of this, up front. Did they even know what was happening?

Beside him Phillimore stood up. He reached for his bag, which was on a rack near the ceiling.

'Get down!' Sherlock yelled.

Phillimore ignored him. He pulled the bag down to the bench and opened it. A bullet zoomed past his head, but he ignored it. From the bag he pulled a revolver with a long barrel. Turning, he pointed it at the nearest rider and pulled the trigger.

There was an explosion of smoke, fire and noise, and the rider fell from his camel as if pushed. Within seconds he had vanished behind them.

Phillimore took careful aim at the remaining rider. The man tried to train his rifle at Phillimore but the barrel kept waving around. Phillimore, stabilized by the carriage floor, was in a better position. He fired again, missing the rider but hitting the camel's right ear. The camel, already spooked by the noise and the train, veered sideways, running out of control. Within moments the camel and its rider were vanishing into the distance and the heat-haze.

'You've got a gun!' Sherlock said. He immediately cursed himself for saying something so obvious, but it had been a surprise.

'I thought this trip might be dangerous, especially based on what happened back in Arundel,' Phillimore said. 'So I packed my gun, and a good thing I did so.'

'How did you get it past Customs in Alexandria?'

Phillimore looked at him as if he'd said something else stupidly obvious. 'I didn't tell them,' he said.

The door at the end of the carriage suddenly burst open. The third black-robed man – the one Sherlock had seen climbing on board the train – filled the opening from side to side and top to bottom. He was carrying his rifle ready for use, and his hawklike gaze scanned the carriage looking for his targets.

Phillimore raised his revolver and fired.

The bullet hit the man in his right shoulder. He fell backwards, out of the carriage, screaming. The train chose that moment to sharply jerk as its wheels hit a bump, or some kink in the track, and the man abruptly rolled sideways and, before he could catch hold of anything, fell off the platform.

Sherlock leaned out of the window, and saw a black blur as the man hit the ground and was immediately left far behind.

'That was . . . interesting,' Sherlock murmured.

Matty crawled out from under a bench. 'Is it all over?' he asked.

'Thanks to Mr Phillimore here,' Sherlock said.

The conductor – a dark-suited man with a red hat – hurried into the carriage. He was carrying a rifle of old design. He glanced around. 'Bedouin tribesmen – very rare they make an attack. Is everyone all right?' He spoke first in French, then repeated it in heavily accented English, and again in what was presumably Egyptian. The other passengers emerged from hiding and shakily reassured him that they were, indeed, all right. Some conversation ensued in which he presumably asked what had happened to the attackers and they gave him various contradictory stories. Sherlock gestured to Phillimore to put his gun away before someone started asking difficult questions. Indeed, a few seconds after he replaced it in his bag one of the passengers pointed to Sherlock and Phillimore and said something in voluble French. Sherlock just tried to look innocent. Phillimore, he had noticed, always looked innocent, so that was all right.

The conductor came down the aisle to talk to them, but he only wanted to make sure that they weren't injured, and that the lack of a window wasn't disturbing them. He suggested that they switch to different seats, but Sherlock was quite enjoying the breeze and elected to stay.

'Is it just that bad things always seem to happen to us?' Matty asked once the conductor had gone. 'Or is it that those blokes were aimin' at us?'

'I think they were,' Sherlock said darkly. 'There are, what, four carriages behind us, and yet they rode along the length of the train until they found us. This is the only window they fired through, as far as I can tell. Either they had deliberately chosen us as targets or we are sitting in the unluckiest seats on the train.'

'So someone knows we're here,' Matty pointed out.

Sherlock nodded. 'Difficult to avoid it. The voyage was long, our names were on the passenger manifest, and we had no choice other than to draw attention to ourselves in Alexandria.' He shrugged. 'We'll just have to be alert.'

Two hours later they arrived in Ishmaili. Unlike Alexandria, which was obviously a very old city before the Suez Canal was even thought of, no building in Ishmaili seemed to be more that ten years old, although the sun and the wind had weathered them. Ishmaili looked like it had been built purely as a base from which the canal could be built. As the train wound its way through the town and slowed as it approached the station, Sherlock observed that there were two very different parts to the city, separated by the train track itself. On one side the houses looked native: earth-coloured single-storey buildings that were barely more than huts or shacks, presumably occupied by native Egyptians who were working as builders. On the other side the buildings were several storeys high, made of whitewashed brick, with solid tiled roofs in a variety of colours. They were the kind of houses that wouldn't have looked out of place in Malta, or Gibraltar, where their ship had stopped on the way to Alexandria: European-style dwellings. This was obviously where the managers and the engineers lived – in more comfort.

In the distance, on the workers' side of the tracks, Sherlock saw a line of green vegetation running along in a straight line for as far as he could see. That, he suspected, was the canal, and the vegetation was growing there because of the water soaking into the ground. There were also what looked something like large steam trains lined up along the side of the canal: huge machines made out of iron with gantries and girders coming out of them in all directions like the legs of vast insects.

One house, bigger than the rest, on a slight rise in the ground and surrounded by palm trees, was, Sherlock thought, probably where Ferdinand des Lesseps lived.

The train stopped and they disembarked, with the contrite and sincere apologies of the conductor ringing in their ears.

''Otel?' Matty asked, and then, hopefully, 'An' food?'

'No,' Sherlock said. 'We go straight to see Monsieur de Lesseps.' At Matty's crestfallen expression he added, 'But if we see anyone selling food from a roadside stall on the way we can get some.'

Ishmaili was obviously a popular destination, and there was a bustle of activity around the station with donkeys, carts and even camels being used to ferry people to where they were going. It was cooler there than it had been in Alexandria, and the air was fresher.

Sherlock was prepared to have to find someone to translate for them, or to have to somehow indicate via sign language that they wanted to visit the big man in the canal company, but the driver of the first cart that they found spoke French – a language of which Sherlock had learned enough to get by. He took them on a twenty-minute journey through the European section of town, although Sherlock was fairly sure it could have been accomplished in ten.

They stopped outside the large building on a small hill that Sherlock had seen from the train. Sherlock tried to pay using the Egyptian money he had picked up on the *Princess Helena*, but the driver shook his head regretfully.

'Only company money,' he said. 'Nothing else can be used in this town.'

'Company money?' Sherlock questioned.

Phillimore nodded. 'It's common in large construction projects like this,' he explained. 'The company print their own money and pay the workers with it. The company money is only usable in the company shops and in the company town, which means that the workers have to stay there and the company get their money back again.'

'That ain't fair,' Matty said. 'It's like slavery, only you get paid for it.'

'It's the way of the world,' Phillimore said. 'Large projects such as this would not be completed on time and to budget otherwise.'

Matty delved in his pocket and pulled out a handful of paper. He looked at it, nodded, then handed one of them to the driver. He in turn inspected it carefully and then tucked it inside his robe. With a nod to them, he drove off.

'Where did you get that?' Sherlock asked.

'Don't ask,' Matty responded. At Sherlock's dark glance he added: 'Let's say one of them blokes at the station is goin' to get a shock when 'e tries to pay for somethin' 'ere.'

Matty started to head towards the building, but Sherlock caught his shoulder.

'Wait a little bit,' he said.

'Why?'

'Because it's not four o'clock yet.'

Matty frowned. 'We ain't got an appointment, 'ave we? Don't matter *what* time we turn up.'

Sherlock checked his watch. '*We* know we haven't got an appointment, but *they* don't. If we turn up dead on four o'clock, then it looks like maybe we *did* have an appointment but they forgot, or maybe they didn't write it down. If we turn up at thirteen minutes to four, then we're just an unwelcome and unexpected nuisance.'

They stood there for another ten minutes in the shade of a large tree. Nobody seemed to pay them any attention – Europeans were obviously a common sight in the area.

The building was surrounded by a low metal fence, but had little other security. Sherlock, Phillimore and Matty walked up the paved pathway to the front door. Sherlock pulled the bell-pull, and deep inside the house something chimed sonorously.

'Wipe your forehead in a minute or so,' Sherlock said to Phillimore.

'Actually,' Phillimore replied, 'the breeze and the shade here are very refreshing.'

'Just do it – please.'

The door opened, revealing a footman in full livery – tailcoat, tight trousers and waistcoat. He looked them over critically.

'*Oui?*'

'We have an appointment,' Sherlock said confidently.

The footman raised an eyebrow. 'I do not think so,' he said in heavily accented English.

'Monsieur de Lesseps's office in Alexandria arranged it.' Sherlock made a show of looking annoyed. 'They were very firm about the time. They said it had to be today, and that it had to be here in Ishmaili, because that's where Monsieur de Lesseps was working. We have had a long train ride to get here.'

Without making any demands that could be rejected, Sherlock left it to the footman to make a decision, but he did step back and stare at the man expectantly.

The footman frowned, bit his lip, and glanced over his shoulder.

Phillimore took a handkerchief from his pocket and mopped his brow theatrically.

Eventually, as Sherlock had known he would, the footman gave in.

'Please – come in. I will consult with Monsieur de Lesseps's secretary.'

He led them through a cool and shadowed hallway filled with potted plants, down a corridor lined with photographs of the construction of the canal to a room at the end that was obviously set aside for people to wait in. There were European newspapers and magazines lying around – all of them dating from before Sherlock and the others had left England.

'How do we get past the secretary?' Matty hissed.

'We don't – we go around him,' Sherlock said. He waited until the footman's footsteps had died away, then gestured to Matty and Phillimore to follow him back into the hall. He positioned the three of them behind a large potted palm, and waited.

After a few minutes the footman came back again with a harried-looking, prematurely bald man in a dark suit – presumably de Lesseps's secretary. They went down the corridor towards the waiting room. Quickly Sherlock led the way to the corridor from which the two men had emerged.

'How do you know that Monsieur de Lesseps is down

here?' Phillimore wanted to know. 'His office might have been back near the waiting room, further up *that* corridor.'

'Not so. De Lesseps is an important man. His office will be at the *end* of a corridor, not the middle. It will also be at the far side of the house, because that is where the best view of the canal occurs, and he will want to see it every day. Oh, and his secretary will be near him, not far away.'

Sherlock went straight through the door at the end of the corridor. It led, as he had suspected, to the secretary's office – small and cluttered with files. There was another door on the far side, lined with green leather. Sherlock knocked twice, opened the door and entered. Phillimore and Matty followed.

The room was large and airy, with French windows at the back that gave out on to a surprisingly luxurious lawn, considering the blistering sun. As Sherlock had predicted, the verdant bank of the canal and the construction machines lined up along it were clearly visible. An enormous oak desk covered in papers and rolled-up maps dominated the room. Behind it sat a bulky man in his sixties with a bushy grey beard and very little hair. He was fussily dressed in a black suit and waistcoat. He looked up at them calmly as Sherlock quietly closed the door again.

'Monsieur de Lesseps, my name is Sherlock Holmes. These are my friends, James Phillimore and Matthew

Arnatt. We have something serious to which we need to alert you.'

De Lesseps nodded slowly. He leaned back in his chair, revealing an expansive stomach pushing at the seams of a cotton shirt. 'Phillimore,' he said. 'I know that name.'

'My brother Jonathan is an engineer on your canal,' Phillimore said, stepping forward. 'He has disappeared, and I have come to find him.'

De Lesseps reached forward and placed his hand on a piece of paper. 'I have the report here,' he said. 'He was a good man. Difficult to replace.'

Sherlock was about to mention the possibility of sabotage directed against the canal when the door opened and the secretary rushed in, wild-eyed. '*Monsieur!*' he exclaimed, '*Mon dieu! Est-ce que tout va bien?*'

Matty backed up to the desk in apparent surprise. He leaned back, hands on the desk's leather surface, as if trying to get as far away from the secretary as possible.

De Lesseps raised a calming hand. 'In English, please, François, for our guests.' He glanced at Sherlock and smiled. 'I presume that you did *not* have an appointment. François here is very particular about my schedule, and he always knows who is visiting and why.'

'I apologize,' Sherlock said. 'But this is important.'

'So you said. Now, let me see if I can guess what it is that you want to tell me so urgently. There is a plot to sabotage my canal, and this engineer who disappeared – Mr Phillimore – had discovered it.'

Sherlock winced. 'You received a communication from Alexandria.'

'I did – a telegram. We do have *some* amenities here. I was told of your visit.' He leaned forward and retrieved a piece of paper from his desk. 'I also received a telegram from England – from your Foreign Office, apparently. I have checked with your Consul here, and he assures me it is genuine.' He pulled a pair of spectacles from his pocket and slipped them on. 'If man and two boys appear with tales of plot to sabotage canal, please disregard,' he read. 'They are fantasists. Someone being sent to bring them home safely.' Glancing up, he said, 'The telegram was in English, of course. You English assume that everyone in the world speaks your language.'

'Who sent the telegram?' Sherlock asked, although the dull ache in his heart told him that he already knew the answer.

'It is signed by a man named "Mycroft Holmes". I have never heard of him.' De Lesseps frowned. 'You said that your name is Sherlock Holmes. Is this man a relative?'

'My brother,' Sherlock replied dully. So – Mycroft knew that he wasn't in Oxford.

'And he is working for the Foreign Office?' De Lesseps nodded. 'You have interesting relatives. Interesting also that he wished to warn me not to believe you.' He sighed. 'The constant attempts of you English to stop construction of the canal or to influence our investors to withdraw their money used to be amusing, and is now pathetic. You obviously want to raise concerns that the canal is not safe for ships so that our business will fail. It is –' he sighed – 'tiresome. Please leave. The opening of the Suez Canal will occur in just a few weeks, and I have an entire ceremony to prepare. There will be royalty and dignitaries from all corners of the globe. I do not have time for your . . . *fantasies.*'

'But –'

'*Tout de suite, s'il vous plaît*, before I call the authorities in.' He shook his head sadly. 'And please do not think that you can trick them as you have apparently tricked my secretary, or make them believe your ludicrous story. The police in this town are recruited by, and paid for by, the Suez Canal Company. They will do as I tell them.'

Sherlock held his hands out in a gesture of apology and conciliation. 'We will go,' he said, 'but please – check the canal for sabotage.'

'How do you sabotage a body of water?' de Lesseps asked. He waved away Sherlock's attempt to say something. 'No. Please – just go. Leave me.'

The three of them were hustled out of the building and escorted down to the fence. 'Do not,' the secretary said, 'pass this point. If you do you will be arrested, and you will never see the light of day again.'

He turned on his heel and stalked off.

'Did you get it?' Sherlock asked.

Matty nodded.

'Get *what*?' Phillimore asked, confused.

'The report on your brother's disappearance,' Sherlock said. 'It was on the table in front of Monsieur de Lesseps. I was hoping that Matty would take the opportunity to remove it when the secretary burst in, and he did.'

Phillimore stared at Matty in horror. 'But that is *theft*!' he exclaimed.

Matty frowned at him, then looked over at Sherlock. ''E does know that he shot a couple of blokes wiv a gun 'e smuggled through Customs?'

'That,' Phillimore said stiffly, 'was a matter of self-defence.'

'And this,' Sherlock said, tapping Matty's shirt and getting a papery, rustling sound from underneath, 'is a matter of trying to save your brother's life, if he is still alive.' He looked around. 'Now let's find a cafe, or a restaurant or something, sit down and look at these papers.'

# CHAPTER FOURTEEN

They found a French-style cafe in the centre of Ishmaili, near the station. It had metal tables shaded with umbrellas outside on the pavement of a wide and dusty street lined with palm trees. They sat, and ordered food and cups of tea, which came without milk but with slices of lemon. The sunlight on the sheets of paper in the thin file was almost blinding, and Sherlock had to squint to read them.

The cafe was occupied almost entirely by Europeans, almost certainly associated with the Suez Canal Company, but several of them were smoking from long pipes which were connected by tubes to large metal flasks on ornate stands.

'What's that, then?' Matty asked, pointing.

'It's a "hookah",' Sherlock replied. He smiled, remembering back to England, and Oxford. 'It's a device for smoking where the tobacco smoke passes through water to cool it down and change the taste. I remember that Charles Dodgson wrote about one in his book *Alice's Adventures in Wonderland*. The character of the Caterpillar was smoking a hookah.'

'I never read novels,' Phillimore said.

Sherlock and Matty shared a long-suffering glance.

Sherlock turned his attention back to the file.

'Apparently the local police investigated your brother's disappearance,' he said. 'He was living in rooms in the European side of town – not the area where Monsieur de Lesseps lives, but one a little less exclusive. He didn't turn up for work one morning. By lunchtime his colleagues were worried, and they raised the alarm.' He glanced up at James Phillimore, who was leaning across the table, listening intently. 'He was, apparently, very punctual, very reliable.'

'Of course he was. He was my brother.'

'The police were called. They broke down his door, on the assumption that he might have fallen ill or . . . or had a heart attack, or something.'

'But he wasn't there.'

Sherlock nodded. 'That's right. There was no indication of foul play, or anything untoward.'

'Should we talk to the police?' Phillimore asked.

'I don't think that would help,' Sherlock replied. 'All they know is in here, and the last thing we want to do is to cause trouble. They'll tell the Suez Canal Company right away, and we would be removed from Ishmaili.'

'Maybe that's what 'appened to Jonathan Phillimore,' Matty observed darkly. He was eating a meat-filled pasty from a plate that they had ordered. 'Maybe he caused too much trouble, and got run out of town by the company.'

Sherlock shook his head. 'If that's all that had happened, then he would have found a way of contacting his brother. And I don't think that Monsieur de Lesseps was keeping anything from us. He seemed to be reacting genuinely.' He flicked through the papers in the file. One, at the end, caught his attention. 'Oh, this is interesting.'

'What?' Phillimore asked.

'Well, there's a final statement appended to the file. Apparently a local cabbie turned up at the police station a few days later claiming that he took a customer somewhere, but the man disappeared without paying his fare. He'd asked for the cabbie to stay, so that he could make a return journey, but he never came back. When the cabbie went looking for him, he had vanished. He wanted to make a complaint, and get his fare paid.'

'And that customer was my brother?'

'The cabbie didn't get a name, but his description sounded like your brother, so a copy of the report was attached to the file.'

'Where did 'e get taken?' Matty asked.

'Either the cabbie didn't say, or it wasn't written down in the report. To be fair, someone only made the connection after the cabbie had left, which is why the copy was attached later. Nobody bothered following it up. Well, it was several days after the disappearance that the cabbie made his complaint.'

'I fink,' Matty observed, 'that we need to 'ave a chat wiv this cabbie. 'As he got a name?'

'Abdul Aziz. There's an address here.' Sherlock looked around. 'Although I'm not sure that this place has many street signs – at least, not in the native quarters.'

They hailed a passing native cab. Aware of the possibility of cosmic irony, Sherlock made sure he checked the cabbie's name. It wasn't 'Abdul Aziz', and neither did he know anybody of that name.

The address turned out to be a kind of collective garage that the Egyptian carriages operated out of, rather than a man's house. It was a long, low building with an open front and a corrugated iron roof that seemed to absorb the sunlight and re-radiate it in multiplied form. Many cabbies were operating out of it, or just sitting around outside it, drinking small cups of black coffee or smoking hookahs like the ones back in the cafe. They seemed to be ubiquitous around the town – perhaps the country. Their donkeys were corralled in stalls inside the building, seemingly sharing the space with the cabbies.

Sherlock assumed that in a town that was at least half European, at least *one* of the cabbies would speak French. They were in luck – they found one who spoke English.

'My name is Mohammed Al-Sharif,' he announced proudly. 'I learned English very well many years ago, when I was in the Egyptian Army.'

'You fought with the British?' Phillimore asked.

He shook his head, smiling. 'We fought with Ottomans against British,' he replied, 'but we took prisoners. I learned from them.'

Al-Sharif took them to Abdul Aziz – an old man with a leathery brown skin and only a few teeth still left in his mouth. He seemed happy to talk.

'Do you remember a complaint you made to the police about a man who didn't pay you for a journey?' Sherlock asked, through Al-Sharif.

Aziz spoke at length, gesticulating and on one occasion spitting on the ground. Al-Sharif turned back to Sherlock after a while.

'Yes, he remembers. He says that the man looked like him.' He pointed to Phillimore. 'He says that if this man is the brother of the man who did not pay his fare, then the debt falls to him. That is the way of the world.'

'We *will* pay the fare *if* he can tell us where he took the man – where he disappeared.'

A deal of discussion ensued back and forth between the two men.

'He tried to inflate the price,' Al-Sharif said eventually. 'I forced him back down to the right amount.' He smiled, revealing nearly as many gaps in his teeth as Aziz. 'You pay me half the fare for translating, yes?'

'Yes,' Sherlock said quickly, aware that Phillimore was about to protest.

'He says that he took the man to the tombs outside Ishmaili, near where the canal is being dug.'

'Tombs?' Matty asked cautiously.

'Places where our people used to bury the dead, very many years ago. Like the pyramids, but smaller. If you were a pharaoh, you got a pyramid. If you were a rich man, you got a tomb. If you were a poor man –' he shrugged, indicating himself modestly – 'you were put in a hole in the sand and left there.'

'What was he looking for in these tombs?' Phillimore asked. He glanced at Sherlock. 'He never showed any interest in tombs or graveyards when we were children.'

Al-Sharif asked Aziz the question in Egyptian. Aziz shrugged. Al-Sharif turned to Phillimore and repeated the shrug.

'How far away are the tombs?' Sherlock asked.

The translator looked at the sky and shrugged. 'We start after sundown,' he said, 'when it is cooler. We arrive at sunrise. Six hours.'

'Yes, but how *far*?'

'Distances, I do not know. Time for journey, I know.'

'Can you take us to this tomb *now*?' Phillimore asked urgently.

'At night. Easier for donkeys; easier for you.'

Sherlock glanced at Phillimore and Matty to check their agreement, and nodded reluctantly.

The translator revealed his gappy smile again. 'You pay in advance,' he said. 'In case you disappear like the last man.'

Al-Sharif assembled a team of donkeys and arranged for bottles of water, coconuts, fruit and packages of cooked food wrapped in palm leaves to be supplied from someone he knew nearby. He assured them that there were no roads to the tombs, and that donkeys were the only practicable means of travel.

The last thing Al-Sharif did was to fetch from storage somewhere a long package wrapped in cloth. He laid it on the ground and carefully unwrapped it, revealing four swords with curved blades. They were old, but still sharp. They had obviously been cared for.

'Used by you British against the Ottomans,' he said. 'I have kept for many years. You take them now, for protection.'

'Protection against what?' Matty asked, looking around nervously.

Al-Sharif shrugged. 'Animals. Bandits. Who knows?'

'Not these Ottomans, then?'

Al-Sharif stared at Matty, frowning. 'No – not today I think.'

Sherlock reached out and took a sword. It felt familiar in his hand after the many days of practice with Mr Reilly on the *Princess Helena*. He slipped it into his belt, where it banged against his leg. Matty did the same, as did James Phillimore, after a few seconds' thought.

As the sun dropped towards the horizon, casting their shadows ahead of them like long, clutching fingers, they prepared to leave. The moon was already in the sky, illuminating everything with a ghostly silver light. The donkeys were lashed together with long ropes, and with Al-Sharif on the lead one, Sherlock, Matty and Phillimore cautiously mounted up and began to move. The last donkey in the line was carrying several packages – food and other things.

'I could *walk* faster,' Matty called from behind Sherlock.

'Yes, but for how long?' Sherlock called back.

As darkness fell the donkeys took them through the native part of Ishmaili and out into what might have been described by a romantic as the desert, or by a practical man as a constant scrubland of sand, stones and bushes. There was nothing but darkness around them, and a profusion of stars from horizon to horizon. It was also getting significantly colder, in the absence of direct sunlight, and Sherlock found himself shivering. They seemed to be moving roughly parallel to the canal: every now and then, through gaps in the small hills of stones and piles of sand that characterized the landscape, he could see, on their left, the line of vegetation – black in the moonlight – that marked its banks. For a while the path they were taking – if it was a path rather than just a trek across country – actually led them along the top of a low ridge, and Sherlock could look down into the canal itself. It was basically a straight slash across the landscape, dug out of the sand and the rock by massive steam-driven dredging and digging machines that had been left alongside the canal every mile or so. In the darkness and the moonlight they looked like bizarre, nightmarish sculptures.

Each machine was different from the others. They all shared characteristics in common, of course: a large pressure chamber for the steam; another chamber for the coal-driven furnace; long metal girders that had belts running along them with lots of buckets attached, which would presumably dig into the desert sand one after another in a never-ending line; jointed arms with pistons and much larger single buckets at their ends for specific excavations. Strangely, however, each machine was also different from the others – the buckets were designed differently, or the belts were arranged differently, or the whole thing was a different shape. It was as if each one had been designed and made in different factories, but to do the same job. They were even painted different colours.

Sherlock was also amazed to see that the canal already had water in it, sparkling in the light of the moon. Somehow he had assumed that the opening ceremony for the canal would involve some kind of ceremonial smashing of a large dam at each end of the canal – Port Said on the Mediterranean and Suez on the Red Sea – and that the waters would rush along, irrigating and filling this channel through the desert, until they met in the middle and fountained up in some massive explosion of water, but that wasn't the case. As each section of the canal was finished, it looked as if the water was introduced into it. The opening ceremony would probably, then, just be a line of French ships heading from Port Said to Suez to prove that the canal was navigable. Something of an anticlimax, Sherlock thought. At least there should be fireworks.

They passed other travellers on their journey. Some were on donkeys, like them, and some on camels. Some were obviously European and some were Egyptians. The polite thing seemed to be for the travellers to wave at each other as they went past, but not to say anything to break the hush of the desert.

Most of the time they were walking on sand, but sometimes they found themselves on stretches of hard rock. When Sherlock looked sideways, at the canal, he discovered that it flowed in a channel that had been carved right through the rock. That, he thought, must have been a quite incredible feat of engineering.

He must have fallen asleep at some time, while still sitting on his donkey. The regular plodding motion was certainly soporific. Every now and then he would jerk awake, but it seemed as if the landscape around them hadn't changed at all. It was like being trapped in a recurring nightmare, and he wondered briefly if Al-Sharif was leading them around in a big circle, telling them that it would take six hours to get to the tomb even though it was only an hour away. He had to check the position of the moon and the stars to convince himself that they were travelling in a straight line.

He looked around, entranced. On the *Princess Helena* there had always been something in the way to block a view all around – a cabin, a mast, a bulkhead. Here he could literally see the horizon all around him, and the entire bowl of the sky overhead. It was a humbling sight.

He felt as if they were all the size of insects crawling across some massive rumpled bed sheet, uncertain if they would ever get to the other side.

But they did. Eventually their path diverged slightly from the line of the canal, and Sherlock realized they were heading for a small hill whose top appeared to be ragged and broken, like jagged black teeth silhouetted against the night sky, blocking out the stars. There were other hills nearby, each with their own set of broken rocks on top. For a while, as they approached the nearest hill, he thought that the broken top was just a feature of the local geography, but as they got closer he realized that this was a cluster of very old stone buildings that had been dug into the earth.

The sky in the east had begun to take on a rosy hue as dawn approached. Al-Sharif halted his donkey.

'The tombs,' he said, indicating the buildings ahead. 'There are many of them. I will stay here and wait.' He looked over to where the line of the canal was still with them, an ever-present part of the landscape. 'There will be plants there for the donkeys to eat. I will rest.'

'You are not going to accompany us into the tombs?' Phillimore asked.

'I own donkeys. I am not a tour guide.'

'But . . . it will be dark in there!'

Al-Sharif went to the last donkey in the line and took a package off its back. Returning, he unwrapped it to reveal several oil lanterns and a glass bottle filled with oil.

'You wish to buy these from me?' he asked, smiling.

Ten minutes later the three of them were heading for the tombs, carrying lit lanterns.

'We should split up,' Sherlock said. 'There appear to be several different tombs, and we need to cover as much ground as possible as quickly as we can. Remember – Mr Phillimore's brother was here investigating something, but we don't know what. He might have had an accident, or someone might have done something to him. Either way, be careful.' He looked around for the black shadows that indicated openings. 'Matty – you go over *there*, Mr Phillimore *there*, and I'll take the nearest one to the canal.'

Sherlock trudged through the sand and stones towards the black opening that he had chosen. The tomb was more like a small hill that had a doorway and some walls built into it than an actual tomb. Before he went inside, he decided to check on top, in case Jonathan Phillimore had gone up there to get a better view, fallen over and broken a leg or something.

The sun was above the horizon now, pushing a blue haze ahead of it, and Sherlock could feel the desert beginning to heat up. He had to use his hands to help pull himself up the mound of sand and stone, and he was slightly breathless by the time he reached the top. Looking round, he could see the canal and the insectile digging machines less than a mile away. He could also see several other tombs nearer at hand, and Al-Sharif with his donkeys a little further away, but he couldn't make out either Matty or James Phillimore.

Closer at hand, there was something left piled up on top of the tomb, covered with a tarpaulin. He uncovered it to have a look. There, in the pile, were what looked like several circular mirrors on poles. The poles had folding stands built into them so that they could be set upright, and pivots so that the mirrors could be swivelled around but also tilted up and down. The mirrors themselves were about the size of his chest.

He looked at the mirrors, then looked out at the horizon. Signalling devices? It made sense, but who would be signalling, and what would they be saying? In fact, who was it who had left them there in the first place? There were still too many unanswered questions about this whole business.

Beside the mirrors was a brass telescope in an oiled cloth sack. He assumed that would be used for scanning the horizon and locating whoever it was in the far distance to whom the signals would be sent.

Reluctantly, he left the mirrors and the telescope where they were and scrambled down the side of the tomb to where he remembered the entrance was. The light from the rising sun only penetrated a few feet into the entrance, and he held the lantern as he went in.

The air in the tomb was warm. The stone obviously absorbed the heat of the sun during the day like a sponge absorbed water. It smelt old and dusty, and slightly rancid as well. The corridor – actually more of a tunnel, he decided – sloped gradually downward as he walked. The lantern's light showed him walls and a ceiling made of crumbling old stone and a floor of hard packed earth. Some of the stonework had faded images on it: figures, animals and strange signs. Ahead of him was a patch of darkness where the light did not penetrate, and behind him the dwindling shape of the doorway into the tomb.

Suddenly the light shone on a wall directly ahead, made of the same crumbling stone. The patch of darkness was now on his right: a turn in the corridor. He followed it, and now the light from the doorway had vanished and he was in a bubble of light about ten feet across that moved wherever he moved.

He walked for about a minute, and then another wall appeared ahead of him. He had the strange impression that the darkness covering the wall was *moving* just as the light hit it, but when he stared at it he saw nothing but the stones, and the gaps between the stones.

There was darkness to his left this time. He turned and kept walking at the same pace. The tunnel still sloped downward, and he thought by this time he was actually below ground level.

A dark patch on the ground attracted his attention. He stopped to look at it. Something seemed to have been spilt there. His heart missed a beat for a moment as he thought it might be blood, but when he bent to check it didn't *look* like blood. It wasn't red, but black, and it glistened in the light. He bent down and reached out to touch it, and discovered that it was *sticky*. When he brought his hand back and rubbed his thumb and fingers together they *slid*. This was *oil*, but what was oil doing on the floor of a corridor in a tomb?

Another puzzle to add to the rest.

He straightened up, but something suddenly skittered across the wall to his right. He jerked away instinctively before he realized that it was a black beetle about the size of his thumb, running away from the sudden illumination. Another beetle appeared to his left as he moved forward, also running away. Sherlock had the sudden horrible sensation that there was an entire army of beetles moving ahead of him, just beyond the limits of the light. He tried to listen for the sound of them moving, but his breathing and his footsteps were too loud. He stopped, and held his breath, but his imagination started telling him that there was an army of beetles *behind* him as well, just outside the lantern's range. He felt like he was surrounded. A sudden surge of panic welled up within him. What would happen if the lantern suddenly went out? He would be in complete darkness, surrounded by beetles, and listening to the sound of their legs brushing against the stone, as they got closer and closer to him. It seemed to be getting hotter in the corridor: he could feel beads of sweat prickling on his forehead and all the way down his back. His fingers were slick on the metal of the lantern handle.

This was stupid. He took a deep, slow breath. He was

in a stone corridor underground and there were some insects around. There were always insects underground – it was where they liked to live. There was nothing strange about this, nothing unusual, and the insects were more frightened of him than he was of them.

He breathed out, and in again, feeling his heart slow and the terror subside.

Something in the darkness ahead of him moaned.

# CHAPTER FIFTEEN

Sherlock's hand twitched in surprise, almost making him drop the lantern. He tried to tell himself that it was the wind gusting through a gap in some stones, but he was below ground. Where was the wind coming from? And besides, he hadn't felt any breeze on his face.

He knew what Matty would have said: this was a tomb, and tombs had dead things in them.

Every instinct in his body told him to go back, but logic told him to go on.

So he went on.

Another moan, louder this time.

He almost turned to run. Instinct was telling him that the body of some dead Egyptian, desiccated by the heat of the desert and the passing centuries, and animated by some ancient sorcery, was shambling towards him along the tunnel, moaning, but logic told him that Jonathan Phillimore was lying somewhere up ahead, injured and in pain. He gritted his teeth, swallowed the panic and kept walking.

Suddenly the floor of the tunnel vanished. He stopped, thinking there was a hole or a shaft leading downward, but in fact the tunnel floor just dropped a foot or so, and the walls on either side widened out. There was a room there. He held the lantern up and shone it into the room, trying to illuminate the far side.

The room was no bigger than his bedroom back in Holmes Lodge, and there was an opening in the wall on the far side leading deeper into the tomb, but the thing that absorbed his attention was the man lying tied up on the floor. He was European, wearing a white suit that was crumpled and stained. A long scarf-like length of cloth had been tied around his head in order to gag him, but he seemed to have worked it loose by rubbing his cheek against the floor. He looked like a younger version of James Phillimore.

His eyes were screwed up against the lantern light. 'Please, God, no more,' he cried in a cracked voice.

'Jonathan Phillimore?' Sherlock asked. 'My name is Sherlock Holmes. I'm here with your brother to rescue you.'

Phillimore opened his eyes in disbelief. 'Is this some kind of trick?' he asked weakly.

'No trick. Let me help you.'

'No!' Phillimore cried as Sherlock stepped into the room and walked closer. 'For God's sake, don't touch me!'

'It's all right,' Sherlock said reassuringly, but as the lantern illuminated Phillimore more brightly, he saw something moving on his clothes. For a moment he thought it was the beetles again, and was about to brush them off, but then he saw that these things were more like spiders, with swollen segments on their legs, massive pincers on either side of their heads and a tail ending in a vicious stinger that curved over their backs, ready to attack. He'd seen something like this before, in a glass case in Ferny Weston's house outside Oxford. He hadn't known what it was then, but Ferny had told him afterwards that these creatures were called 'scorpions'!

Sherlock withdrew his hand slowly. There was a scorpion on Phillimore's chest, another on his shoulder and a third on his leg. Sherlock suspected that there were others hidden in the folds of his suit. They didn't seem to be scared of the lantern's light in the same way that the beetles were – they weren't scuttling away. The light just seemed to be annoying them, making them flex their tails as if they were preparing to strike. He pulled the lantern back to try and calm them down.

'They're tied to me with cotton threads,' Phillimore said in his cracked voice.

'Why?' Sherlock asked.

'So I don't move. So I don't try to escape. And to terrify me into talking. I have been assured that their stings aren't fatal – just incredibly painful.'

Sherlock could see the thin threads now, tied around the bases of the scorpions' tails, keeping them from moving too far from Phillimore. They were tied to the buttons on his suit. 'That's appalling,' he said. 'Who did this?'

'George Clarke.'

'He's the man you wrote to your brother about.'

Phillimore's eyes opened wide. 'You read my letter? My *brother* read my letter?'

'And he's here. We came to help you.' Sherlock set the lantern down and pulled the sword from his belt. 'Stay very still – I'm going to cut through the threads.'

'No!' Phillimore cried, 'you'll provoke them!'

'Not if I'm careful.'

'Just kill them! You've got a sword!'

'They've got hard shells, and besides, I might miss them and stab you – which would be a bad thing. No, the safest course of action is to allow them to leave, and then give them a *reason* to leave.'

Sherlock reached for the nearest scorpion. Without touching it, or pulling on the thread, he gathered the thread into a loop. He held the loop closed with two fingers while he slipped the blade of the sword into it with his other hand and sliced through the thread. The scorpion stayed where it was, unaware for the moment that it had been freed. 'One down. How many are there?'

'Five, I think.'

Sherlock did the same thing with the cotton on the second scorpion. 'That's two.' He moved the lantern closer, forcing the creatures to flee from the light, chasing them down Phillimore's body until they ran on to the packed earth and scuttled away.

The third scorpion was larger than the first two. Sherlock could see the glitter of multiple eyes on its blunt head. Its pincers twitched as Sherlock got close.

He repeated the trick with the thread, but this thread was shorter than the others, and he had to get his fingers closer to the scorpion. Just as he was about to cut the thread he saw the thing's tail stiffen. Quickly he moved the blade of the sword, intercepting the stinger as it arced forward above the scorpion's head and plunged downward. The stinger hit the metal of the blade, leaving a smear of poison. Before the scorpion could try again, Sherlock sliced through the thread and then, inserting the sword blade beneath the scorpion's body, flicked it away.

The fourth scorpion was hiding beneath Phillimore's jacket, on his shirt. Sherlock had to pull the jacket further open to find it. The creature's stinger would have injected poison just above Phillimore's heart if it had struck, and Sherlock suspected that – despite what this George Clarke had said – that would have proved fatal. Once Sherlock had cut through the thread holding it, the creature tried to take refuge in the darkness between two of his shirt buttons, but Sherlock blocked its path with the blade of the sword and instead it moved on to his jacket. Again, Sherlock flicked it away into the corridor.

Phillimore didn't know where the fifth scorpion was, and Sherlock couldn't see it. Eventually he had to slice the ropes on Phillimore's wrists and ankles and help him very slowly into a sitting position. Even then he couldn't see it. He moved the lantern all around the man, trying to work out where it was, but there was nothing.

He was almost about to believe that the scorpion had got loose by itself and scuttled away when Phillimore said in an overly calm voice, 'There is something moving on my head.'

Sherlock looked closer. The scorpion was moving through Phillimore's hair, near his ear.

'Please, remove it,' Phillimore said. His voice sounded close to cracking.

'I can't,' Sherlock admitted. 'I don't see where the thread is. I think it's somehow wound the thread in with your hairs.'

'If you don't remove it *now*, I will smash my head against the wall to kill it.'

'Don't do that.' Sherlock put his blade down and reached gingerly for the scorpion's tail. In order to distract Phillimore, he said: 'Did you discover what George Clarke's plan actually is?'

'I did. He intends to set the Suez Canal on fire.'

Sherlock closed his finger and thumb on the end of the scorpion's tail, being very careful not to let the stinger itself touch his skin. It felt hard, and yet slightly squishy beneath his fingertips.

'Did you warn Monsieur de Lesseps?' Phillimore whispered.

'We tried,' Sherlock admitted, 'but without any knowledge of the actual plot we couldn't convince him.'

Sherlock pulled the scorpion away from Phillimore's

head. Its eight legs and two front claws waved vainly, trying to get a grip, but it came away easily. Sherlock could see the cotton thread now – longer than the others had been, and tied to a button on Phillimore's collar. He picked the sword up with his left hand, pulled the thread taut by holding the scorpion as far away from Phillimore as it would go, and then sliced through it.

'Done,' he said as he threw the scorpion into the darkness. He felt, rather than heard, Phillimore's heartfelt gasp of relief.

'Let's get you out of here,' he said, standing up and extending a hand to the man on the ground. Phillimore took it gingerly. His hand was dusty, and Sherlock could feel it trembling.

'Do you have any water?' Phillimore asked as he stood stiffly upright.

Sherlock passed him the flask that he had hanging on a strap around his neck. 'Don't drink it all,' he warned. 'Sip it, otherwise your stomach will rebel and you'll bring it all up again.'

Phillimore nodded, and gratefully drank some water. He closed his eyes in bliss. 'I have dreamed of this,' he said.

'How on earth was George Clarke going to set fire to the Suez Canal?' Sherlock asked, his mind finally getting to grips with what Phillimore had said.

'He has had his own workers lining some of the deeper rooms and corridors of these tombs with metal,'

Phillimore replied, and took another sip of water. 'They have been converted into *tanks*, and he has filled them with oil.'

Sherlock remembered the black stain on the floor of the tunnel that he had noticed earlier. 'And he intends, what? Somehow getting this oil to the canal and then setting it on fire? That seems like a plan that could go wrong in so many ways.'

Phillimore shook his head. 'No, he has thought it through very thoroughly. The tanks took over a year to construct, and another six months to get the oil transported here in hundreds of barrels. It's a special kind of oil, one the Greeks used to use in warfare to set enemy ships alight. "Greek fire" it was called by the ancients. Once started, the conflagration cannot be put out.'

'But how would he get the oil from the tomb here to the canal?'

'His workers have laid their own pipes in secret from the tomb to the canal. They are buried beneath the sand. One of the steam-powered digging machines standing on the banks of the canal has been built to Clarke's specifications, not Monsieur de Lesseps's. Clarke will use the steam engine to pump the oil out of the tomb and into the canal, where it would spread across the surface.'

Sherlock shook his head. 'But not all the way down the canal – that would take too long, and there can't be enough oil in the tomb, surely?' He remembered the mirrors and the telescope on top of the tomb, the ones he had found earlier. 'Of course!' he said, hitting his forehead. 'He has similar oil tanks in similar old tombs all the way down the length of the canal. His men, once they are in place, will signal to each other and release the oil at the same time. The whole canal will be covered, from Port Said down to Suez!'

'And that's when they will use Chinese fireworks to set the oil aflame – almost certainly at the moment that the canal is declared open and the first official convoy of ships passes through.' Phillimore shook his head. 'It will burn for days, weeks, even months. The damage to ships would be huge, but the damage to the reputation of the Suez Canal Company would be . . . infinite. The canal would be a catastrophic, monumental failure.'

There was silence in the tomb for a few moments as they both imagined the sight if the oil was released and set aflame.

'Then we have to stop it,' Sherlock said quietly.

Phillimore sighed. 'I tried. After my attempts to warn the company failed, I investigated Clarke's activities myself. I broke into his office and examined his receipts and work orders, and I followed him here, but he heard me and took me prisoner. He wanted to know how many people I had told, and what I knew, but I wouldn't tell him.' He drew himself up: proud despite his crumpled and dirty appearance. 'I wanted him to believe that other people out there were working to stop him. He was torturing me with the scorpions to find out the truth.'

He looked around. 'We should get out,' he said weakly. 'Alert the authorities.'

Sherlock shook his head, realizing that the gesture was almost invisible in the darkness. 'No – I want to see the oil reservoirs first.'

'Don't you believe me?' Phillimore seemed affronted.

'I believe you, but I always like to see the evidence for myself.'

Phillimore nodded in resignation. Instead of heading back towards the way out, he led the way across the room where he had been imprisoned and into the dark doorway on the other side. Sherlock followed with the lantern.

The tunnel split into two a little way along its length, and then again a little way later, but it always led downward, and Phillimore always knew which way to go. Sherlock kept an eye out for the scorpions, but the only things he saw moving away from the light were beetles. He wondered idly, as they walked through the warm dark air, what the beetles ate. Each other?

After a while Sherlock realized that he could smell something: a warm, heavy odour with a pungent edge. It became more intense the further they went.

The tunnel ahead of them gradually broadened out into another room – much wider and deeper than the one Phillimore had been tied up in. That had been a lobby: this was a chamber. Stairs led down into it from the corridor, but the floor beneath wasn't visible. The chamber was filled, right to the level of the last step, with a black liquid that sucked in the light from the lantern. Cast-iron pipes descended from holes in the stonework of the ceiling and plunged into the blackness.

Sherlock knelt down and touched the surface of the liquid. It was sticky, and left a black residue on his fingertips. It smelt faintly sharp, like pine needles.

'Greek fire,' Phillimore said. 'The weapon invented by the Byzantine Empire and used successfully for centuries, lost for even more centuries, and somehow rediscovered by George Clarke.'

'Oh,' a voice said from behind them, 'I cannot take full responsibility. Apparently the secret recipe was written down in papyruses held in the archives of the British Museum.'

Sherlock and Phillimore turned around. There, behind them, was a small man with a mass of black hair that stuck up, like a brush. His expression was calm, almost serene, but he was holding a revolver which was pointed loosely in their direction.

'The papyruses were only translated three years ago by a scholar in Oxford,' he went on. 'When it was realized what they said, the British Government declared the whole thing a state secret, and hid it away again.' He smiled at Sherlock. 'I do not believe we have been introduced. My name is Clarke – George Clarke.' He nodded at Phillimore. 'Jonathan and I are already acquainted, of course.'

Sherlock glanced at Phillimore. The man seemed

hypnotized by Clarke, terrified by his very presence. 'So the British Government are behind all this?' Sherlock asked.

Clarke shrugged. 'Parts of it are. Not the whole thing. The British Government is a vast and slow bureaucracy. There are bits of it that operate entirely independently of other bits. I work for one of those bits.'

Sherlock straightened up, wondering whether he could pull his sword from his belt and lunge for Clarke before the man could pull his trigger. He was pretty sure he wouldn't make it. Despite the casual way the man was handling his gun, Sherlock thought he could bring it to bear pretty quickly. 'And you're just following orders?' he asked. 'You're going to set fire to one of the great wonders of the world, the biggest engineering project since the Pyramids, and you don't have any regrets, any concerns?'

'You're trying to appeal to my better nature,' Clarke said, nodding. 'Understandable. I would do the same in your circumstances. What you don't understand is that I don't have a better nature. I am being paid so much – into a secret, untraceable bank account – that I had it surgically removed.'

Sherlock raised an eyebrow. 'Seriously?'

Clarke shrugged. 'You're right – I jest. Actually, I have never had a better nature. I cheated at school, I cheated at university, and I cheat in my work. It's what I do.'

'People will die,' Sherlock pointed out. He was looking

around Clarke for some advantage, something that could be used, but he couldn't see anything.

'Probably. The most effective time to pump the oil out into the canal and set fire to it would be when the inaugural column of ships is passing through. That will grab the newspaper headlines. More importantly, that will grab the attention of the investors. They will sell their shares in a panic, the Suez Canal Company will collapse, and the British Government will quietly buy up those shares. Eventually they will control the canal – whether it reopens quietly in a decade or whether they keep it shut. The French will have no say in the matter, and the British Empire will still control half the world.'

'And you will retire happy – where?' Sherlock asked. He looked sideways at Phillimore, to check he was all right. The man's eyes were wide, and his face was white. He was either going to pass out or launch himself at Clarke. Either, Sherlock thought, would be bad. 'The South Seas? The Caribbean?'

'Oh no. I have had too much of hot temperatures. I was thinking of trying my luck in the Antarctic. There are several engineering projects there that I could help with.' He made a little gesture with the gun. 'The two of you, of course, will be retiring here, I'm afraid. You will never leave this tomb.'

'What about finding out who Jonathan Phillimore has told about your plans?' Sherlock asked rapidly, aware that Clarke's gun could fire at any moment.

Clarke laughed. 'I think we have established by now that nobody knows anything in the Suez Canal Company, and anyone in the British Government who has any idea will keep very, very quiet about it.'

Phillimore twitched. Sherlock reached out to take his shoulder, trying to hold him back. He didn't want the man to be killed needlessly. Having said that, he realized that he had no real idea how to stop either of them being killed needlessly. That would require some thinking, and he didn't have much time. Seconds, in fact.

Something moved on Phillimore's jacket, emerging from the folds of the gag that was still loosely tied around his neck and scuttling over his shoulder.

It was one of the scorpions – the largest one. Sherlock hadn't managed to flick it away after all. It had found a convenient fold and stayed where it was.

As it emerged into the light, Sherlock slid a finger beneath it and flicked it at Clarke.

The scorpion flew through the air in a shallow arc that ended at Clarke's face. Sherlock had a confused impression of its legs folding up beneath it and its tail clenching to strike. Clarke saw something and raised his free hand to his face, but too late. The scorpion struck, and struck.

Clarke screamed. He dropped the gun and raised both hands to his face, back arching. The scorpion dropped to the ground and scuttled away, but the damage had been done. There was blood on Clarke's cheek.

Clarke was staggering around now in agony, clawing at his eyes. Sherlock bent and snatched his gun from the ground, but it wasn't needed. Clarke stumbled past Phillimore, still screaming. Phillimore moved aside to let him pass.

And Clarke fell into the oil.

He missed his footing where the tunnel ended in a step, and toppled forward. Water would have splashed, but the oil just seemed to accept him, closing up around his body as if nothing had really happened.

Sherlock and Clarke stared in horror for perhaps a minute, but his body didn't float back to the surface. A lone bubble eventually rose from the depths and very slowly popped. That was it. That was the last of George Clarke – engineer and saboteur.

Eventually Sherlock turned to Phillimore. 'We need to destroy this,' he said.

'Why? The man is dead.'

'There might be others. There *are* others. He wasn't working alone.' Sherlock thought quickly. 'The best thing to do would be to set fire to the oil, burn it all up. The trouble is, if we use the lantern to do that, we'll never make it back to the surface. There are mirrors up there, and a telescope. If we can arrange the mirrors to reflect the light of the rising sun all the way down the tunnels, then we might be able to use the lenses from the telescope to focus the light on to the oil, heat it up and cause it to catch fire.'

Phillimore reached up to the cloth gag that was still around his neck. 'Or,' he said, we can use this, soaked in oil.'

Sherlock looked at him for a long moment. 'Or we can do that,' he said.

It took them less than a minute to tear the gag into strips, tie the strips into a long rope of cloth, dip the rope into the black, viscid oil, and then lay it in a trail along the hard-packed earth floor. It led in a wavery black line all the way to the point where the corridor split.

Phillimore looked at Sherlock. Sherlock looked at Phillimore.

'The lantern?' Phillimore asked.

Sherlock nodded. He knelt, picked up the end of the cloth, raised the glass shield on the lantern and touched the cloth to the flame.

It caught fire in a flash of blue flame which began to travel slowly along the cloth towards the pool of oil in the chamber.

'Time to go, I believe,' Phillimore said.

They ran back up along the tunnels, past the junctions, through the lobby where Phillimore had been imprisoned, around corners and towards the blinding daylight shining through the doorway of the tomb. Sherlock's breath rasped in his throat as they ran. The fresh scar on his ribs was burning with pain. Phillimore's thin arms and legs waved wildly as he sprinted beside Sherlock. They reached sunlight at the same time, throwing themselves outside the doorway, hitting the sand.

And behind them, the tomb shuddered.

A gust of hot wind followed them out of the doorway, dissipating in the fresh air outside.

Somewhere in the distance, on the other side of the hill that contained the tomb, rocks and stones sprayed into the air, followed by a thin plume of smoke.

Sherlock stood up, and pulled Phillimore to his feet.

And then the entire hill shuddered and seemed to lift up into the air. As Sherlock fell he could have sworn that he saw cracks open momentarily in the earth, revealing red hot fire beneath, and then the hill settled back, sealing the cracks again. Dust drifted across the tomb – the only sign that anything had happened far below.

'The oil will keep burning, underground,' Sherlock said, climbing to his feet again. 'If what you said about Greek fire is correct, then nobody will be able to put it out.' As he spoke he found himself wondering what Matty and James Phillimore, in their own tomb, would make of the explosion. He hoped that it hadn't dislodged any stones and trapped them.

'There are other tombs, and other reservoirs of oil,' Phillimore pointed out, running a hand through his hair. 'They will need to be destroyed as well, otherwise they could be used to set fire to the canal.'

Sherlock glanced over at him. 'Then you and your brother will have your work cut out for you,' he said. 'Just as long as you know you're doing the right thing, and making the world a better place.'

It was at that point that a sound drifted across from the direction of the canal: a chugging, chuffing noise, like a steam train setting off from a station.

'What's that?' Sherlock asked.

Phillimore frowned. 'It's one of the dredging machines,' he said, frowning, 'but the canal has been finished here for weeks. Why would anyone be starting up one of the dredgers now?'

'Because it's the dredger that George Clarke supplied,' Sherlock said grimly, 'the one that's connected to the oil reservoir in the tombs. Someone is trying to pump the oil out before it all burns away!' He pushed Phillimore away. 'Go and find your brother – he's somewhere in the other tombs. Find my friend Matty as well. Tell them what's happening.'

'What are you going to do?'

'I'm going to stop that pump!'

Sherlock ran towards the distant verdant line of the canal, leaving Phillimore and the tomb behind him. He didn't know what he was running towards, but he knew that he couldn't leave things the way they were. After everything he had been through, to leave someone pumping that oil out into the canal would have been wrong.

By the time he got to the canal, and the nearest of the dredging machines, he was exhausted. So much had happened that his energy reserves were spent. There was nothing left.

The metal machine towered over him: a central series of metal tanks and units bolted together with big rivets and painted a rusty red. Girders and strange metal arms led away from the main body, sticking up into the air. Pipes – like the ones that he'd seen below the ground, in the tomb – emerged from the sand and plugged straight into the underbelly of the machine.

He walked to the front, overlooking the Suez Canal.

It reached from the horizon on his left to the horizon on his right – a deep groove in the ground that might have been made by a sword-cut inflicted by the gods, filled with sparkling blue water. Green bushes and reeds lined its banks. Sherlock had seen canals back in England – Matty had spent a large part of his life travelling on them – but this was different. This was so wide that he couldn't have thrown a stone to the far bank, and so deep that whales could have swum in it. The Suez Canal was an unequalled feat of human engineering.

Beneath him, in the sandy, pebbly bank, there were several round openings where the pipes from the tomb ended. No oil was pumping out yet, but it was only a matter of minutes.

Who, he wondered desperately, had started the pumps? One of George Clarke's men? Some unknown conspirator?

Or . . . ?

'Sherlock,' a voice said. 'I'm sorry it had to be this way.'

He turned around. There were several 'last people in

the world' it could have been, standing there in the hot Egyptian sun, facing him. Amyus Crowe . . . Virginia Crowe . . . his brother Mycroft . . .

In the end, it was Rufus Stone.

He stood with the pumping machine behind him, holding a cutlass. The breeze blew his black hair back from his face. His mouth was open in – not a smile, but a grimace. The sun shone on his single gold tooth. His expression was . . . regretful. Even sad.

'Following orders?' Sherlock said, pulling the sword from his belt – the one that Mohammed Al-Sharif had given him.

'I have a job to do,' Rufus said. 'It's one of the problems with being an adult – we don't get a choice. There's always someone telling us what to do.'

'In your case, it's my brother.'

'And in his case,' Rufus pointed out, 'he has his superiors. And they have their superiors. And their superiors have their own superiors. And so on. And so on.'

'Where does it end?' Sherlock asked, taking up a guard stance. 'The Prime Minister? The Queen?'

Rufus adopted a similar stance. 'I don't know,' he said. 'It's above my pay grade.' He paused, sighing. 'I don't want to be here, Sherlock, but I've been told what needs to be done. You have to be stopped from destroying the oil. If that proves impossible, the oil needs to be immediately pumped into the canal and set on fire.'

'Mycroft told you to kill me? I don't believe that he would do that.'

'Mycroft told me to stop you from alerting the Suez Canal Company to the sabotage. He sent a telegram to them to warn them about you, and tell them that you were a fantasist. He told me that if you continued to look for the actual sabotage itself, if you actually *found* the sabotage and tried to prevent it from happening, then I was to stop you. He didn't say how, and he didn't give me any limits or boundaries. He trusts me to find a way to get you to stop without killing you, but frankly that's up to you. If you try to get past me then I will fight you. If we fight then I will beat you. If I beat you there is a chance that I might accidentally kill you. The best way to avoid that is for you not to get past me. Let it be, Sherlock. Let events occur as they will.'

'It's wrong, Rufus.'

'It's life, Sherlock.'

Sherlock instinctively felt his body lower its centre of balance in anticipation and preparation, the point of his sword aimed towards his friend. 'Amyus Crowe warned me to be careful of you,' he said. Somewhere inside him he knew that there was a twisting, roiling core of disbelief, but on the surface he was calm. He had to be. 'Amyus told me that Rufus Stone wasn't even your real name. It's a place in Hampshire.'

'I found it on a map,' Rufus said, also leaning forward and extending his blade. 'I'm warning you, Sherlock –

don't make me do this. If it comes to a fight I can't guarantee that I can injure you without killing you. Sharp blades are dangerous, unpredictable things.'

'You taught me to play the violin. You were my friend.'

'I taught you the violin, but I didn't teach you sword-fighting. There was a reason for that.' His eyes seemed to cloud over momentarily. 'And yes, I was your friend.'

Sherlock looked at the pumps, then looked at the distant hills beneath which the oil was waiting to be pumped. He looked back at Rufus Stone, whose face was strained and unhappy.

He had no choice.

Sherlock sprang forward, his sword slashing down at Rufus's arm, hoping to disarm him with only a small injury. Rufus immediately pronated his guard into the 'guard of quinte' and parried.

Remembering the lessons that Reilly had taught him on the SS *Princess Helena*, Sherlock kept slashing his sword towards Rufus, trying to force his friend to back away, or get him to drop his own sword. Together they moved back and forth across the sand: slash and parry, lunge and block. Gradually the fight shifted so that Rufus was on the attack rather than in defence. He had obviously realized that Sherlock wasn't going to give up.

Sherlock's entire attention was focused on the next few seconds. He couldn't spare any thought for the future, any consideration over what was going to happen next. He had to restrict himself to blocking Rufus Stone's blade every time it came flashing towards him.

He couldn't counter-attack. He tried, but he just couldn't. Rufus was his friend. Rufus had saved his life more times than he could count.

But that wasn't stopping Rufus. Face grim, he was pressing Sherlock back, closer and closer to the bank of the canal. His blade seemed to appear from nowhere – above, below, left, right, it kept forcing Sherlock to retreat. All of his energy was being poured into defending himself.

Logically there was no way out. If he wasn't prepared to attack, then Rufus would eventually wear him down. And he wasn't prepared to attack. He couldn't hurt his friend.

Each time their blades clashed, the impact vibrated up Sherlock's arm, weakening him, sending pulses of pain through his shoulder and chest.

Slash and parry. Lunge and block.

The lessons that Maestro Reilly had drilled into him, the exercises the two of them had been through, hour after hour on the ship – that was what he fell back on. The mechanics of fighting, the intuition of protecting his body with the numerous guards. But his heart wasn't in it. He didn't want to win. Not against Rufus Stone.

The trouble was, if he couldn't win, then he was going to lose. That was the inexorable logic of the fight.

Rufus's sword flickered like the tongue of a snake: always just where he wasn't expecting it. Instinct kept his sword flashing to the right place to intercept Rufus's blade each time, but where Rufus's movements were smooth and flowing, Sherlock's were becoming clumsy and rough. He knew that he was going to lose. It was just a matter of time.

And all the time they were fighting, he could hear the *chug-chug-chug* of the pump, pulling the viscid oil from the black depths of the tomb. It didn't matter that far below, the oil was on fire – that was just on the surface. The oil beneath the surface was still viable – for now. Even if some of the burning oil was pulled through the pipes, it didn't matter. That was what Rufus's masters wanted, after all – burning oil, floating on the surface of the Suez Canal.

His attacker's relentless strength, coupled with the effort and strain of parrying and absorbing the repetition of blows, pushed Sherlock in retreat. In the end, Sherlock's foot caught in a tuft of reeds close to the bank of the canal. He fell backwards, his head actually emerging from the vegetation and hanging above the glittering surface of the virgin waters. His hand let go of his sword, and it fell, turning and turning, until it hit the water and sank.

Rufus stood above him, his blade pointed at Sherlock's throat.

'Every part of me wishes that things were not this way,' he said. His cheeks were wet with tears. 'But they have to be. We all do what we have to do.'

'We do what we choose,' Sherlock said. His hand was beside him, and for some reason he found that it was reaching into his pocket. He felt his fingers close on something: a mass of cloth. He pulled it out and held it up: a red handkerchief that he had forgotten about, given to him by Mrs Loran back on the SS *Princess Helena*.

He held it up. The cloth shone like a flame in the light of the morning sun.

'Turn around,' a voice said. He recognized the voice. It belonged to Maestro Reilly: the man who had taught him swordsmanship on the *Princess Helena*. The man who, he now realized with crushing despair, was an agent of Mrs Loran, of the Paradol Chamber, placed on the ship to prepare him for what had to inevitably happen.

Rufus Stone looked over his shoulder. Sherlock couldn't see Reilly from where he lay, gazing up at the blue sky, but he saw Rufus moving away.

There was a great deal of clashing of metal. Somewhere off to one side. Sherlock just lay there, staring upward. Virginia Crowe had betrayed him, his brother had betrayed him, and Rufus Stone had betrayed him. Friends meant betrayal. Best, he thought tiredly, not to have any friends at all. If he got out of this, he promised himself that he would be on his own, forever.

Clashing of metal, louder and softer as they moved closer and further away. Sounds of heavy breathing. Two evenly matched swordsmen.

And then silence.

After a long, long while, Sherlock decided that he needed to stand up. After a much longer while, he decided to do something about it. He eventually rolled over, every muscle in his body protesting. He used his hands and his feet to push himself up. Eventually he was standing.

The sunlight glittered on the surface of the canal. There was no oil out there, and the noise of the pump had stopped.

He turned around.

K. James Marius Reilly – his erstwhile sword tutor – was standing with his sword pointed at the ground. At the far end of his sword, Rufus Stone was lying on the ground. The sword had penetrated about half an inch into Rufus's chest, directly above his heart.

'You need more lessons,' Reilly observed calmly to Sherlock. 'Your defences were acceptable, but you lacked the conviction to attack.'

'There's a reason for that,' Sherlock said. He started to walk past Reilly.

'Would you like me to kill him?' Reilly called to him.

Sherlock thought for a moment. 'No,' he said. 'It's always best to know who your enemies are. Leave him. Let him live.'

He walked towards the dark red bulk of the dredging machine. It was stationary now, no longer pumping. There were three people standing by its base. As he got closer he saw that it was the two Phillimore brothers –

very similar in build, but one a lot thinner and dustier than the other – and Matty.

'We stopped the pump,' Jonathan Phillimore observed.

'Good,' said Sherlock. He realized that he was intellectually pleased that the threat to the Suez Canal had been stopped, but emotionally he was dead. There was nothing there. He didn't care.

'What now?' Matty asked. He was staring at Sherlock in concern. 'Where do we go? Back to England?'

'No,' Sherlock said, surprising himself. 'There's nothing for me there.'

'Then where?' Matty's face was folded into a mask of concern and puzzlement. 'Where do we go now?'

'India isn't too far away,' Sherlock said calmly. 'I thought we could go and find my father.'

# AUTHOR'S NOTE

It's funny, but I always find this bit of the book the most difficult to write. That's probably because I can't hide behind anything, like a particular writing style, or exciting events, or fast-moving action ('Quick, look over there! Don't look at me!'). It's just me, talking. And those of you who've seen me talk will know that I get embarrassed doing that, and tend to shy away from it.

The first thing to say, I guess, is that I'm sorry it's taken me eight books to get around to introducing Sherlock's sister, and his old family home. In the books from *Death Cloud* onwards I wanted Sherlock to feel disconnected from his roots – a loner; someone who had nowhere comfortable to live and who only had his brother, Mycroft, to fall back on, and often not even that. All the time, however, I knew that I wanted Sherlock to eventually go home, but at a point when it wasn't really home any more. His mother is dead, his father is missing in action, and his brother has finally shown that his work comes before family and indeed morality. The older, adult Sherlock Holmes that Arthur Conan Doyle and so many other authors have written about never talks about his past and obviously has a difficult relationship with his brother, and that's what I've finally been able to get around to addressing in my books. Now you know why he is the way he is.

There are still some things for Young Sherlock to do before he becomes Old Sherlock, of course. The spectre of his father, which has been haunting him since *Death Cloud*, needs to be put to rest once and for all, and there are still some things he needs to learn (or learn better) – particularly chemistry and the art of theatrical disguise. He also needs to resolve his rather complicated relationship with the Paradol Chamber – is he working for them, or fighting against them, or both? Oh, and I think that Amyus Crowe and Virginia Crowe need to turn up again, just to give him something else to complicate his life. So, if there is a ninth book (and that's out of my hands, I'm afraid), then you can probably expect it to be set at least in part in India, with Sherlock going after his father and coming up against the forces of the Russian Empire (they were very active in India at the time, fighting both secretly and openly against the British).

While I'm here, however, I need to give you some kind of historical context for this book – because I don't just make things up, you know. The Suez Canal is a real thing, and it was built in the way I've described in this book. At the time it was probably the most impressive engineering project that the world had ever known. I have to admit that I have fudged the date of completion a little bit, just for literary purposes. But that's okay; I'm allowed to do that. The stuff about the British Government being very much against the construction of the canal, which was pushed through by the French, is however completely accurate.

Most of the research for this book was done using only two volumes:

*Parting the Desert: The Creation of the Suez Canal* by Zachary Karabell (John Murray, 2003) – this book tells the whole story of the political and engineering challenges that dogged the construction of an artificial channel between the Mediterranean Sea and the Red Sea – the kind of project that, these days, would either be deemed too difficult or too expensive or both;

*Victorian Women visiting the Pyramids* by John Theakstone (available from Amazon for Kindle) – this collection of diary extracts from real Victorian women who had visited the pyramids in Egypt was invaluable in giving me a flavour of what it was actually like to be there in the 1870s. *I* would think twice about going now (too hot, too many insects), but these indomitable ladies managed it when the only choice of transport in going from Cairo to the pyramids was by donkey or camel.

So, there we are. Maybe I'll get the chance to talk to you again, or maybe Sherlock will be left here, desperately worrying about the fate of his father. Who knows?

I hope we talk again.

# ABOUT THE AUTHOR

Andrew Lane is the author of the bestselling Young Sherlock series and of Lost Worlds. Young Sherlock has been published around the world and is available in thirty-seven different languages. Not only is Andrew a lifelong fan of Arthur Conan Doyle's great detective, he is also an expert on the books and is the only children's writer endorsed by the Sherlock Holmes Conan Doyle estate. Andrew writes other things too, including adult thrillers (under a pseudonym), TV adaptations (including *Doctor Who*) and non-fiction books (about things as wide-ranging as James Bond and Wallace & Gromit). He lives in Dorset with his wife and son and a vast collection of Sherlock Holmes books, the first of which he found in a jumble sale over forty years ago.